More Than We Know

Rachel Hyde

DayLily Press
Copyright © 2014 Rachel Hyde
www.rachelhyde.net

ISBN 978-0-9909511-0-0

Cover design: Jill Breitbarth
Interior design: Alida Castillo
Cover photo: Jessie Brown
Daylily photo: Corinna Vanderspek

This is a work of fiction. Names, characters, places and
events are the product of the author's imagination or are used
fictitiously. Any resemblance to actual persons, living or dead, or
to actual business establishments, events, or locations is entirely
coincidental.

for my daughters

CHAPTER 1

L aura felt her daughter's hand slip through her fingers and then Jessie disappeared through the open doorway. Other children were clinging to their mothers but Jessie walked into the classroom as if she'd done it a hundred times. She was just like her father, Laura thought: confident, optimistic. How did she manage that? Laura's chest was so tight with sorrow she could hardly breathe.

She leaned forward and peeked into the room. Jessie was already sitting at a table—with children she'd never met before—constructing a collage out of sequins and feathers. It was exactly the kind of project she loved; she'd gone through more gluesticks at home than Laura could count.

The teacher smiled at Laura and flashed a discreet thumbs-up. I know, Laura thought, her throat aching. It's time for me to leave.

She backed into the hallway and made her way past the row of cubbies toward the front door. It's only nursery school, she told herself, but she knew nothing would be the same after today. The life she'd been living, wrapped completely around her children, was moving toward its inevitable end. When she spotted Jessie's purple sweatshirt on the hook in her cubby, dangling over her miniature backpack, Laura's pent-up tears burst out and started running down her cheeks.

Nearly blinded, she stumbled out the door and crashed into another mother just arriving. The woman grabbed Laura's arm, to keep them both from falling. Her hand was firm and warm on Laura's skin.

"I'm so sorry!" Laura said, mortified, hastily wiping her eyes.

"It's OK," the woman said. "Is your child having a rough start?"

"No, she's fine," Laura said. "I don't know what's wrong with me."

She looked up into the woman's eyes. They were light brown with little flecks of green, full of kindness and compassion.

"There's nothing wrong with you," she said. "It's just the first day. Don't feel bad." She squeezed Laura's arm and reached down to take the hands of two little girls who stood on either side of her, staring up at Laura.

"I'd better get them inside," she said. "We're late, as usual. Will you be all right?"

Laura nodded and watched her walk toward the school. She had a confident stride, like an athlete, her calf muscles outlined in close-fitting leggings.

What a nice woman, Laura thought. Why did I have to be such a mess? She probably thinks I'm a basket case. Laura tried to remember if the woman had been at the parents' meeting a week ago, but all those new faces had merged in her mind. Her family had barely moved into this town before school started.

She wouldn't even have had Jessie registered in time if her husband hadn't pressed her. Laura's first impulse had been to resist the idea but Peter had been surprisingly stubborn.

"Jessie's ready," he'd said, and Laura had to admit that he was right. Even if Laura wasn't ready to let her go.

She went back to the car, studied the map Peter had drawn for her, and navigated the unfamiliar streets back to the house. At least she still had Mark, the baby, to go home to. That was some consolation but it was painful to think about how soon she would have to give him up, too. The brief window of time when the children were small and belonged to her was already starting to close. And then what? Laura wondered. What will I do? Who will I be then?

Peter was sitting on the living room floor, playing with Mark. He'd stayed home with him that morning so Laura could concentrate on Jessie in case she had a hard time separating.

Laura leaned down to kiss the top of Mark's head, comforted by the feel of his soft baby hair against her lips.

"How did she do?" Peter asked. He turned to look at Laura, his blue eyes clear and untroubled.

"Fine," Laura replied. "She just marched right in."

"That's our Jessie," he said. "School is going to be so good for her."

"I know." Laura swallowed. She didn't want to cry in front of Peter.

"It'll be good for you, too," he declared. "Think about what a pain Jessie can be. Now you get the whole morning free of whining."

"I know," Laura said again but she wasn't thinking about Jessie's recent storminess; she was remembering how she used to hold her infant daughter for hours, gazing at her perfect little face.

Peter unfolded his long legs and stood up. "I should go," he said. "I'll try not to be too late getting home."

"I'm sure Jessie will be happy to see you tonight."

"I hope you will, too," he said. He caught her eye and winked.

Laura looked back down at Mark. She used to be charmed by Peter's little signals but lately they didn't seem to do much for her.

Peter lifted Mark off the floor, gave him a kiss, and set him down on his feet. "Take care of Mommy, big guy," he said.

Mark toddled to the couch next to the window and clambered up. Laura followed and they both watched Peter get in his car and drive away. She didn't really want him to stay home but somehow it was hard to watch him leave.

Now she'd be alone again, isolated in a strange town. Over the six years of her marriage, she and Peter had moved five times.

Whenever his company opened a branch in another city, Peter was the person responsible for getting the new office up and running. He was well suited to his work: easygoing and trustworthy—the same traits that had made him seem like ideal father material.

Laura had left her own job to devote herself to caring for the children, immersing herself in the daily rituals of nursing, diapers, naps, making dinner as they crawled around her feet. They had been the anchor in her nomadic life, a distraction from her loneliness. But of course that couldn't last forever.

Mark pointed out the window, shouting "Tuck, tuck, tuck!" A garbage truck lurched down the street in front of the house.

Laura glanced at the boxes of books still stacked in a corner. She really should unpack them and put them away, although sometimes it seemed so pointless: how long would they be living here before they had to pack up and move again?

"Come on, Mr. Marco, let's go out," she said. She scooped him into her arms. "Let's get a new diaper and go out for coffee."

Predictably, as soon as his diaper was off, Mark's chubby hand reached down to grab his penis. Watching him, Laura found herself wondering what it would feel like to have one of those; she'd had the same thought when she and Peter were making love. Her son was a constant reminder of what a mystery boys—and men— were to her. She had no brothers and her father had been a marginal presence in the family. Even after she started dating, boys seemed like an alien species. When prenatal ultrasound revealed that a boy was growing inside her body it had seemed even more astonishing than having a girl in there.

After Mark was dressed again, Laura packed a snack for him in the diaper bag. On the way to the nursery school she'd passed a café in the center of town; she could sit down with a cup of coffee while Mark drank juice and ate animal crackers. She used to take Jessie out for what they called "ladies' tea" before Mark was born: Laura would buy herbal tea for them both, with plenty of milk, and they'd sip slowly, pinkies extended, while Jessie asked questions about everything under the sun.

But Jessie was no longer interested in just sitting and talking to her mother. Her world was expanding in all directions—and, young as he was, Mark's was, too. Laura wouldn't be the focus of their lives for much longer, whether or not they remained at the center of hers.

As she eased into a parking space, she realized Mark had become suspiciously quiet. She turned around to look; sure enough, he was fast asleep, his mouth slightly open, his hands resting on his knees. Sleeping children always look like angels, Laura thought.

She could drive back home, put him in his crib, and unpack those books. But the thought of being alone in the house, without even the baby to talk to, made her feel unbearably lonely.

She took the stroller out of the van, unfolded it, and put Mark down in it. As she prepared to maneuver it through the door of Carole's Coffee Shop, an arm appeared from behind her and pulled the door open. Startled, Laura turned and found herself looking at the mother she'd bumped into at the nursery school.

"Oh, it's you!" she said, a little disconcerted. "Thank you."

The woman followed her inside. "I see you have a little one," she said.

"Yes, this is Mark. And I'm Laura."

"I'm Julia." The woman put out her hand. She smelled ever so faintly of roses.

"Who did you drop off at the nursery school?" she asked.

"My daughter, Jessie. Her very first day. Did you leave both of yours?"

"Yes. Now I can finally have a peaceful cup of coffee. Will you join me?"

Laura felt a familiar shyness spreading over her. She considered saying she was just picking up coffee to go—but really, what was the sense of being so cautious? Didn't she want to make a friend?

"Oh . . . yes . . . sure," she said.

"I'll get it," Julia offered. "You sit here with the baby." She walked up to the counter. Her straight blonde hair swung across her chin when she turned to look at Laura.

"Just coffee?" she mouthed.

Laura nodded and a few minutes later Julia came back with two steaming mugs.

"I drink mine black, do you want anything in yours?" she asked.

"Yes, actually . . . two sugars and . . . here, I'll do it." Laura carried her cup back to the counter. As she stirred in cream and sugar, she glanced toward the table; Julia was looking down at Mark with a tender expression on her face.

"He's lovely," she said, when Laura returned. "I'll bet he keeps you busy."

"I'll be glad to have the distraction, now that Jessie's gone," Laura said.

"I felt that way last year when Emily started school. But lately she and Sara have been fighting so much I'm glad to get rid of them."

It was a little shocking to hear a mother admit that. Jessie had given Laura plenty of rough moments, too—refusing to put on her shoes, balking about the car seat, yelling at Mark if he touched her toys—but all she'd thought about this morning were the sweet times.

"Now that they're both in school, I don't know what to do with myself," Julia went on. "I don't really want to just clean my house, though it could certainly use some attention."

"Mine, too," Laura confessed.

"At least you have the baby to give you an excuse. I'm assuming you don't have a job, either, since you're sitting here drinking coffee in the middle of the morning," Julia said.

"You're right, I don't. I mean . . . I guess my job right now is being a mother." Laura was seized by the familiar awkwardness that arose whenever someone asked her what she did or where she worked.

"Exactly," Julia said. "And there doesn't really seem to be any place for women like us."

She was expressing Laura's own thoughts; it was as if she'd

read her mind. The relief and surprise of feeling so understood brought a lump into Laura's throat. She took a sip of coffee and swallowed hard.

The classical music that had been drifting out of the ceiling speakers was abruptly replaced by Patsy Cline's distinctive voice, belting out "Back in Baby's Arms." Laura sat up straight, listening.

"Somebody's shift must have ended," Julia said. She peered at Laura. "You really like this, don't you?"

"I love country music," Laura admitted. She knew it showed on her face. She also knew some people, especially here in New England, didn't appreciate country music but she'd loved it since she was a teenager growing up in Indiana. She loved the wail of the fiddles, the moan of the dobro, the sobbing catch in the voices of the singers.

"I do, too," Julia said. "Just listen to that voice!"

"I know. Patsy really was the queen."

Mark stirred and his blue eyes—so much like Peter's—opened slowly.

"Hello, my sweet boy," Laura said, lifting him into her arms.

"Mine never wake up that mellow," Julia said. "You're lucky."

"How old are your children?" Laura asked.

"Four and three—thirteen months apart."

"That must have been intense." As much as she treasured the experience, Laura could only think about doing it all a second time—pregnancy, labor, the cracked nipples, the sleepless vortex of life with a newborn—after Jessie had stopped nursing and started to give up diapers.

"No kidding. Sometimes I thought I would lose my mind," Julia said. "To make it worse, we moved here just a year ago. Greg—my husband—was offered a job in Boston and I had decided to stay home with the children so it was a good move financially. But I felt totally uprooted for a while. I still haven't made many friends here—everyone's either working or way too young."

So there was something else they had in common: Julia had

experienced the same upheaval, the same isolation, that Laura had. Laura's throat felt tight again.

"We just moved here two weeks ago," she said.

"Oh, gosh, I know exactly how you feel."

Julia reached across the table and put her hand over Laura's. She looked into Laura's eyes, her gaze direct and intimate, and Laura was afraid she really would start to cry. She hadn't realized how starved she was for the kind of conversation women have with each other. It had been so long since she'd made a really close connection with another woman; the weight of her accumulated loneliness was becoming insupportable.

"Why don't you bring the children over for lunch after school?" Julia suggested. "I have peanut butter and jelly and kid-friendly white bread."

Laura hesitated. As much as she yearned for a friend, she'd grown used to living inside the snug cocoon of her family. It felt a little risky to emerge.

"If today isn't good, you can pick another," Julia said. "It's not as if I have a million things scheduled. Your kids aren't allergic to peanut butter, are they?"

"No . . . and we'd love to come," Laura said.

"Great." Julia slung her purse over her shoulder. "It'll be time to pick up the kids before you know it. I have a couple of errands to do; I'll meet you back at school."

"Wait! I should give you money for the coffee," Laura said.

"It's OK, you can get it next time." Julia smiled and walked out the door.

After she left the room seemed empty and Laura was struck again with the reality of Jessie's absence. Reluctant to go home to the quiet house, she took Mark to a playground not far from the nursery school.

She put him in a baby swing and stood in front of him, pushing him by the soles of his feet. As he swung toward her, she pretended he was about to bump into her, crying "Uh-oh!" with mock concern. This produced a torrent of giggles, and after that he expected her to do it over and over. It was amazing what children could get you to do in the name of entertainment; they gave you an excuse to be silly but they could also be tyrants about letting you stop.

Mark pointed at something behind her.

"Docky!" he cried. It was his word for dog—his second favorite thing in the world, after trucks.

Laura turned around to see a group of young women pushing strollers toward the playground. They looked too young to be mothers, Laura thought—they were probably nannies, on an outing together. A shaggy golden retriever, the late summer sun lighting up its reddish coat, trotted beside them. Mark watched the dog and Laura watched the women, as they chatted and laughed and tossed their hair over their shoulders. She'd never been part of a group like that; for her there had been nothing sociable about having a baby.

She finally pulled Mark out of the swing. "Come on, Mr. Marco. It's time to get Jessie."

In front of the nursery school a long line of minivans waited like a patient herd of elephants. A clump of parents and nannies had formed outside the school door; soon after Laura arrived, Julia showed up.

The door opened and children streamed out. Jessie made a bee-line for Laura.

"Mommy, can I have a playdate?" she asked.

Laura gazed at her daughter, envious of the way she launched herself, headlong, into her new life. She'd probably made a whole crowd of friends already.

"You're in luck, sweet pea," Laura said. "We're going to Emily and Sara's house for lunch."

She loaded the children into their car seats and then followed Julia's minivan into a new neighborhood and parked behind her in the driveway. She was relieved to find that Julia's house looked a lot like hers inside: there were toys strewn around the living room floor and books scattered across the couch.

Mark walked over to the couch and picked up a book. It was *Goodnight Moon*, one of his favorites.

"Moon book," he said.

"He wants me to read it," Laura told Julia.

"Go right ahead, make yourselves at home." Julia pushed aside the other books to clear a space on the couch. "Come on, Jessie, I'll show you the playroom. Emily and Sara are already in there."

"My girls have about a million Barbie dolls," she said to Laura, a little sheepishly, when she returned.

"Jessie's favorite toy," Laura replied.

"I never believed my daughters would play with Barbies," Julia said. "I was sure they'd be above such sexist nonsense."

"They're hard to avoid. My mother sent one for Jessie's birthday."

"Greg's mom gave one to Emily but Sara lusted after it so much I bought her one, too. A fine example of selling out for the sake of a little peace."

Laura laughed.

"Moon book," Mark said again, patting the book on her lap.

"I'm afraid he's a little impatient," Laura said.

"He's a kid." Julia shrugged. "You read to him and I'll go make some sandwiches."

Laura opened the book and Mark turned the pages while she recited the text, committed to memory after countless readings. She was listening to the voices of the girls in the playroom and the sounds of Julia moving around in the kitchen. Being in a house full of other people felt cozy and pleasant.

At the end of the story, she closed the book and took Mark into the kitchen. Julia had several slices of bread spread out on the counter and was slathering them with peanut butter.

"I'm assuming your kids like plenty of peanut butter," she said.

"They do," Laura said. "But Jessie likes just a little bit of jelly."

"My girls like a lot. So much that it squeezes out of the sandwich and falls onto their clothes. It's not enough jelly if it doesn't get on their clothes."

"I never tried those stain remover sprays until I had kids," Laura said. "Laundry was never been such a big part of my life."

"How did this happen?" Julia asked, scraping the peanut butter knife on the edge of the jar. "Two perfectly intelligent women, spending our days thinking about laundry."

"What did you do before?" Laura asked.

Julia dipped the knife in the jelly jar and scooped out a glob of jelly. "In my other life, you mean? I was a lawyer. That's how I met Greg—we were working on opposite sides of a case. It wound up settling out of court so we were doing a lot of talking and negotiating and I guess one thing just led to another."

"Is Greg still practicing law?"

"Yes, he's a partner now. That's what pays the mortgage and keeps us all in peanut butter and jelly," Julia said. "What about you?"

"I met my husband at work, too, sort of."

"Sort of?" Julia turned around and leaned back against the counter. Her lively eyes focused on Laura in a way she wasn't used to; it made her feel flattered and a little unnerved.

"I went to an office party with someone I was dating at the time, and Peter was there. We wouldn't normally have crossed paths; he's a vice president and I was in HR."

"So you ditched your date and hooked up with him instead?"

"The guy I went with was a jerk anyway. He was always canceling plans, or forgetting we even had plans. I would never have wanted to have kids with him. Before I met Peter, I'd just about given up on finding a man who was really dependable."

"They're not exactly a dime a dozen, are they?"

Emily stomped into the kitchen.

"Mommy, Sara's taking all the shoes," she reported furiously.

Julia sighed. "Those Barbie shoes are going to send me over the edge," she said to Laura. "If the girls aren't fighting over them, they're constantly getting lost. I'd like to vacuum them all up and be done with it but, no, I've actually stopped the vacuum cleaner to dig around in the bag full of dust and save those stupid shoes."

"Make her give them back," Emily demanded.

"Let's deal with this after lunch," Julia said. "It's all ready to eat."

"Lunchtime!" Emily shouted and the other girls came running.

"I get to sit by Jessie!" Emily said.

"No, I do!" Sara argued.

"You can each sit on one side of her," Julia suggested.

Jessie seemed perfectly comfortable being the center of attention. Maybe most kids were, Laura thought; maybe it was only when you grew up that you got too self-conscious to just enjoy it.

The girls ate quickly, talking to each other with their mouths full. Jessie remarked on the strawberry jelly, which prompted a spirited debate about the relative merits of grape and strawberry.

Emily asked for another sandwich but by the time it was made she'd lost interest. The girls slid out of their chairs and Julia gave their faces a quick onceover with a wet cloth. Both her daughters had jelly smears on their clothes; Julia pointed to them silently, rolling her eyes.

"I guess I'll eat the sandwich myself," she said. "That's a mother's job, isn't it?"

"I probably eat more peanut butter and jelly now than I ever did as a kid," Laura agreed.

"Are you sick of it? Shall I make you something different?"

"No, I actually like it," Laura said. "Besides, you have strawberry jelly." She grinned and Julia smiled back.

Mark climbed down out of his chair and Julia opened a low cupboard full of pots and pans for him to play with. He began to pull them out and arrange them on the floor.

"Do you mind if he empties that cabinet?" Laura asked.

"Whatever keeps him happy," Julia said.

They sat down together at the table. After the clamor of all the kids it seemed oddly quiet. Laura tried to think of something to say.

"The girls don't seem to be fighting over the Barbie shoes any-more," she remarked.

"It won't last. They can always find something to fight about. It's just what sisters do."

Laura thought about the mixture of annoyance and affection she felt for her own sister. Christine, five years younger, was always trying to catch up to Laura. Laura remembered Christine tagging after her as she walked to school; Laura had shooed her off as if she were a puppy.

Laura had been walking with Michelle Dooley back then. She and Michelle had been the best of friends, practically inseparable, from first grade to sixth. They pricked their fingers and swore to be friends forever; they planned out their futures together: they would marry handsome men and raise happy, clever children in houses with adjoining yards.

But when they entered junior high, all the plans derailed. Michelle abandoned Laura for a new group of girls—girls who wore makeup and called up boys and lied to their parents. They sat together in the lunchroom, whispering and giggling, and left no room at their table for Laura. Michelle's betrayal was one of the hardest things Laura had ever experienced; it was like losing a piece of herself. She had never again felt so completely loved—or so painfully rejected. After all these years, she'd never quite gotten over it.

The three girls reappeared in the kitchen doorway.

"Can we have paper?" Emily asked. "We want to draw."

Julia settled them at the dining room table with paper and markers. As she came back to the kitchen, Jessie called after her, "Can we have scissors?"

Julia grimaced. "How about just coloring for now?" she re-plied.

Laura heard Emily telling Jessie, "Sara's too little for scissors."

"I am not!" That was Sara's voice.

"She is, too," Julia whispered to Laura over the kitchen table.

Mark stood up and came over to Laura, leaving his array of

pots on the floor. He leaned against her knee.

"Are you tired, little bean?" She picked him up and called into the dining room.

"Jessie, we need to go soon. We have to get Mark home for his nap."

"Babies are such a bother," Jessie declared.

"Our big girls have something in common," Julia said. "The unbearable nuisance of a younger sibling."

"I kind of felt that way about my little sister, too," Laura admitted.

A shriek of laughter burst out of the dining room.

"What's going on in there?" Julia called.

"Sara's cutting off her hair!" Emily crowed.

"What?!" Julia jumped out of her chair. Laura followed, carrying Mark.

Sara was holding a pair of scissors in one hand and a lock of hair in the other. Her suddenly uneven haircut and the gleam in her eyes gave her a slightly demented appearance.

"What do you think you're doing?" Julia seized her daughter's wrist and pried the scissors out of her fingers. "I told you no scissors, didn't I?"

"Jessie wanted them," Emily replied.

"I'm so sorry!" Laura said in dismay. Everything had been going so well.

"This wasn't your fault," Julia assured her. "Or Jessie's, either."

She stood by, holding the scissors, as Laura herded her children out the door.

"I feel so dumb . . . I don't know how to get home from here," Laura confessed.

"I remember that feeling," Julia said. "Where do you live?"

It turned out Laura's house was not far away; she was home in less than ten minutes.

At the end of the afternoon, Peter called from work.

"How about if I come home early and we'll order pizza?" he suggested. "I'll stop and pick up a movie on the way."

Laura and Peter never went out to the movies anymore. Laura didn't want to leave the children and Peter had given up trying to persuade her. But sometimes they would rent one and watch it at home.

After the children were in bed, Peter opened a bottle of wine and poured two glasses. Laura took the DVD out of its bag; Peter had brought a romantic comedy. She looked at him in surprise; he usually preferred action films.

"I guess I'm trying to get you in the mood," he said, handing her a glass.

"Am I that hard to get through to?" she asked, but she knew it was true. After the children were born, her focus had shifted; being a mother felt simpler, more natural, to her than being a wife. The neediness of children was so straightforward, so easy to fulfill.

Peter pulled her down beside him on the couch. The woman in the movie looked a little like Julia, Laura thought, remembering Julia's lively face across the kitchen table that afternoon. Peter put his arm around her; Laura could smell his aftershave and then his wine-tinged breath when he leaned over to kiss her after the movie was over.

"So . . . did it work?" he asked, as they headed upstairs.

"I just have to check on the children," Laura said.

"Don't make me wait too long," Peter teased. "I might fall asleep."

Laura went down the hallway and into Jessie's room. Jessie lay in the middle of her bed, the covers tangled around her feet. Her arms were flung out: one above her head, the other to the side so that her hand, open as a star, dangled over the edge of the bed. Laura picked it up and Jessie's fingers curled unconsciously around hers. As an infant, Jessie's hands were like little monkey fists, grabbing Laura's fingers with enough strength to hold her own weight. The sensation of those hands, hanging on for dear life, had made Laura feel needed in an elemental way, as if the whole purpose of her existence might come down to only this: that a tiny helpless creature depended on her.

She pulled the blanket free of Jessie's feet and covered her, although she knew she'd be uncovered again by morning. Laura backed toward the door, her eyes on her daughter. She hoped she would always be able, by looking at Jessie's sleeping face, to see the baby in her.

Across the hall, Mark was asleep too, lying on his tummy. When he was born, Laura had been advised to put him down on his side, but he always managed to scooch around until he dislodged the rolled-up blankets intended to brace him. The sounds through the baby monitor gave him away: a few minutes of rustling and snuffling, followed by his quiet breathing as he sank into sleep.

At first, Laura would go back to his room to rearrange him, although Peter tried to talk her out of it.

"Leave him alone, he's comfortable," he would say.

Her efforts were useless anyway. She finally learned to be satisfied with checking on the baby frequently, putting her hand on his back to assure herself that it was moving up and down.

She still did this, out of habit, relishing the sensation of his small sturdy body under her palm. From the height of the crib rail she inhaled his baby odor: part soap, part sweat, part the faint ammonia scent of his diaper. It wasn't really the sweet smell people attributed to babies but it was the fragrance of her beloved child.

When she walked into her bedroom Peter was lying on his back with his eyes closed. He began to snore abruptly, so she knew he was only pretending.

As Laura slid in beside him she could see the hair on his chest; he was naked under the covers. He reached over, took her hand, and placed it against his pulsing erection. He turned toward her then and opened his eyes.

"I thought you'd never get here," he whispered.

"Well, here I am," she whispered back.

He put his hands on her breasts as she closed her eyes and tried not to picture her children nursing, their infant mouths wide around her nipples.

CHAPTER 2

The next morning Jessie was up early. She got dressed without prompting and bolted down her breakfast, chattering about school the whole time. When she arrived, she skipped into the classroom and greeted her teacher with a jubilant smile.

"It's great to see her look so happy," the teacher murmured to Laura. "Some children are still having a tough time."

"We're lucky, I know," Laura said, lunging after Mark as he headed into the classroom after his sister. She took him outside and let him wander around the schoolyard while she watched other parents arrive and leave. The procession of minivans was almost over by the time Julia drove up. She hurried toward the school, a girl hanging onto each hand.

"Hi, Laura!" she sang out. "Can you wait five minutes while I drop them off?"

She emerged a few minutes later, her arms swinging, hair blowing in the breeze.

"I'm so glad you're here," she said, with unabashed pleasure. "Do you have plans? Want to go out for coffee?"

"We'd love to," Laura said. She'd already packed Mark's diaper bag with snacks just in case.

"I'll meet you at Carole's—I have to stop at the bank first,"

Julia said.

Laura was sitting at a table with Mark on her lap when Julia came through the door, a burst of cheerful energy.

"I'll get the coffees . . . you stay here with him," she said. "You like lots of cream, right?"

"Yes, and two sugars. But you have to let me pay," Laura said.

"OK. This time." Julia grinned.

Laura handed her wallet to Julia, who went to the counter and returned with two coffees, one black and one pale brown with cream.

"Does that look right?" she asked.

"It's perfect," Laura said.

"Would you like something to eat?" Julia asked. "I didn't have any breakfast."

"Oh . . . sure."

Julia left again and brought back two fat raisin scones.

"Those look yummy," Laura said.

"They are," Julia asserted. "Lowfat, too, if you care."

"I try not to," Laura said. "I think it's tiresome to worry about that stuff."

"I knew you were my kind of woman," Julia exclaimed. A little thrill of pleasure shot through Laura.

Julia sat down across the table. She looked like she burned off all the calories she consumed anyway. Her body was lean and wiry, her stomach nearly flat, despite having gone through two pregnancies. Laura was well aware that motherhood had altered her own shape. She was rounder all over now, her belly and breasts bigger than ever. Peter liked her new proportions; Laura was less pleased but she was determined not to obsess about her weight. That seemed like a poor model for her daughter—bad enough that Jessie was playing with Barbies.

She broke off a piece of scone for Mark and he pushed his finger into it, picking out the raisins. Laura watched him put a raisin in his mouth, open his fingers to release it, then pull them out between his lips before closing them. There was something almost miraculous about the way children learned to feed themselves: they started out so helpless, able only to suckle instinctively, but somehow they learned how to chew, to take bites, to manipulate a spoon into their mouths.

A woman opened the door and held it open for a blind man and his guide dog. The dog was a husky, with pale blue eyes and cream-colored fur, impeccably groomed.

"What a beautiful dog," Julia said quietly. "How ironic that his owner can't see him."

The man sat down and the woman trailed her hand lightly across his shoulder, then turned and went to the counter.

Julia's eyes met Laura's. "I wonder what it would be like to make love with a blind person," she said.

"Do you think they're married?"

"No, they're lovers," Julia said.

Laura stared at her. "Do you know them?"

"No, I'm just making this up," Julia admitted. "But think about it: what would it be like? Or suppose you were blind yourself . . . do you think that would make it more sensuous, like being blind-folded?"

"Is that more sensuous?" Laura asked.

"Don't you think so?"

"I guess I wouldn't know." Laura felt herself coloring.

"Oh . . . oops!" Julia grinned impishly. "I'm making all kinds of assumptions today."

Laura wasn't sure what to say. She didn't talk about sex with anyone except Peter and even that was rare, especially after the children came along. She found it difficult to reconcile mother-hood and an ongoing sex life; having children meant less time and less privacy, but it wasn't just that. She felt as if her role had changed irrevocably, and it was hard—sometimes too hard—to find her balance.

Laura watched as the woman brought two cups of coffee and a biscotti to her table and sat down. She dipped the cookie into her coffee, took a bite, then placed it in the man's hand and he did the same. They passed it back and forth until it was gone.

"That was pretty sexy," Julia whispered.

"I guess you were right about them," Laura conceded.

The couple sat face to face, leaning toward each other, as if they were gazing into each other's eyes. The dog sighed, under the table.

Mark slid out of his chair and started toward them.

"No, Mark, don't touch the dog." Laura jumped up to grab him.

"Docky," he said, straining against her.

"Mark, that's a working dog," Julia tried to explain. "You mustn't bother him."

"Docky," Mark said again, on the verge of tears. He'd been perfectly content a moment ago, eating his raisins, and now he sounded as if his world were falling apart.

Suddenly the man spoke. "Do you want to pet the dog?"

Mark stared at his unseeing face, turned not quite in their direction.

"Are you sure you don't mind?" Laura asked.

"I'm sure. It's fine." The man leaned down over the dog, his hand on its collar.

"Thank you," Laura said.

"No problem. Let him smell your hand first and then pat him."

Laura guided Mark's hand, clasped in hers, toward the dog's face. The dog reached its neck forward a little to sniff them.

Mark opened up his hand, his fingers barely touching the dog's fur. Laura glanced at the woman across the table, then put her own hand on the dog's head and scratched behind its ears.

"You have a beautiful dog," she said.

"He's a good pal," the man said. "His name is Taylor. And I'm Jim Darling." He stuck out his hand and Laura reached over to take it.

"I'm Laura Donovan. My son's name is Mark."

"Hi, Mark. Always ask before you pet a dog, OK?"

"Thanks again," Laura said.

"I love kids," John Darling said, but Laura had already turned back toward Julia. He and the woman resumed their private conversation and the dog lay down again, its head resting on its crossed forepaws.

"Wasn't it odd how that woman didn't speak to you?" Julia said. "I bet she's jealous because her boyfriend's so friendly. And she doesn't want children because she wants him all to herself but he'd like to have kids but he won't insist because he thinks it would be unfair because he's blind . . ."

"You're making all that up," Laura said, laughing.

"I know." Julia beamed at her. "Isn't it much more fun than just wondering?"

"I just wish all dogs were that well-trained," Laura said. "When Jessie was Mark's age, a huge dog ran up to us and put its paws right on the edge of the stroller. Jessie screamed until the owner came over and pulled the dog down." Laura shivered, remembering.

"How awful!" Julia exclaimed.

"The stupid woman kept saying 'It's OK, he's just being friendly.' I wanted to slap her. Jessie's still terrified of dogs."

"Not like Mark, I guess," Julia observed.

"It's the only thing Jessie is afraid of."

"What a shame." Julia's compassionate gaze washed over Laura. Even Peter, when she described the incident to him, hadn't been so deeply understanding. Julia seemed to actually experience Laura's feelings right along with her.

Mark reached for Laura's scone. She gave him another piece, then wrapped the rest in a napkin and tucked it into the diaper bag.

"I should take him outside," she said. "He loves the playground, and we won't have many more of these beautiful days. Winter is right around the corner."

"Don't remind me," Julia said. "I turn into a lunatic in the fall, planting bulbs like crazy so I can look forward to spring."

"I've never understood a thing about gardening," Laura said.

"You don't have to understand anything. That's what's fun about it. You just stick things in the ground and they grow—or sometimes they don't. You have to take a chance."

As they walked back to their cars, Laura felt reluctant to say goodbye.

"Would you like to bring the girls over this afternoon?" she suggested. "The kids can all play outside in the yard."

"That sounds like fun," Julia said.

"After all, we owe you an invitation," Laura added, and promptly regretted it. She didn't mean to sound like she was keeping score.

"Well, you'll have to offer us lunch another day," Julia said. "I promised to buy sneakers for Sara right after school. How about if we show up around two?"

"Anytime. We'll be there."

Laura was tempted to straighten up the house, but she remembered how reassuring it had been to find Julia's house a little messy, so she restricted herself to putting the dirty dishes in the dishwasher and cleaning off the kitchen counter. She was upstairs changing Mark's diaper when Julia arrived; Jessie opened the door and Laura came down to find Julia standing in the living room, holding a paper bag.

"Welcome to my house," Laura said.

Julia held up the bag. "I brought you some crocus bulbs. I thought we could plant them while the kids are playing."

"Plant them?" Laura repeated.

"Yes, silly. You'll be so glad in the spring when they come up and bloom for you. I don't suppose you have a trowel?"

"I don't think so."

"Luckily you have me to think of everything. I stuck mine in the car."

The little girls took off into the back yard and Mark tagged along with the two women as they walked around trying to decide where to plant. They finally settled on a spot by the front walk; they knelt down and took turns digging holes in the stony soil, while Mark made a little pile of the rocks they set aside.

The girls reappeared as Julia was taking the bulbs out of the bag.

"Can we help?" Jessie asked.

"Isn't that always the way?" Julia remarked. "We do all the work and then they want to do the fun part."

"I don't mind," Laura said, so Julia showed the children how to place the bulbs in the holes, the tiny hairy roots facing down, and then cover them with dirt.

"Now you just have to wait for the flowers to come up," she said.

"Are they going to be flowers?" Jessie asked. She'd been satisfied just to put bulbs in the ground, without thinking about the future.

Julia looked at Laura. "She's never planted anything?"

"I never thought of it because I never know how long we'll be in one place. We move a lot; Peter's job sends him to a new city every year or so."

"Oh! I didn't realize . . .That must be hard." Julia sat back on her heels and gazed at Laura. "Well, now that we've planted bulbs, maybe you'll stay here awhile." She smiled. "Shall we get some hyacinths tomorrow?"

Laura felt a lump forming in her throat. She'd forgotten how good it felt to have someone appreciate her company for its own sake, without expecting anything else from her. No doubt Peter and the children loved her, but they had needs which they depended on her to fulfill; Julia just wanted to be friends.

She swallowed. "How about something to drink?" she suggested. "I think it's snack time."

"Snack time!" Jessie scrambled to her feet. "Can we have cookies?"

Laura had intended to offer something healthy, but all three girls were looking at her expectantly.

"Do you mind?" she asked Julia.

"Of course not." Julia grinned. "As long as we get some, too!"

The children wolfed down lemonade and cookies in the kitchen and then the girls took off for Jessie's room. Mark sat down to play with the trucks he'd left in the middle of the floor as the mothers lingered at the table.

Julia picked up an Oreo and pulled it apart.

"I still love these," she confided.

"If I were a good housewife, I'd have baked homemade cookies," Laura said.

"Housewife—don't you hate that word? It sounds as if you were married to a house, not a husband. Although I certainly spend more time with my house than with my husband."

The mention of Julia's husband was oddly jarring, like an intrusion on the conversation. It struck Laura that she knew nothing about him, except that he was a lawyer.

"What is Greg like?" she asked.

"Well, he's ridiculously handsome," Julia said. "That's always the first thing women notice about him."

"Really? What is he like as a father?" Laura asked.

"He's totally into it. Sometimes I think he's out to prove something about fatherhood."

Laura hesitated a moment. "How about as a husband?" she asked.

"Well, he's better than my first one," Julia declared. "I got married back in law school, when I was too young to know better."

"What happened?"

"He started sleeping with my best friend—my maid of honor, for crying out loud. How tacky is that? I walked in on them six months after we were married."

"Oh, Julia." Laura's heart ached with sympathy. It was so painful to be let down by someone you trusted with all your heart. Laura had held back nothing from Michelle; after losing her she'd never again been so unguarded.

"I felt like such a fool," Julia went on. "I didn't think I'd ever get married again. It was a long time before I even dated anyone. Although I told Ron—my ex—that I was sleeping with our contract law professor, just to get revenge. I disguised my handwriting and wrote love notes to myself and left them where Ron would find them. I came up with lots of juicy details for him to picture."

"Good for you." Laura remembered Julia inventing a sex life for the blind man and his companion. Her fantasies were quite convincing.

"What about Peter?" Julia asked. "Is he a good husband?"

"Oh, sure. He's kind of a workaholic, though—that's why his company loves him so much."

"Do you ever think about going back to work?" Julia asked.

Laura almost choked on her lemonade. There it was: the question she always dreaded.

"Not really," she said. "Mark's still just a baby. It all goes by so fast—I don't want to miss even a minute. What about you?"

"I don't know—sometimes I feel like I can't even construct a coherent sentence anymore. It's all just 'Stop that,' or 'Hurry up,' or 'Don't touch.' Not the most intellectually stimulating conversation."

"Not like being a lawyer?"

"No. I wouldn't go back to that, though. That was my father's dream for me. My brother and sister are both doctors."

"Do they have children?"

"Yes, they do. Totally raised by nannies, I might add."

"So you're the rebel," Laura suggested.

Julia laughed. "We do lead a very cutting-edge lifestyle, don't you think?"

"Yes, sometimes that's exactly what I think," Laura said. "And sometimes it seems very weird and lonely."

"That's why I'm glad we found each other," Julia said. Their eyes locked for a moment.

"Mommy!"

Jessie and Emily thumped down the stairs.

"Emily called me a bossy Betsy!" Jessie whined.

"No, I didn't!" Emily shouted.

"Look: they're as close as sisters already." Julia rolled her eyes at

Laura. "Maybe this playdate has reached its natural end."

"Will you come again sometime?" Laura asked.

"Of course," Julia declared. "You're not getting rid of us. Just for the rest of the day."

Laura stood on the porch, watching them go. Julia waved as she drove away, her hand fluttering gracefully out the driver's window.

Julia and her girls did come again and Laura and her children went back to Julia's house, too. Several afternoons a week they'd all wind up together and in the mornings, after dropping the girls off at school, Laura and Julia would meet for coffee at Carole's or at one of their houses. They never discussed this in advance; it felt spontaneous each day, but it became a predictable ritual.

One morning, chasing Mark down the sidewalk outside the school, Laura missed Julia's arrival. She corralled Mark and drove to Carole's anyway, confident that Julia would show up. She bought coffee and a raisin scone and sat down to wait, but even after she and Mark had eaten the entire scone, Julia still hadn't arrived.

Laura went back home and called her.

"Hi!" It was Julia's cheery voice on the answering machine. "Sorry we can't talk to you now. Please leave a message."

Laura hung up the phone. Julia was out, doing something without her.

She loaded Mark back in the car and drove to the grocery store, hoping to at least accomplish something useful. She walked up and down the aisles, brooding, so distracted she kept forgetting things on her list and having to go back after them.

Mark thought riding around aimlessly in the shopping cart was great fun.

"Cookie!" he declared, pointing a chubby finger, as Laura plodded past the shelves.

"Sure," she answered dully and threw a box into the cart. She was annoyed with herself for feeling so disappointed—she and Julia hadn't exactly had plans. When she went back to school to pick up Jessie, she didn't even expect to see Julia but suddenly there she was, with her clean rose scent and her exuberant energy, as if the sunlight had been turned up a notch.

"I forgot to tell you I couldn't have coffee today," Julia said. "I'm sorry—I meant to say something. I went to have a massage."

Laura intended to reply, indifferently, "You don't have to explain anything," but instead she heard herself say, "You did? Really?"

"Yes. It was heavenly."

"I've never had one," Laura admitted.

"Oh, Laura, you should! It's a great present to yourself."

"Isn't it weird to have some stranger touch you like that?" Laura asked.

Julia laughed. "I've had people a lot weirder than massage therapists touch me! It wasn't nearly as relaxing, either!"

Laura thought of Darren, the man she'd been dating when she met Peter. His touch had become downright irritating but she'd put up with it anyway. It had never occurred to her to question him; was that just because he was a man?

"I really missed our coffee date this morning," Julia said, as the school door opened and children began to emerge. "Let's do it tomorrow, for sure."

"Yes, absolutely." Laura felt buoyant, as if a weight were dropping away.

The next morning, as Laura was settling Mark into his car seat outside the school, Julia ran up to the van.

"It's silly to drive two cars," she said. "Why don't I leave mine here and ride with you?" She opened the door and climbed into the passenger seat.

"There we go," she said, buckling her seatbelt. "Isn't this better?"

"Oh yes," Laura agreed. "This makes a lot more sense."

But the way it felt to have Julia sitting beside her was less about logic than just plain happiness. After the years of loneliness, it felt so good to have a companion, someone to share the long day with her, while the husbands were off in the distant realm of offices and neckties and paychecks.

Julia leaned back in her seat.

"It's nice not to be driving for a change," she said. "You don't mind, do you?"

"No, I'm used to it. I could practically drive this van in my sleep."

"Who drives when your husband is around?" Julia asked.

"He does—although he thinks the minivan is boring."

Julia chuckled. "Sounds like a typical midlife reaction. How old is Peter?"

"Funny you should ask." Laura pulled the car into a parking spot. "He's turning forty in a week—and I can't figure out what to do for him," she confessed. "I don't even know what he'd like."

"What about a party?" Julia suggested.

"We don't know anyone," Laura said. "Except for you."

"Take him out to a fancy dinner? I'll bet you never get out alone together. I'll give you my babysitter's name—she's terrific."

"But if we use your babysitter, you and Greg couldn't come," Laura said, to her own surprise.

"You want us to come?"

Laura hadn't thought of it until she said it but now it seemed like a great idea. It would make the birthday special, more festive somehow.

"Would you want to?" she asked.

"I'd love to meet Peter," Julia said. "I'll see if I can find babysitters for both of us. You can have Mrs. Nixon—she's great with babies—and I'll rustle up someone else for my girls."

"That's so generous of you," Laura said.

"It'll be fun. We hardly ever get out either," Julia said.

"Well, thank you." Laura hadn't realized how much the upcoming birthday had been weighing on her until the dilemma was solved.

They opened their car doors at the same time and got out. Julia waited as Laura extracted Mark from his car seat and then the three of them walked into Carole's together.

CHAPTER 3

Over the next week, Laura and Julia read restaurant reviews, picked out a place, called for reservations. Julia arranged for Laura to meet Mrs. Nixon, a plump, white-haired woman who bustled into the house and proceeded to entertain Jessie with a puppet she'd brought in her purse, then sat down and drew pictures of trucks for Mark. Laura described the children's evening routines as Mrs. Nixon nodded knowingly, with the air of an experienced grandmother.

Laura sometimes thought it might be nice to have a grandmother around—to babysit and be a source of wisdom and support. It was only a fantasy, though: both of Peter's parents had died before Laura met him and her own mother's energy was used up taking care of Laura's father and his advancing lung cancer. She only saw her grandchildren when Laura and Peter took them to Indiana, which wasn't very often. Going back there made Laura feel edgy, as if her life were somehow in danger of regressing.

"We love it when you come to visit," her mother had told her wistfully the last time they were there, the summer after Mark was born. She and Laura had been sitting on the porch swing, sipping iced tea, as the evening air gradually started to cool down.

"I don't like it when Daddy smokes around the children," Laura said.

"Honey, he just can't seem to stop," her mother said. "His doctor has ordered him, I've begged him, but it doesn't do any good."

"Daddy never paid attention to you," Laura was tempted to say, but she resisted. "The smoke is terrible for babies," she said instead.

"It didn't seem to hurt you or Christine," her mother said.

"We don't really know that, do we?" Laura retorted. She counted on her mother's reassurance but found it irritating at the same time. Her parents' lives were so limited, so simple.

Laura waited until the day before the birthday dinner to tell Peter about it. Julia had urged her to make it a surprise but Laura was afraid he might decide to work late or take off suddenly on a business trip.

"You planned a party for me?" Peter seemed a little nonplussed.

"Is it OK?" she asked, suddenly uncertain. In the fun of planning everything with Julia she'd thought more about her own enjoyment than Peter's.

"Yes, of course," he said agreeably.

The next evening Laura put on a black dress and a string of pearls, while Jessie watched, fascinated. Mrs. Nixon rang the doorbell right on time. Laura had already written down a long list of instructions she knew were unnecessary.

"You two just have fun," Mrs. Nixon said warmly.

"Can I have three bedtime stories tonight?" Jessie asked.

"You can have as many stories as you want." Laura scooped up Mark and squeezed him.

"Be good, little bean," she said. She was starting to feel choked up. Julia had given her a pep talk about this very thing, though, pointing out that if she never left her children they'd eventually make it impossible. She was lucky they weren't putting up a fuss now.

She made herself put Mark down.

"We won't be late," she said to Mrs. Nixon. "Goodbye, sweeties."

"Bye, guys," Peter said, closing the door behind them. Leave-taking was routine for him.

He reached for Laura's hand as they walked to the car. Laura was reminded of the days before they were married, before there were children in the picture. Peter had been quite courtly then, picking her up at her apartment and seeing her safely home—unlike Darren, who always wanted to just meet up somewhere. The first time Laura spent the night with Peter, he got up and made her breakfast in the morning.

She'd been unaccustomed to that kind of attention and not entirely at ease with it. As soon as Jessie was born, Laura slipped readily into the role of family caretaker. Besides, these days Peter left early for work; most mornings he didn't even eat breakfast at home.

As soon as they arrived at the restaurant, Laura's impulse was to call home, but she restrained herself. It was only fair to let Mrs. Nixon settle in with the children, without the interruption of a phone call.

"Shall we have a drink?" Peter suggested.

"A glass of wine would be nice," she replied.

There was one empty stool at the bar; Laura sat down and Peter stood beside her, looking handsome in his dark suit and the silk tie she'd given him last Christmas. When he leaned forward to speak to the bartender Laura could feel the warmth of his body under the open suit jacket. He put his hand on her shoulder and looked down at her.

"You don't think we should have just gone out alone?" he asked.

"I thought it would seem more like a party if we had some other people," she said. "You don't mind, do you?"

"No, it's fine," he assured her.

Their drinks arrived: chilled white wine for her and a vodka and tonic for him. They picked up their glasses and clinked them together.

"Happy birthday," Laura said.

She glanced past Peter to the door. Julia was just coming in. Laura felt a thrill at the thought of seeing her at night; it seemed so different from their daytime mommy selves. There was also something a little unsettling about the prospect of meeting each other's husbands. They hadn't been a part of the friendship up to now.

Julia spotted Laura and came toward her, followed by a tall, drop-dead gorgeous man, with wavy blond hair and green eyes sparkling under long, dark eyelashes. Laura instantly understood Julia's description of her husband as "ridiculously handsome." He was one of those people whose charisma is almost palpable—and the two of them together were truly striking.

"Hi, Julia, you look great," Laura said.

"You do, too," Julia said, clasping her in a brief embrace. She stepped back and said, "This is my husband, Greg."

Peter put out his hand; Greg shook it and then took hold of Laura's. His hand was so big that hers felt engulfed in it.

"I'm glad to meet you," he said. "I've heard a lot about you."

"I'm glad to meet you, too," she said. She felt tongue-tied, like a teenager in high school confronted with the football star. He smiled at her, his teeth so straight and white that Laura wondered if they were capped.

"This is Peter," she said, belatedly.

"Of course—the birthday boy." Julia gave him a quick peck on the cheek. "Happy birthday! This is the Big One, isn't it?"

"That's right." Peter laughed. "It's all downhill from here."

"Surely the best is yet to come," said Julia.

"Well, that's what I hope," Peter said. "Would you two like drinks?"

Greg and Julia both ordered martinis.

Laura looked at Julia. "A martini?"

"This is a special occasion," Julia said. "It's not as if I have one every day."

"Maybe that would be a good idea," Laura mused. "It might make that awful late afternoon time go more smoothly."

"That is a terrible time, isn't it?" Julia agreed. "The kids at the end of their rope and no daddy in sight."

"Maybe we should start a Moms' Happy Hour," Laura said.

"Oh yes." Julia laughed. "Mothers all over town pouring themselves drinks before dinner. We could go out on our porches and toast each other for having made it through another day with the kids."

"Except there really aren't that many like us," Laura said. "We're a dying breed."

"Then we just have to make a lot of noise so we can hear each other." Julia touched her glass to Laura's.

The husbands stood by, staring off vaguely into the restaurant. They didn't know each other, Laura reminded herself; she and Julia should pay some attention to them.

"Honey, Greg is a lawyer," she said. "He and Julia met on opposite sides of a case."

"No kidding," Peter said. "Who won?"

Greg grinned, flashing his perfect teeth. "I did, of course. I got the girl, didn't I?" He put his arm across Julia's shoulders.

"The case was settled out of court," Julia added, rolling her eyes at Laura.

"What law firm are you with?" Peter asked, and then he and Greg launched into the kind of predictable conversation people have with each other about work, the kind of conversation Laura felt unequipped for, now that she had no job. She felt a little annoyed, even though she was the one who'd gotten them started.

She tried to focus on Greg while he was talking but he had a way of looking at her so intently it made her uncomfortable. He and Julia had this intensity in common, but somehow it felt different to be in Greg's high beam than in Julia's. Some women probably chose to take his attention personally; if he were homely and radiated that kind of energy it might be seen as intrusive but from this gorgeous man it could seem flattering.

Laura wondered how it felt to be married to the sort of person who made heads turn. She wondered what it was like for Julia, then found herself wondering what it was like for him to be married to her. Did they appreciate each other?

Their table was ready just as they finished their drinks. Laura excused herself to call home and, when she joined the others, a bottle of wine had already been ordered. Julia raised her glass and said, "To Peter, on the unmentionable birthday."

He looked amused; he was finding Julia's charm irresistible, too. Over appetizers, he asked her if she was still practicing law.

"No, I left all that behind when I had children," Julia said.

"So you're a housewife . . . homemaker . . . whatever the right word is—like Laura," he said.

"To quote the bumper sticker: every mother is a working woman," she answered, smiling sweetly.

"My mother stayed home when I was growing up," Peter remarked. He turned to Greg. "Would you ever have guessed you'd wind up living the lifestyle of your parents?" he asked.

"My life is nothing like my parents," Greg replied brusquely. For the first time there was no sign of his dazzling smile.

"Oh?" Peter said mildly, managing to seem curious but not nosy.

Greg took a swallow of wine. "My father abandoned my mother with two little boys," he said.

"I'm sorry," Peter said, at the same time Laura said, "How awful," and Julia laid her hand on Greg's arm for a moment without a word.

He lifted his head and turned on his smile again. "We should be talking about happier things," he declared. "This is a birthday, after all."

They ordered another bottle of wine with the main course. Now the conversation shifted easily from one subject to the next: Peter's work, Greg's latest case, the reputation of the local school system, the universal stubbornness of children. By the end of dinner Laura felt intoxicated, from both the alcohol and the heady pleasure of being served and sitting still for the length of an entire meal.

The waiter appeared with a dessert menu.

"You have to come to our house for dessert," Laura said quickly. "I made a birthday cake."

When the bill arrived, Laura reached for it but Greg got to it first.

"We'll take care of this," he said.

"Oh no, you mustn't!" Laura exclaimed. "I invited you to come out to dinner—you can't pick up the whole tab."

"Of course we can," Greg said, flashing his amazing smile. "It's our birthday treat."

Dismayed, Laura looked at Julia but she just shook her head.

"It's not worth arguing about," she said. "He's made up his mind."

Laura turned to Peter. "Honey, help . . ." she began, then drew in her breath abruptly. There was a hand on her knee under the table. She looked at Greg, but one of his hands was holding the bill and the other was pulling out his wallet. Of course it wasn't Greg's hand on her knee; she must be drunker than she'd realized.

Peter squeezed her leg gently.

"Thank you," he said to Greg. "We'll just have to take you two out some other time."

They drove back to Laura's house and Laura went upstairs to look in on the children.

Jessie was fast asleep, arms and legs spread across the bed. Laura kissed her and pulled the covers back over her.

When she went into Mark's room, he sat up, suddenly awake.

"Mama?"

She picked him up and sat down in the rocking chair next to his crib. He snuggled against her as she hummed a made-up lullaby, remembering how she used to nurse him in the middle of the night. He'd stopped nursing after his first birthday and sometimes she still missed it: the weight of his warm head in her elbow, the rhythmic pulling on her nipple, and the sensation, unlike anything else, of her milk flowing down through her breast. She'd experienced a profound kind of peace while her babies were nursing, a feeling she sometimes wished she could recapture.

She stopped humming and listened to Mark's even breathing; he was asleep again. It was time to get back to her abandoned guests. She put Mark down in the crib and he promptly rolled to his tummy. Laura checked to see that the monitor was on and went downstairs.

Peter was starting a pot of decaf in the kitchen. Greg stood in the doorway, nearly as tall as the doorframe, talking to him.

"How about that cake?" Peter asked.

"Go wait in the living room. I'll get it," Laura said. "Julia, will you help me?"

She took the cake out of its hiding place in the cupboard, and arranged birthday candles in the shape of the numerals 4 and 0. Then she and Julia lit them together, laughing as they tried to get to them all without burning each other's hands.

Julia ran back to the living room and turned off the light. Laura held the cake with both hands, heat from the flaming candles rising into her face. Julia started singing "Happy Birthday" as Laura proceeded at a stately pace, slow as a bride down a church aisle, and set the cake on the coffee table in front of Peter.

"Don't forget to make a wish," Julia reminded him.

He blew out the candles and Laura suddenly felt a pang that the children hadn't been part of the celebration. Maybe she should have done it differently—but it was too late now. She'd be sure the children got some cake tomorrow.

"This is delicious," Greg declared.

Julia made appreciative humming sounds as she ate, her pleasure as artless as a child's.

Peter looked perfectly content. He was so easy to please; he really didn't demand much.

Julia scraped up the last bit of icing from her plate and licked it off her fork.

"Did you get any fabulous presents?" she asked Peter.

"I just got taken out for a fabulous dinner," he replied.

Laura stood up. "Wait—there's more," she said. She collected the plates and carried them to the kitchen, then ran upstairs and came back with Peter's present.

Julia looked on, her eyes sparkling; she already knew what it was. Laura had a hard time deciding what to get for Peter, who never seemed to want anything he didn't already have. But forty was a milestone: it deserved something special. Laura watched him open the package.

Inside was a leather jacket, buttery soft, the color of milk chocolate, lined in a subtle paisley silk. She'd found it in the sort of store she wouldn't usually enter, one morning when Jessie was in school and she and Julia had gone shopping in the city. It was unlike her to come up with anything so luxurious and she felt excited to have bought such a thing at all.

"Wow," Peter said. He looked at Laura in surprise and lifted the jacket out of the box. Then he stood up and put it on, zipped it, stroked its sleeves.

"That's a beautiful jacket," Julia declared.

"Do you like it?" Laura asked.

"It's great, honey. I love it." Peter put his arms around her. She could smell the rich leather and feel its smooth surface, like a soft, fine animal.

He leaned down to kiss her but she turned her head, acutely conscious of Julia and Greg sitting there. Peter seemed to have forgotten them already.

"We'd better go now," Julia said cheerfully. "I expect you two are ready to be alone."

Laura felt oddly forlorn as she watched Greg and Julia put on their coats.

"Thank you again for buying dinner," she said.

"When we turn forty, you can take us out," Julia replied. Laura wondered fleetingly if they'd still be living in the same town.

She stood in the open doorway, watching them go. Julia slipped her arm around Greg's waist and his arm settled across her shoulders. They walked to the car like that, pressed tightly against each other, looking like one huge person with two heads. Greg unlocked the passenger door and opened it.

Julia turned and waved.

"Drive carefully," Laura said quietly, almost to herself, as she waved back.

She closed the door and turned to Peter, who was still wearing the jacket.

"Did you have fun?" she asked him.

"Oh yes."

He pulled her toward him and began to kiss her hungrily. She wrapped her arms around him; he unzipped her dress and lowered her onto the couch. She lay back as he pulled off her shoes, hoping the children would stay asleep until afterwards.

Peter stood up and began to remove the jacket.

"Don't take it off," Laura heard herself whisper.

He stared at her, startled. "What?"

"Leave it on," she said. "Just to be different."

She was as amazed as he was at the idea. Peter watched her, his eyes wide, as they took off the rest of their clothes. Laura fondled the smooth leather of the jacket, breathing in its unfamiliar smell, feeling suddenly, violently aroused. They fell back onto the couch and made love, as the smell of leather mingled with the smell of sex.

CHAPTER 4

"You weren't lying," Laura commented to Julia over coffee the next morning. "Your husband is such a hunk."

"Not you, too," Julia groaned. "Somehow I hoped you'd be immune."

"I'm sorry . . . I didn't mean . . ." Laura floundered.

"It's OK," Julia said. "I told you: women can't help noticing. His female clients are all crazy for him—I just hope he isn't fooling around."

Julia's face had a dreamy, faraway look; it occurred to Laura that maybe she was a little turned on by the idea. Perhaps the thought provided some kind of spark between her and Greg.

If Laura ever suspected Peter of cheating, she was sure she'd completely lose interest in sex. Even now, she sometimes had to work herself into the mood, but she'd never be able to get past infidelity.

"He's going away on business over Columbus Day," Julia said. "His firm schedules this trip every year. The most beautiful autumn weekend in New England and they all go off to Florida."

"Peter's going to be gone then, too!" Laura exclaimed. "He's going to Chicago—his first business trip since we moved here. I suppose I should be grateful he stayed put for over a month."

"I hate it when Greg goes away on weekends," Julia said. "No school to break up the day . . . just me and the kids all day long."

"Shall we get the kids together?" Laura suggested.

"That's a great idea," Julia said. "Why don't you all come spend the night on Sunday? We can order pizza and have a pajama party."

Laura felt an odd jump in her stomach. She hadn't been to a pajama party since junior high; the idea made her excited and a little bit nervous.

As Laura helped Peter pack for his trip she realized that something felt different: she didn't have that vague feeling of uneasiness she used to get whenever Peter went away. She didn't feel abandoned this time; she had something to look forward to.

Before he left, Peter kissed her and the children and promised to call home every evening.

"We'll be at Julia's on Sunday," Laura reminded him. She couldn't imagine being alone in a hotel, away from her children. She watched Peter swing his suitcase into the trunk of the taxi and settle into the back seat, looking—as always—relaxed and in control.

Late that evening, long after Peter had called, the phone rang again. Laura was sitting on the couch, watching TV, and trying not to eat cookies.

She picked up the telephone. "Hello?"

"How is it going over there?" Julia asked.

"Pretty peaceful. The kids are sleeping."

"You have to teach me your secret," Julia said. "It's such a struggle around here. Sara pops out of bed for one thing after another—it can go on for hours. And it's worse when Greg is away."

"Maybe she feels insecure when he's not around," Laura said. "Or she picks up on your higher stress level, maybe?"

"Or she wants to torture me for no reason. What makes you think my stress level is higher when he's gone?"

"I just assumed it," Laura said. "Sometimes when Peter goes away I start inventing things to worry about."

"Mommy?" she heard through the phone.

"Speak of the devil," Julia said. "I'll have to go upstairs again. I just called to ask if you'd like to go to the beach tomorrow."

"The beach? In October?"

"It's beautiful then. And no crowds. It's too cold to go in the water but around here that's practically true all year. How about if we pick you up around ten? We can have a picnic up there."

"See you then. Good luck with Sara." Laura hung up and pictured Julia walking Sara up the stairs, tucking her in, smoothing her hair, blowing a kiss from the open doorway, just exactly as Laura would have done.

The next morning Laura had the children dressed, their faces sunscreened, and a picnic basket packed by nine. It was a glorious day, with brilliant sunshine pouring out of the sky.

Laura moved her car seats to Julia's van and Julia turned on a kids' music CD as they drove out of town. The music came out of only the rear speakers so it felt as if there were a children's zone in the back of the car and a mothers' zone in the front.

"It would never have occurred to me to go to the beach once the summer was over," Laura said. "I would have just waited until next year."

"Oh, that's much too long," Julia declared. "I try to get to the beach at least once every season."

The huge parking lot was nearly empty; Julia parked and they unloaded children and picnic baskets. Julia hoisted a knapsack full of beach toys onto her back. Laura slung the diaper bag over her shoulder, picked up her picnic basket, and followed Julia up the path through the dunes. Tall grass waved on both sides of her, yellow-green under the deep blue sky.

The three girls trudged between them, their sneakered feet sinking into the sand. Mark tried to keep up but he was unstable on the soft terrain. He turned to Laura to be lifted and she scooped him into her arms. Julia plodded along steadily, under the weight of the knapsack.

They walked over a little rise in the dunes and suddenly, spread out in front of them, was the ocean, the cobalt water sparkling in the sunlight. The water was bright, the sand was bright, the very air was bright. Laura stopped for a minute to take it in.

"Look, Mr. Marco, there's the ocean," she said. "The Atlantic Ocean—on the other side of that is Europe."

Julia and the girls had gone ahead but they waited where the path opened onto the wide flat beach. A little way to the left, an elderly couple sat on folding beach chairs, their faces obscured by the broad, floppy brims of their sun hats. Sweaters wrapped tightly around them, they looked out over the water. There was something peaceful and companionable about their battered chairs facing the water, side by side, as if they'd been doing this for uncountable years.

To the right, the beach was deserted. Julia headed that way and set down her load. Laura put Mark down and helped Julia spread out a big blanket. The girls rummaged in the knapsack for sand toys, then moved a few feet away and started filling their pails with sand. Julia sat down on the blanket and kicked off her shoes.

"This is the life," she said. She reached into the bag of toys, pulled out a shovel and a sand wheel, and showed Mark how to scoop sand through the top to make the wheel spin. Then she lay back on the blanket and closed her eyes.

Laura watched Julia's chest move up and down with her breath and listened to the voices of the girls playing, the cries of gulls overhead, the shushing sound of the surf against the beach. A cool breeze blew in off the water but the sunshine was warm. It was one of those moments when everything seemed to be exactly in its place. Laura sat suspended in perfect contentment.

Julia lay still for a long time, long enough that Laura began to wonder if she was asleep. The girls were having an unusually pro-longed period of harmony; it was only when Mark crawled over to examine their construction that the balance was upset.

"Mom!" Jessie yelled. "Mark's going to mess up our castle!"

Laura doubted he would do more than look at it, but, for the sake of preserving the peace, she got up and brought him back to the blanket.

"Let's take off our shoes and walk in the sand," she suggested. Mark pulled off his shoes and Laura helped him tug the socks off his chubby feet. Julia stretched and sat up.

"We're going for a little stroll," Laura told her.

"Have fun."

Julia waved at Mark. He clung to Laura's hand, still uneasy about the sensation of sand shifting under his feet. Laura led him to where the sand was damp and packed hard, thinking he'd like that better, but the damp sand was cold and after a few steps he stopped and held up his arms.

"Mommy hold," he said.

She lifted him, looking down to admire his tiny footprints. It seemed like only yesterday that Jessie's feet had been that small.

She looked back at Julia sitting on the blanket and the three girls, their heads bowed over their sand structure. Then she walked down the long sweep of beach, watching the waves, mesmerized by their regular breaking, until she began to feel how heavy Mark was in her arms. When she turned again, the others looked far away.

"Let's go back, Mr. Marco," she said.

He was willing to walk now but only on the dry sand, so they made their way slowly back to the blanket. By the time they arrived the girls were clamoring for lunch.

"I was trying to hold them off until you got back," Julia said. "Isn't this a gorgeous beach?"

"It's the most beautiful beach I've ever seen," Laura said. She hadn't been to all that many beaches but she couldn't imagine anything more perfect than this.

She sat down and watched Julia's hands moving busily as she unpacked sandwiches and chips and passed them around. She found herself wondering what it would be like to be alone with Julia on a beautiful empty beach like this, the sky blue above them, with a picnic of bread and cheese and wine. It was an odd thought; she and Peter had never even done that. For their honeymoon, they'd taken a tour of Europe: six cities in fourteen days.

"What did you and Greg do on your honeymoon?" she asked Julia.

Julia raised her eyebrows. "Well, what do you think?" she said. "You don't want me to go into detail in front of the children, do you?"

"Oh no, I didn't mean that," Laura said hastily. "I meant where did you go?"

"Of course you did." Julia laughed. "We went to one of those couples-only resorts in the Caribbean: very unreal, lots of American couples with plenty of money but none of it changing hands because everything was already paid for. Nothing to do but lie on the perfect beach, drink rum drinks, and stare at each other."

"Sounds pretty ideal for a honeymoon," Laura said.

"What's a honeymoon, Mommy?" Jessie asked.

"It's a special trip that a husband and wife take together after they get married."

"Why?"

Laura glanced at Julia, who snickered softly.

"To get to know each other better and to rest after the wedding," Laura said.

"Good answer," Julia murmured approvingly.

After lunch Julia took a turn going down the beach, the muscles in her legs flexing as she walked on the sand. Laura built a sand castle with Mark, looking up occasionally to watch Julia getting farther and farther away until she disappeared around a curve of the dunes. All at once it seemed as if she'd just walked out of their lives, as if all along she'd been only a figment of Laura's imagination. Laura took a long deep breath, staring at Julia's empty shoes next to the blanket. Then, as suddenly as she'd disappeared, Julia appeared again, walking back along the water's edge, the waves lapping over her bare feet. Laura recognized her at first only by the shape of her haircut and the fluid motion of her arms and legs swinging rhythmically as she came closer, until she finally stood again above the little group sitting on the sand.

"How much longer do you want to stay?" she asked.

All my life, Laura thought, and said, "We can leave any time."

"I'm just thinking it takes a while to drive back and we're going to want to get all these kids into the bath before we order pizza."

"You're right. We should probably go."

But it was hard to leave. Julia sat down again; she and Laura gazed out over the water. A little inlet of tidewater was forming between them and the edge of the sea.

"Mark, do you want to put your feet in the water?" Julia asked him.

He took her hand and went with her to the shallow pool. Laura watched him put his toes in, back out hastily, then try again. Julia stood in the water, ankle deep, coaxing him on.

The girls dropped their shovels, and ran over. Jessie and Emily kicked off their shoes and splashed in. Sara struggled with her sneaker and Laura bent down to help her. As soon as it was loose, Sara flung it aside and hurried into the water.

"Mommy, it feels good!" Jessie exclaimed. "You should come in too!"

The water was surprisingly warm, the sandy bottom soft beneath their feet. They walked around, lifting their feet and putting them back down deliberately, as if on strange lunar terrain.

All of a sudden, Sara fell in. Laura didn't see it happen—she'd been looking out at the pale horizon—but suddenly Sara was sitting down in the water, soaked to the waist.

"Mommy, I'm all wet!" she wailed. Emily and Jessie giggled.

"I guess we really have to get out of here now," Julia said. She lifted Sara and carried her back to the blanket.

"I wasn't smart enough to bring a towel," she said, rubbing her shivering daughter with a corner of the blanket. "Let's take off your wet things, honey, and you can wear . . ." she paused to think. "I'll wrap you up in my shirt."

She took off her shirt to reveal a snug-fitting tank top underneath. Her nipples stood out under the soft, white jersey.

"I was afraid you were just going to have a bra on," Laura said. "This beach is pretty empty but it's not completely deserted."

"I don't think even I would have the nerve to stroll back to the car in just a bra."

Julia took off Sara's wet clothes and put the shirt on her. It dragged along the sand behind her, the sleeves flapping empty below her hands. She looked like a tiny ghost, or an angel.

Julia collected the sand toys while Laura folded up the blanket and they began the slow procession back through the dunes. The older couple they'd seen earlier had left but now a group of young men was throwing a Frisbee around. It was a good thing Julia wasn't just in her underwear.

When they got back to Julia's house Mark was fast asleep. So was Sara.

"We can let the little ones sleep in the car while we wash the older ones," Julia suggested.

They coaxed Jessie and Emily out past their sleeping siblings.

"You get to have a bath before the others," Julia told them. "Take off your shoes and go straight upstairs to the bathroom. Don't go anywhere else: you're covered with sand."

The girls, pleased to be first with anything, headed up the stairs while Laura and Julia took off their own shoes and shook the sand out of them.

"I thought we'd pop the girls in the tub together," Julia said. "I'll go start the water. On second thought, why don't you go? I'll deal with Sara's wet clothes and the leftover food."

In the bathroom, Emily and Jessie were already taking off their clothes. They were still too young to be shy about getting undressed together. Laura remembered the misery of the locker room in junior high, all the girls desperate to cover their developing bodies. When she and Michelle had first become friends, they'd been as uninhibited as Jessie and Emily were now but by sixth grade it wasn't safe to even look at each other.

Laura turned on the water and held her hand under it to check the temperature.

"Can we have bubbles?" Jessie asked.

Emily brought over a bottle from the crowded bathroom counter. Laura poured some in, stirred it with her hand, and adjusted the temperature again. When she turned back around, both girls were completely naked. Laura felt a burst of adoration for their little girl bodies: their perfect four-year-old proportions, their smooth skin, their silken locks of hair—no longer the fuzz of babyhood but without the weight and sheen it would acquire as they grew older.

"Anyone need to go potty?" she asked.

They both declined, but as soon as they got into the water they were desperate to go. Laura helped each of them, slick with soapsuds, out of the bathtub and back again.

Julia appeared in the doorway.

"Everything all set in here?" she asked.

Laura moved aside so Julia could see the girls' heads and shoulders emerging from the pile of bubbles in the bathtub.

"They're so cute," Julia said.

"How are the little ones doing?" Laura asked.

"Still sound asleep," Julia assured her. "Do you want to go see for yourself? I can take over in here."

Julia's van sat serenely in the driveway. Laura peeked through the tinted back window at the sleeping children, tipped over toward each other in their car seats. She returned to the house, where the sound of girlish laughter, mingled with Julia's grownup voice, floated down the stairs.

Laura went to the CD rack and found a cluster of country music CDs. Those had to be Julia's; she'd told Laura that Greg didn't like country music. He had that in common with Peter, who didn't really care for it either. Laura pulled out a Patsy Cline recording and slipped it into the CD player.

"Hey, turn that up!" Julia called down from the bathroom.

After a couple of songs Laura went back out to the driveway. Mark was looking around the inside of the car in confusion. How

odd it must be for little kids, never knowing where they were going to wake up. They fell asleep wherever they were, dropping like
puppies, only to find themselves transported somewhere else, as if
by magic. But they seemed to accept that uncertainty; it was seeing
a familiar face when their eyes opened that mattered most.

Laura lifted Mark out of the car. He smelled of sunscreen and
salt air.

She brought him into the house and they waited until the girls
came downstairs. Jessie was wearing an unfamiliar outfit.

"I get to wear Emily's clothes," she announced.

Julia followed them down. "I didn't want to put them back in
their sandy things," she said.

"I brought extra clothes but I can see Jessie's getting a big kick
out of this."

"It's probably only the beginning," Julia said. "Didn't you used
to trade clothes with your friends?"

Laura remembered the time she and Michelle had switched everything they were wearing, even their underpants, one day in the
bathroom at school. That evening, on the phone, they had dis-
solved in helpless giggles as they described the looks on each of
their mothers' faces when they got home.

She carried Mark upstairs and filled the tub. He was wide awake
by the time she put him in, splashing and grabbing his penis, slippery as a little fish.

Julia took Sara into the shower with her, then Laura showered
alone, and after everyone was clean, they ordered two pizzas: plain
cheese for the children, olive and anchovy for themselves.

"I can't believe you like anchovies," Julia exclaimed. "No one
else I know will eat anchovy pizza. We must be soul mates or
something."

Laura nodded, wordless, filled with happiness.

At bedtime, Jessie and Emily wanted to wear each other's pajamas. A cloud came over Sara's face as her lower lip started to
protrude.

"I think everyone needs to wear their own pajamas," Laura said quickly. Julia shot her a grateful glance.

When Emily and Sara began competing over whose room Jessie would stay in, Julia put a stop to the squabbling by announcing that they could all sleep on the floor in the guest room.

"You and Mark can have our bed. It's huge," she said to Laura. "You don't mind sleeping with him, do you?"

"Oh no, we do that a lot. But where will you sleep?"

"I'll take one of the girls' beds."

"Sleep in my bed, Mommy!" Emily said, followed by Sara, "No, mine!"

Julia rolled her eyes. "I can't win, can I?"

At last the girls settled into sleeping bags on the guest room floor, Jessie sandwiched between Julia's daughters. Julia turned on a nightlight and both mothers blew kisses from the doorway. After a few minutes of whispering the room was silent; they were all too tired to keep each other awake.

Laura put Mark in the center of Greg and Julia's king-size bed. She read *Goodnight, Moon*, then lay down beside him and watched his eyelids droop and close. By the time Julia peeked in, he was sound asleep.

The two women tiptoed downstairs and collapsed onto the sofa. Julia leaned back and put her bare feet on the coffee table. She folded her arms behind her head and sighed.

"I can see all the cobwebs on the ceiling," she remarked. "But I'm not going to do anything about them." She turned to Laura. "Does Peter do any of the cleaning at your house?"

"Not really," Laura said. "I guess we both assume it's up to me since I'm there all day."

"But you're there with a baby," Julia pointed out. "That takes as much time and energy as any job, if not more."

"That seems to be hard for other people to understand."

"Does Peter?"

"No. But at least he doesn't complain about the house. To be honest, I don't think he notices."

"Greg does. Even if he doesn't say anything, I can tell he's looking at the dust bunnies and inspecting the state of the toilet."

"Does he do any cleaning?" Laura asked, pretty sure she knew the answer.

"Oh, once a year he might clean out the garage but he doesn't do any of the routine stuff. If I don't empty the dishwasher, it just stays full, you know what I mean?"

Laura turned her head to look directly at Julia. She wanted to ask other questions about Greg, but she didn't know exactly what they were.

"Did Greg's father really abandon his family?" she asked.

Julia sat up. "Yes, he did. I think that's why Greg is so fanatical about being a good father."

"If his family matters so much, he's not going to fool around and take a chance on wrecking that," Laura said. "Even if his clients throw themselves at him."

"You're right. I don't really believe he would," Julia admitted.

"Then why would you even say it?"

"I suppose I was feeling jealous because you were so taken with him."

"Me?" Laura was astonished. "I only said he was a hunk."

"See?" Julia covered her ears.

Laura took hold of Julia's hands and pulled them off her ears. "Listen," she said, her heart pounding, "I think you are beautiful, too, don't you know that? And not just on the outside—on the inside, too. Greg must know he already has the best."

Nearly breathless, Laura could feel the hot flush in her cheeks. She dropped Julia's hands.

"Well, thank you," Julia said softly. "You are so sweet." She pushed her hair back with her fingers. "Hey—you want to start a business together?"

"You and me?"

"We could open a coffee shop. That's where we like to spend our time anyway. We'll only play country music and we'll call it L & J's Country Music Cafe."

"Will we get any business with a name like that?"

"Who cares? If there aren't any customers, we can just dance." Julia got up, put on a Hank Williams CD and started dancing around the room. She reached toward Laura, still sitting on the couch, and then the phone rang.

Julia answered and handed it to Laura.

"It's for you," she said. "Your hubby." She went back to dancing by herself.

"Hi, sweetheart. How's it going?" Peter asked. "What are you up to?"

"Just sitting around," Laura said, watching Julia's hair swing across her mouth. "The kids are asleep. We wore them out at the beach."

"You went to the beach? In October? A little chilly for swimming, isn't it?"

"Well, we didn't actually swim." Laura pictured Sara, wrapped in Julia's shirt. As if the memory had conjured her, Sara appeared at the bottom of the stairs, blinking in the light.

"Oops, one of the children is up," Laura told Peter. "I have to go."

"What's the matter?" Julia asked, putting her arms around her daughter. She turned back to Laura and whispered, "Didn't I tell you?"

"I can't sleep," Sara said. "I'm lonely."

"Oh, honey, how can you be lonely? You have all that company in there."

"Emily and Jessie are sleeping."

"You should be too," Julia said. "Let's go try again." She took Sara's hand and led her back upstairs.

Laura stared at the phone. She'd forgotten all about Peter's nightly call. She used to wait to hear from him every day when he was gone, but tonight it had almost seemed like an interruption. She sat in the living room, listening to Hank wailing on the stereo, and thought about Julia upstairs with all the children.

The CD was over by the time Julia reappeared.

"She's down again," she reported. "I hope it lasts this time."

Your kids are such good sleepers, Laura, you're so lucky."

"Jessie's first two years were pretty rough but then she came around. Mark's always been a good sleeper."

"I'm jealous," Julia said.

"Sara will grow out of this," Laura assured her.

"It's always worse when Greg's away but when he gets back it takes her awhile to adjust to that, too. I'll tell you, it can be hard on our sex life."

"Has she ever woken up when you and Greg were . . . ?" Laura had always worried about that, although it had never happened to her.

"Oh my, yes. Luckily we have a lock on the door so she just stands outside knocking."

Laura giggled, embarrassed and fascinated. "Who gets up to take her back to bed?"

"Depends on how far along we are. Whoever can actually stand up at that moment."

They were both giggling now, like little kids sharing a dirty joke. Laura felt all stirred up somehow, thinking of Julia and Greg in bed together. It was a feeling she liked and didn't like at the same time.

Julia walked over to the CD player. "How about Dolly Parton?" she suggested.

She put on a CD, then sat down on the couch next to Laura. She stretched out her long legs in front of her.

"Look at those poor, naked toenails," she said. "Now that sandal weather is over I keep forgetting to polish them."

"I've never polished my toenails," Laura confessed. "Just my fingernails, when I was in elementary school." She and Michelle used to trade nail polish colors in fifth grade, the final year of their friendship.

"There's nothing sexier than nice bright toenails," Julia declared. "Hey! Want to do each other's?"

"Why not?"

Julia went upstairs—quietly so as not to wake Sara—while Laura took off her shoes and socks and tucked them under the couch. The skin on her feet tingled with anticipation.

"OK, here we go." Julia came back carrying several bottles of polish and a box of cotton balls. "You first."

Laura set her feet on the coffee table; Julia knelt on the floor and tucked bits of cotton between her toes. It tickled a little and Laura shivered. Julia looked up, the ends of her hair nearly brushing the tops of Laura's feet.

"For your first time, I think it has to be bright red, don't you?" she said.

"Whatever you say."

Julia shook the bottle and twisted it open with her slender fingers. She put one hand on top of Laura's foot to steady it, then slowly painted shiny red polish on each nail as Dolly Parton's clear, childlike voice filled the room.

"Isn't that beautiful?" she said. She bent her head to blow on the wet polish. Laura shivered again.

"We could do your other foot a different color," Julia suggested.

"No, don't change a thing," Laura said softly.

Julia painted and blew on the other foot, then closed the bottle and stood up.

"Don't move yet," she instructed. "They're not quite dry. Would you like a cookie? Cup of tea? Brandy?"

"I'm fine," Laura said, but Julia went to the dining room and took a bottle of brandy and two snifters out of the china cupboard.

"Once I thought of this, I really wanted some," she explained, setting everything on the table by Laura's newly-splendid feet.

She poured two brandies, handed one to Laura, and sat down with the other, swirling the amber liquid around in the glass.

"My ex-husband—that pretentious bastard—used to drink an after-dinner brandy," she remarked. "I actually like the stuff, though," she went on. "It's probably the one good thing he introduced me to."

"Surely an after-pizza brandy isn't too pretentious," Laura said.

Julia turned her warm gaze on Laura. "The company is a whole lot better now, too."

They sat there for a while, sipping brandy and listening to the music. Then Laura set down her glass.

"Now it's your turn," she declared.

She started to kneel on the floor the way Julia had done, but Julia cried, "No, you'll wreck your polish!"

So Laura sat on the coffee table, her feet flat on the floor between it and the couch, and took Julia's foot onto her lap.

"What color would Madame like today?" she asked in a fake French accent.

Julia grinned. "How about ze orange?"

"As you weesh." Laura picked up the bottle, shook it, opened it, then stroked the polish over Julia's toenails, one at a time.

Julia let out a sigh of pleasure. "This is the life," she said, just as she had at the beach that morning.

Laura set the finished foot beside her on the coffee table and cradled the other foot in her lap. When she was done with that one, she just held it there, feeling the weight of it against her thighs.

"This has been so much fun," Julia said.

"I haven't had such a great day since I don't know when," Laura said, truthfully.

The music ended but neither of them stirred. The brandy shimmered in the snifters.

"I think Sara is finally down for the count," Julia said. "We probably should think about going to bed. You know they'll all be up at some ungodly hour in the morning."

Laura didn't want to move. She felt as if she could sit there all night. But, after another minute Julia pulled her foot out of Laura's lap, lowered both feet to the floor and stood up.

"You can have the bathroom first. I'll take the glasses to the kitchen and lock up," she said.

Laura went upstairs to Julia's bedroom. Mark was fast asleep, exactly as she had left him, a small shape in the middle of the great big bed. She fished around for the toothbrush in her overnight bag.

As she brushed her teeth, it occurred to her that Julia and Greg hadn't spoken on the phone that day at all. It was funny, how different couples lived out the details of their relationships in different ways, significant or trivial.

She changed into her pajamas—a pair of sweatpants and an old tee shirt of Peter's—and started to climb in next to Mark, then changed her mind and went back to the guest room.

The nightlight shone on the faces of the three girls on the floor. Jessie had managed to wiggle halfway out of her sleeping bag but Laura left her alone; adjusting her might disturb the others. Laura stood in the doorway, drinking in the sweetness, and suddenly Julia was there beside her. They smiled at each other in the semidarkness, then turned the smiles on their unconscious children.

CHAPTER 5

When Peter came home he was amused by Laura's painted toenails.

"What's all this?" he said, laughing, as she took off her socks.

"Julia gave me a pedicure," Laura told him. "Does it drive you wild with desire?"

He laughed again. "I'm just glad to be back," he said, reaching for her. He was always ready for sex after being away, although Laura sometimes found it hard to change gears, to adjust from single parenthood to having him back in the house.

With eager hands he pulled off her shirt and unfastened her bra. As they began to make love, Laura watched for glimpses of color on her feet. They made her feel sexier, just as Julia had promised.

The next day she told Julia that Peter had been unimpressed by the pedicure.

"Did Greg have a more satisfying reaction?" she asked.

"I don't think he even saw my feet," Julia replied. "He was too focused on other parts."

"What is it about these business trips that gets them so . . . interested?" Laura mused.

"It's probably the cable porn channel they've been watching in their hotel rooms."

"You are so bad."

Julia grinned. "Hey, maybe instead of a cafe we should open a nail salon," she said.

"Oh, right. And will we just play country music there, too?"

"Funny you should mention that . . . did you know Tammy Wynette is coming to Boston?" Julia asked.

"I wouldn't have thought many people around here would go to see her."

"You'd be surprised. They'll be coming out of the woodwork for this."

"Wouldn't that be a heartwarming sight: a whole auditorium full of Tammy Wynette fans," Laura said, dreamily.

"Well, you're going to see it for yourself," Julia declared. "I got us tickets! For your birthday."

"Oh, Julia, you didn't!" Laura clasped her hands. "You are too sweet!"

"That's me," Julia said, smugly. "I even called Peter and told him which night he has to spring you."

"How did you find out it was my birthday?" Laura asked.

"It wasn't hard," Julia said. "It's right there on the calendar of birthdays you have hanging in your kitchen."

"Well, when is yours?" Laura asked.

"I'm not telling . . . you have to find out for yourself," Julia teased. "But yours is coming right up and we are going out!"

On Laura's birthday, Peter came home with a cake. After dinner he carried it into the dining room, ablaze with candles.

"Can I help you?" Jessie asked, crowding in next to Laura.

"One, two, three . . . blow," Laura said, and they blew out the candles together.

"I have something else for you, too," Peter said. He left the room and came back with a little box. "I've been carrying this around in my coat pocket ever since Chicago."

Laura lifted the lid. Inside was a pair of earrings, green and sparkling. She emptied the box into her palm and looked down at them.

"Emeralds! They're beautiful," she said. "Thank you."

"Put them on, Mommy," Jessie directed.

Laura went into the bathroom, took out the plain gold studs that had been in her ears, and put in the emeralds. In the mirror she could see them catch the light.

Mark looked up at them as Laura was changing his diaper at bedtime. Keeping one hand on his penis, he pointed at the earrings with the other.

"Daddy?" he said.

"That's right, Daddy gave me these earrings." Laura leaned down and he put his finger gently on one of the stones.

She kissed his nose, his cheek, his forehead. The thought that he might someday turn away her kisses was almost unbearable. She was determined to get in as many as possible while he was still young and the adoration was mutual.

She read *Goodnight, Moon* and settled him in his crib. He'd always been more amenable to bedtime than his sister. Laura remembered sitting on the edge of her bed, holding her wailing infant daughter, so exhausted she was afraid she might just pitch forward onto the floor, baby and all.

After both children were tucked in, she went downstairs to find Peter loading the dishwasher.

He turned and grinned at her. "Don't get used to it or anything—this is just in honor of your birthday," he said. "Why don't you sit down and relax? Read a magazine or something."

"Oh . . . OK," she said, backing out of the kitchen.

The phone rang as she was walking past it and she picked it up.

"Happy birthday to you . . ." Julia sang.

Laura listened, smiling. "You already wished me happy birthday this morning at school," she said.

"I just wanted to say it again," Julia said. "How is it going?"

"Peter brought home a cake and Jessie blew out the candles. Now the kids are in bed and Peter's dealing with the dishes."

"Sounds good," Julia said. "Well, I won't keep you. Remember we have a date this weekend so don't use up all your celebrating energy."

"Don't worry," Laura assured her. "I'll be in the mood when the time comes."

She hung up the phone, still smiling.

"In the mood for what?" Peter asked.

"For the Tammy Wynette concert," she replied. "The country singer."

It was hard to shift her focus rapidly from Julia to Peter. It made her feel awkward somehow, as if she couldn't quite find her place. Since the night of Peter's birthday, neither she nor Julia had suggested getting them all together again.

When Saturday arrived, Laura couldn't decide what to wear. She hadn't thought so hard about her clothes for a very long time. She'd grown used to having spit-up stains on her shirt or a wet spot above her hip where a diaper had leaked or the smudge marks of grimy fingers on her pant legs. But she wanted to look really good tonight. She pulled things out of the closet, tried them on, and discarded them, until the bed was covered with a pile of rejected garments.

At last she settled on a denim skirt and a white blouse. She put on the emerald earrings and a bright pink lipstick, then considered every pair of shoes she owned. When she finally came downstairs, Jessie looked her over with an appraising eye.

"You look beautiful," she declared.

"Thank you, sweetie." Laura ran her hand over her daughter's head, loving the texture of the soft hair between her fingers.

Mark reached up to be held. Laura checked his hands for dirt before she lifted him against her crisp white shirt.

"You do look good, honey," Peter said. "How come you don't dress up like that for me?"

Laura blushed. "But . . . on your birthday . . ."

"I'm teasing," he said, putting his arms around her and Mark. Jessie wiggled in between their legs. It felt good to be surrounded by her family, but Laura was also looking forward to going out without any of them.

"Can I borrow the leather jacket?" she asked impulsively.

Peter took a step back. "Well, I don't know—that was a present from a very special lady," he said.

"I promise to be careful," she assured him.

"Just don't let any bikers pick you up." He took the jacket out of the front closet. Laura set Mark down and put it on.

It was too big but that made it feel sexier somehow, like when she used to walk around Peter's apartment in his shirt, as they rustled up a late dinner after making love. Laura stroked the smooth leather over her arms. It really was an awfully nice jacket.

The doorbell rang and Laura opened the door.

"Oh my God," she said.

Julia was wearing a long black wig that tumbled over her shoulders and curled around her face. She was so utterly transformed that just for a moment Laura wasn't certain who it was, until she heard Julia's uninhibited laugh.

"Hey, that jacket looks great on you," Julia said. Turning to Peter, she added, "You didn't get to keep it very long, did you?"

"Whatever possessed you?" Laura asked her.

"Oh, the wig? I got it for a Halloween party and I thought it deserved another outing." Julia spun around and the curls bounced against her shoulders. "Do you like it?"

Laura felt a tiny, unreasonable prick of jealousy thinking of Julia at someone else's party. "You look so different," she said.

The children came to the door and Julia grinned at them.

"Do you recognize me?" she asked.

Mark turned to Laura, his face uncertain. She picked him up.

"It's OK, that's Julia, little bean."

"Can I touch it?" Jessie asked.

Julia bent down to her height. "It's just like dress-ups," she said.

"Do moms have dress-ups?" Jessie asked, incredulous. Next to crafts, dress-ups was her favorite thing at school.

"These moms do," Peter said. "And if they don't get moving they're going to be late."

"You're right," Julia said, straightening up.

"Have her back by midnight," Peter said.

"Yes, sir." Julia grinned at him.

Peter lifted Mark out of Laura's arms. "Say 'bye' to Mommy," he said. Laura thought of all the mornings he had waved goodbye to Peter from her arms.

"Bye-bye. I love you," she said, and followed Julia out the door.

It was chilly outside and very windy. Leaves blew off trees in the dark and the two women shuffled through them as they walked to Julia's car. Laura felt nervous and excited, the way she used to feel when she went on a date with someone new. This was the first time she and Julia had been out alone together. Even that night at Julia's house, all the children had been right upstairs.

Julia parked in a garage next to the theater. "It costs an arm and a leg but I don't care," she declared. "If I walk too far in this wind, my wig might blow off."

The lobby was bright and noisy, full of people milling around. Laura hadn't been in a city crowd for a while; she was tempted to cling to Julia like a little child, afraid of getting swept away.

"Let's go to the restroom first," Julia suggested. "It'll be mobbed at intermission."

Inside the restroom, Laura felt as if they'd stepped into their own little world. As they stood in front of the mirror she looked at Julia's reflection, with that extraordinary hair, and started to laugh.

"Here, you try it," Julia said, pulling the wig off her head. A woman standing at the sink beside them gasped softly. Julia's fine blond hair, full of static electricity, swirled across her face as she held the wig out to Laura.

"Go ahead, put it on," she urged.

Laura pulled the wig over her short hair and Julia pushed the stray locks under it, her fingers darting around Laura's ears and the back of her neck.

Then they both looked at her in the mirror. It was amazing how much the wig changed her appearance. The black ringlets looked striking against her white shirt and the emerald earrings sparkled as Laura tossed her head to make the curls bounce and to hear Julia's delighted laugh.

"That's wonderful," Julia exclaimed. "You keep it, it looks much better on you."

Laura started to protest but Julia put a finger to her lips.

"I insist. You look like a country star yourself, in that denim and that glamorous hair. Come on, let's find our seats."

Julia handed their tickets to an usher in the balcony just as the lights went out. The usher turned on a flashlight and Julia grabbed Laura's hand as they made their way down the steep stairs and into their seats.

The concert was terrific. Tammy sang all her old favorites: "D-I-V-O-R-C-E," "I Don't Wanna Play House," "Stand By Your Man." After the final encore, the crowd, like an amorphous cheerful creature, moved slowly toward the exits.

"It's only eleven," Julia said when they got outside. "You want to go have a drink somewhere?"

Laura hesitated. The wind stirred the curls of the wig.

"Are you tired?" Julia asked.

It was already later than she usually went to bed, but Laura felt wide awake.

"No," she said. "Let's go out."

"There's a bar down the street, I think, that's not too sleazy," Julia said. "I've only been in this neighborhood once or twice."

They walked a few blocks through the windy night as Laura held onto the wig. Julia stopped in front of a brick building with a purple door.

"I think this is it," Julia said. "I don't remember that purple door, though. Shall we just peek inside?"

She pushed the door open. The air inside was warm and reeked of alcohol and cigarette smoke.

"It looks OK, what do you think?" she said.

It seemed a little daring to go into a strange bar, but Laura felt safe as long as she and Julia stayed together. They went inside and found two empty stools at the bar.

"What are you going to have?" Julia asked.

"After all that country music, I feel like having a beer, don't you?" Laura said.

"Good idea. And let's drink out of the bottles."

They grinned at each other, ordered two beers, and clinked the bottles together.

"Hey, Loretta," Julia said.

"Who?"

"I think I should call you Loretta tonight. That long black hair makes you look like Coal Miner's Daughter or something."

"Oh, you mean Loretta Lynn. But I really can't sing." Laura laughed.

"So, Loretta, have you noticed anything strange?" Julia leaned over and whispered. "This whole bar is full of women."

Laura looked around. It was true: the patrons, the bouncer, the bartender—they were all women. How could she not have noticed?

"Oh my gosh. Do you think . . . ?"

"I think we walked right into a gay bar," Julia said, her eyes sparkling.

Laura stared at her. "Julia, did you know about this?"

"No, really, I swear. It wasn't like this before."

A painful memory stirred in Laura's mind: the sound of Michelle's voice saying "Are you a lez or something?"

"Don't you love this?" Julia chuckled. "We went from "Stand By Your Man" to a lesbian bar. What do you suppose our husbands would say?"

"We don't have to tell them, do we?" Laura replied. She wondered what Peter would think. He might find the whole story amusing—his wife accidentally winding up in a gay bar—but she didn't really know how he'd react.

"Well, aren't you the wild thing?" Julia said, admiringly.

"It must be the wig," Laura said.

Julia was rocking on her stool to the beat of the music. She looked past Laura toward the dance floor and Laura turned to look, too. Several pairs of women were dancing in the dim, smoky light.

When Laura turned back around, another woman was talking to Julia. She had blond hair—the same color as Julia's—and rows of earrings going up both ears.

"You don't mind, do you, Loretta?" Julia asked.

"Mind what?"

But Julia had already slid off her stool and was heading toward the dance floor.

"Is that your girlfriend?" Laura heard the other woman ask. Julia laughed, but if she said anything, Laura couldn't hear it.

Laura pushed her stool back from the bar so she could see more clearly. Her vision was focused entirely on Julia, like the light at the end of a tunnel. The rest of the bar seemed obscured by darkness, with only Julia dancing, alone in a personal spotlight. Her slim hips swayed, her hair swung back and forth across her face. Laura had a strange fluttery feeling in the pit of her stomach; part of her wanted to get up and go closer but she stayed rooted, stuck to her stool, a little dizzy.

When the song was over, Julia came back, leaving the other woman on the dance floor. Her face was flushed and her intense gaze made Laura's skin feel hot, too, her color rising to match Julia's.

"Come on, Loretta," Julia said, taking her hand. "Come and dance, it's so much fun."

She pulled gently, but persistently, until Laura slipped off her stool. Her legs felt weak and she tilted toward Julia.

Julia put an arm around her, steadying her as they walked to the dance floor. The woman with all the earrings had already found a new partner. Julia kept her eyes on Laura and started to dance.

Laura hadn't danced in what seemed like a million years. She and Peter had gone dancing a few times before they were married but she couldn't remember doing it since their wedding. At her sister Christine's wedding, Laura had been pregnant with Mark, so heavy she could barely move.

It was strange to do it again after so long. There was more weight on her body now than before the children and it felt different. Her breasts actually shook and her behind felt loose and jiggly. The long hair of the wig swung behind her as she began to let herself move.

She looked up into Julia's face. Her eyes were shining and her smile lit up the room. Laura looked back down and watched Julia's pelvis tilting toward her and away, her graceful hands swinging back and forth, the undulation of her torso. It seemed as if she could see through Julia's shirt right to her skin, glistening with sweat. Laura closed her eyes and danced, feeling herself growing hot inside Peter's jacket.

After a few songs the music turned slow and sensual. Some couples on the dance floor melted toward each other, others drifted apart.

Laura and Julia stood for a moment together, panting.

"Are you out of breath?" Julia asked.

Laura nodded. She could feel rivulets of perspiration running down her neck and forehead.

Julia took her hand and threaded them back through the crowd toward the bar. More people had arrived while they were dancing; now the stools were all taken.

"Shall we have another beer?" Julia asked. She reached up to push her hair back and Laura saw the face of her watch.

"Oh my God, it's late," she said. "We'd better get home."

"Are you going to turn into a pumpkin?" Julia teased.

"I didn't think we'd be out this late . . ." The faces of Laura's sleeping children appeared in her mind and she felt suddenly guilty, as if she'd forgotten them, left them behind in a store or something and just walked out without even thinking.

Julia was looking at her stricken face. "It's OK," she said, soothingly. "We'll go now, we'll get you home."

Laura left the jacket unzipped as they walked out into the cold.
Her head was sweating underneath the wig.

She felt shy with Julia now, outside in the night air, after the
intimacy of the bar and the dancing. Julia walked beside her, not
saying anything, and Laura wondered if she was annoyed about
having to leave so abruptly.

But after they got back in the car she turned to Laura, smiling,
and said, "Wasn't it fun, being honorary lesbians?"

Laura flinched as Michelle's voice returned inside her head.
Early in sixth grade, hoping to win back Michelle's attention from
her new group of friends, Laura had invited her for a sleepover.
They used to stay at each other's houses frequently but many
weeks had gone by since the last time. Still, Michelle had accepted
the invitation, Laura had joyfully pulled out the trundle bed, and
she and Michelle lay side by side again, as Christine snored softly in
her own bed across the room. In the old days, Laura and Michelle
would climb into one bed and whisper to each other as the heat of
their bodies warmed the sheets around them. Sometimes they fell
asleep talking and woke in the morning, limbs entwined, their hair
scattered over the same pillow.

But this time—the last time—each of them lay in her own bed
and their conversation was forced and clumsy, as if they didn't really know each other. For five years they had shared every thought
and dream and worry but now there was a huge, painful distance
between them. It felt to Laura as if Michelle had run ahead without her, leaving her behind without an explanation or a backward
glance.

Laura's heart ached with wanting everything the way it used to
be. She reached out her hand to Michelle across the space between
the beds.

"Do you want to get in bed with me?" she asked. It sounded
like a plea; she felt herself blushing in the dark.

"Eww, what are you, a lez or something?" Michelle replied, her
voice tinged with a mocking laughter that felt like needles sticking

into Laura.

Tears burned her eyelids as she whispered back, "Of course not."

All the old feelings poured through Laura now as she sat in the car staring dumbly at Julia, afraid that she would cry if she tried to speak.

"Laura, are you OK?" Julia asked. "Hey, I was kidding, Laura."

"I know," Laura managed to say. "And yes . . . it was fun."

Julia backed the car out of the parking space and guided it through the garage. Laura felt embarrassed, exposed, but she tried to regain her composure, taking out her wallet as they reached the exit.

"Let me pay for the parking," she said.

"No way. This was your birthday present," Julia declared.

"You're as bad as your husband, you know," Laura said, recalling Peter's birthday dinner. It was a relief to be thinking about the husbands now.

"I know." Julia grinned at her impishly.

She was just as adamant about the wig. When she pulled up in front of Laura's house, Laura took it off and tried to give it back but Julia kept both hands stubbornly on the steering wheel.

"No, Loretta, you keep it. I don't need it—I already wore it to the party, and besides, it looks much better on you."

"No, it doesn't," Laura protested weakly, knowing it was useless.

"Keep it," Julia repeated. "It'll remind you of this evening."

They looked at each other for a moment in the quiet darkness of the car. Laura's heart felt full almost to breaking.

"Thank you," she said, finally. "Thank you for everything."

"You're totally welcome. I had such a good time tonight," Julia said, warmly. "Thank you for giving me an excuse to go out like this."

She took her hands off the wheel and, still restrained by the seatbelt, leaned toward Laura. They hugged each other awkwardly and Laura opened her door.

"Thanks again," she said into the car as she stood on the curb, the wig dangling from her hand.

"Happy birthday," Julia said.

Laura walked up to the porch, then turned and waved the wig at Julia, flapping the curls, knowing that would make her smile.

After the taillights of Julia's car had disappeared down the street Laura went inside and took off Peter's jacket. She hung it on the doorknob of the coat closet to let the smoke air out of it. She didn't know what to do with the wig; it felt strange to have brought it into the house. She finally put it on the floor of the closet and kicked it into a far corner, out of sight.

She stood still for a moment, listening to the silence in the house. Then she slipped off her shoes and tiptoed upstairs to look at her sleeping children.

CHAPTER 6

Laura lay awake for a long time, her heart racing inside her. When she finally fell asleep, she dreamed that she was sleeping in Julia's big bed, then woke abruptly, disoriented to find herself beside her husband.

What would he think if he knew his wife had been dancing in a gay bar with Julia? Would he be jealous? Should he be? What a foolish thought, she told herself—it was just an amusing accident, after all. She and Julia were nothing more than best friends.

Best friends. Laura hadn't had a best friend since losing Michelle; she hadn't imagined she would ever have one again. She lay still, listening to Peter's even breathing and thinking about Julia: her intense gaze, her infectious laugh, her supple body swaying as she danced. It was amazing how in a few short weeks this woman had become such a big part of Laura's life.

But what if some unmarked line had been crossed during their night out? Had they disrupted some crucial balance in the friendship—was the ease, the happiness, all over?

By Monday morning, Laura was eager to see Julia again but she was anxious now, too, afraid something might have changed, or been forever lost, between them. Ambivalent, she put off leaving the house and then felt guilty for making Jessie late to school.

The sky was a low canopy of gray clouds, like a dark umbrella over everything. As Laura pulled to the curb, headlights on, she saw Julia's van already parked. She urged her children out of the car and headed toward the building.

She was almost at the front door when it opened and Greg walked out. His outlandish good looks seemed out of place amidst the harried mothers and self-conscious young nannies.

Laura stopped short and Greg strode up to her, smiling his dazzling smile.

"Hello, Laura," he said. "How nice to see you again." The ordinary greeting sounded intimate and personal in his voice.

"These must be your children," he remarked.

"My daughter, Jessie, and my son, Mark," Laura introduced them. "Jessie is in the same class as your Emily."

"Oh, I know. I've heard a lot about Jessie," Greg said. "I've heard a lot about all of you."

Laura felt arrested by his attention, unable to move past him, even though Jessie was already late.

"I'm sorry the four of us haven't gotten together again," he said. "That was such an enjoyable evening."

Laura looked at him blankly.

"Your husband's birthday," he added.

"Oh yes . . . that was nice . . . and you were so generous . . ."

"Nonsense," he said. "It was a pleasure spending the evening with you."

Laura stared back dumbly; was he flirting with her? She wished Julia—or even Peter—were here.

"Come on, Mommy!" Jessie tugged at her hand and Laura allowed herself to be pulled toward the school. Greg hurried back to open the door and ushered her through with a little bow. He seemed to be mocking the deference of a doorman—or was he mocking her?

"Thank you," Laura murmured, trying not to look at him.

She delivered Jessie to her classroom and walked back slowly through the hallway, looking at the children's artwork on the walls.

"Look, Mark, there's Jessie's picture. And look over here, little bean, here's one that Emily made. Isn't that pretty?"

"Pitty," he repeated.

Laura's thoughts kept going back to Julia; despite her uncertainty that morning, now she felt deprived, missing her. Since when did Greg bring the children to school? A thought struck her: could Julia be sick?

"Let's go home and call Julia, Mr. Marco," she said.

They went outside and there was Greg, still hanging around. Laura felt ambushed, as if he'd been lying in wait.

"Hello again," she said warily.

"Hello, Laura," he said. "Hello . . . Mark, is it?" He leaned down and offered his hand but Mark just stared at him, bewildered.

"How is Julia?" Laura asked. "She isn't sick, is she?"

"Oh no." He laughed lightly. "Did you think she caught a chill carousing around in that wind on Saturday night?"

"No . . . it's just . . . I've never seen you at the school," Laura said.

"You're right. I haven't been here nearly enough," he said. "I think it's important for daddies to take the kids to school sometimes, too. After all, we're just as important as mommies."

It was an oddly emphatic assertion, but Laura remembered that Greg had been abandoned by his own father.

"It's so important for children that their families stay together, don't you think?" he went on, looking at her with his queer intensity—so unlike Julia's. Julia's gaze was warm but this was like a searchlight, or the bare bulb of an interrogation room.

"Well yes, of course, I guess so." She wasn't sure how to answer. He seemed to be looking for some particular response but she couldn't figure out what it was.

"Did you enjoy the concert?" he asked.

"It was wonderful," she said, remembering that he didn't like country music. She took a breath and added boldly, "It was sweet of Julia to take me."

"It certainly was," he said.

Nothing in the conversation was out of the ordinary but Laura felt off-balance. She didn't know what to make of this man or what, if anything, he was after. She began to walk toward her car and Greg strolled along beside her.

"I need to get home and do some laundry," she said lamely, to explain her retreat.

"Those little domestic chores—they never seem to be done, do they?" he remarked.

He stood by as she settled Mark into his car seat, her rear end poking inelegantly out of the car as she bent over to buckle the seatbelt.

She turned around to face Greg. "Well, goodbye," she said.

"Give my regards to your husband," he replied.

"OK." Laura walked around her car to the driver's side.

"I'll tell my wife you asked about her," he called after her.

Laura felt drawn toward Carole's, as if Julia might be there, but she drove home anyway, distrustful of her own impulses, and began to collect a basket of dirty clothes. She'd said she was going home to do laundry; she might as well follow through.

The phone rang as she was heading into the basement. She stopped and listened as the answering machine kicked in.

"Hi, Laura, it's Julia. . . shoot, I was hoping you'd be home. . ."

Laura set down the basket and grabbed the phone.

"Julia? Hello, I'm here!"

"Oh, good." The sound of Julia's voice washed through Laura like a wave of warmth.

"We missed you at the school this morning," Laura said.

"Greg took the girls today." Was there annoyance in Julia's voice or was Laura just projecting her own disappointment?

"I know," Laura said. "I ran into him there."

"Oh." Julia paused. "Laura . . . was he weird to you?"

"What do you mean?"

"I got the feeling he had some bee in his bonnet about our night out."

"You mean the concert?" Laura's stomach clenched uneasily.

"Well, I think it was the bar that made him so nutty," Julia said.

"You told him about the bar?" Laura was aghast. "I thought we weren't going to tell them."

"Had we decided that? I'm sorry—I remember you suggesting it but I didn't think we'd promised."

"We didn't promise, exactly," Laura admitted. She felt betrayed, although she knew better.

"You were right, though," Julia declared. "I should never have mentioned it."

"Why did you?"

"I don't know, it was stupid. I guess I thought he'd think it was funny or maybe kind of sexy or something. I didn't think he'd be weird about it."

"Julia! Does he think that we . . .?"

"Oh no, not really. I don't think so. I think the whole idea just pushed his buttons, you know what I mean?"

Laura remembered how ill at ease—almost on the defensive—she had felt with Greg that morning. It made sense now.

"I'm still not going to tell Peter," she said.

"Would Peter be weird about it?"

"I have no idea," Laura said truthfully. She tried to imagine what Peter would say. There was so little that seemed to rattle him, but after hearing about Greg's reaction, she couldn't help wondering. She wasn't even sure of her own feelings.

Julia sighed. "Men," she said. "Why do they have to be so silly? I mean, for heaven's sake, we didn't do anything wrong."

"No, we didn't." The image of Julia dancing, her shirt soaked with perspiration, filled Laura's mind.

"Besides, it wasn't Laura in that bar," Julia said. "That was Loretta, remember? With the long black hair?"

"I suppose you're right," Laura said, uncertainly.

"Good, that's all settled," Julia declared. "Do you want to meet up for coffee?"

Laura looked out at the gray sky. It could start raining any minute. She pictured how cozy it would be inside Carole's: the windows steamed over, a warm cup of coffee in her hands, Julia's radiant smile across the table.

"I'm afraid today isn't good for me," she said, listening to the words come out of her mouth as if someone else were saying them. "I have a few things I need to get done."

"Well, far be it from me to stand in the way of someone actually getting something accomplished." Julia laughed and Laura tried to join her.

"Have a wonderful, productive morning," Julia said. "I'll see you at pick-up time."

Laura stared at the quiet phone, empty of Julia. What was she thinking? What was she afraid of?

She carried the laundry downstairs and stood there watching the washer fill, nearly overcome with sadness. This was silly, she scolded herself; it wasn't as if she'd never see Julia again. But the old anxiety had been awakened: Laura knew how a friendship she'd thought was reliable could disappear and leave her clinging to nothing. After all these years, she could still feel the sting of Michelle's rejection.

Ten minutes before she really needed to leave, Laura drove back to the school. Mark poked around in the yard while she waited nervously for Julia. Denise, a mother whose daughter was in Jessie's class, approached her shyly.

"Megan has been asking me for a playdate with your Jessie," she said. "Do you think she would like to come over sometime?"

"Oh, sure, I guess so," Laura said.

"How about today? You could drop her off . . . or you could all stay and visit. It's nice to have some adult company."

Laura turned to really look at Denise. She was young—even younger than Laura's little sister—and she had big, brown eyes with long lashes that Laura pictured her batting at her handsome young husband. Not that she knew anything about Denise's husband; her imagination was getting as vivid as Julia's.

"I can get out some of Megan's old baby toys for your little boy," Denise offered.

She was perfectly nice—but she wasn't Julia.

"Thank you, but I think we already have plans for today," Laura said. "Maybe some other time . . ." she trailed off.

"Sure." Denise moved away and Laura had a feeling she wouldn't ask again.

Laura was amazed at her own capacity for lying. First she told Julia she was too busy to get together, now she was telling Denise that she had plans which didn't really exist.

Julia arrived just as the school door opened and the children poured out. Jessie ran to Laura, both hands clamped against her crotch.

"Mommy, I have to pee!" she said. "Come in with me!"

"Why didn't you go before you came outside?" Laura cast a rueful glance at Julia and followed Jessie into the school, with Mark in tow.

When they emerged again, Julia and her girls were leaving with Sandy, another mother who had two children in the school. Julia waved across the schoolyard.

"See you tomorrow!" she called.

Laura stood still, watching them go. She tried not to be annoyed with Jessie for having to go to the bathroom at just that moment—but maybe if they'd been outside she could have claimed Julia first. Julia and Sandy might have set this up in advance, but Laura had the sense of a just-missed opportunity.

She didn't want to go home and be alone, knowing that Julia was with someone else. She took the children to the library and read to Jessie while Mark played with the cars and trucks in the children's room. When Jessie insisted that she was too hungry to listen to any more books, Laura checked out a pile to take home and they headed toward the car. Outside, on the sidewalk, a blind man was approaching with a guide dog; Laura realized suddenly that it was the same dog she and Julia had seen in the coffee shop back in September.

Jessie shrank between her mother and the car but Mark shouted joyfully, "Docky!" The dog lifted its head and so did the man. He had told Laura his name . . . what was it?

It came back to her—Jim Darling—and although there was a time she might have let him pass unacknowledged, this time she spoke.

"Hello, Mr. Darling," she said. Jessie cowered behind her as Mark bounced up and down excitedly by her side.

The man stopped. "Hello?"

"I'm Laura Donovan," she said. "We met in Carole's Coffee Shop a few weeks ago. My son wanted to pet your dog, do you remember?"

"Oh yes," he said. "Hey, Mark, would you like to pet Taylor again?" he asked.

The three of them sidled toward the dog and Mark reached out his hand to touch him.

"Jessie, do you want to pet him, too?" Laura asked.

"Jessie?" Jim Darling repeated.

"My daughter is with me today," Laura explained. "She's a little afraid of dogs."

"Mommy!" Jessie whispered, shooting her mother a look of embarrassed fury, like a preview of adolescence.

"Taylor is the nicest dog you'll ever meet," Jim Darling assured her. "He loves little girls—and he can stand perfectly still."

Laura watched the conflicting expressions crossing Jessie's face. It was humiliating for her to be afraid of doing something her little brother could do; still, her fear was real and deep.

To let her off the hook, Laura said aloud, "I guess not today. But thank you, Mr. Darling."

"You're welcome," he answered, cheerfully. He tightened his grip on the dog's harness, preparing to move on.

"Wait, Mommy, I want to do it," Jessie blurted.

Jim Darling spoke to the dog and they both stood still as Jessie came toward them.

"Let him sniff your hand first," Jim Darling advised, just as he'd said to Mark in the coffee shop.

One hand holding Jessie's, Laura demonstrated with the other, holding her fingers under the dog's nose and then scratching behind its ears. Jessie imitated her, frightened and proud.

"Isn't he soft?" Laura asked her.

"Yes," Jessie agreed, her eyes shining in the misty air.

"Thank you so much, Mr. Darling," Laura said.

"No problem. I love kids," he said. "It's nice to have run into you again."

"Nice to see you, too," she said, then felt her face flushing. How could she have said see to a blind man?

He didn't seem bothered. "Take care," he said, and continued on his way.

"Bye, Taylor," Jessie called after them.

"I'm proud of you, sweet pea," Laura said as she unlocked the car.

"Why did that man's eyes look funny?" Jessie asked.

"He's blind," Laura explained. "Something is wrong with his eyes and he can't see with them. But he's lucky to have that smart dog to help him. He's called a guide dog because he can see to guide Mr. Darling."

"If I was blind, would I have a dog?"

"I guess that would be up to you. Would you want one?"

"No. I'd want a kitty," Jessie declared.

"I never heard of a seeing eye kitty," Laura replied. "But I suppose anything is possible."

For the rest of the day and into the evening, Laura couldn't stop thinking about Julia. It had been bad enough wondering all weekend if they'd overstepped their friendship in that bar, but now she was worried about Julia's husband, too. Could his reaction put the friendship at risk?

When Peter came home, Laura reheated his dinner and set his plate in front of him.

"You're awfully quiet," he remarked. "Hard day with the kids?"

Laura shrugged. "I'm just tired, I guess."

"Maybe you should go to bed," he suggested.

She did, but she was wide awake. When Peter came upstairs, she closed her eyes and waited until he fell asleep beside her. She slipped out of bed, went back downstairs, and made her way through the living room to the coat closet. It was pitch dark inside; Laura felt around on the floor for the black wig.

She put it on and turned her head to feel the curls swing across her back, remembering how it felt when she was dancing with Julia. Was that a different Laura? Or just a different version of the same one? How many different Lauras could there be, she wondered, and was there room inside her for them all?

She took the wig off, threw it deep into the closet, and went back upstairs. She tiptoed into Jessie's room and gazed at her, sleeping soundly, her covers in a heap. She was perfectly relaxed; you would never guess by looking at her that she had overcome her greatest fear that afternoon. Could Laura be as brave as her daughter? Could she manage to face down her own old fears?

The next morning Laura took Jessie to school and then sat inside her van, watching the mirror to see whether Greg or Julia arrived with their girls. Her stomach felt all fluttery inside.

When Julia pulled up behind her, Laura grabbed Mark and got out of the car. Julia was hurrying into the school but as soon as she came back out, Laura said, "Will you have coffee with me again?" the words fairly tumbling out of her mouth.

"Of course!" Julia beamed at her and relief flooded through Laura. She looked at Julia through a sudden film of tears, trying to memorize every freckle on her face.

"Laura, are you OK?" Julia asked.

Laura took a breath. "I was afraid . . ."

"Of what?" Julia prompted.

"Afraid we couldn't be friends anymore," Laura said, her emotion as raw as a teenager's.

"Of course we're friends," Julia said. "Why on earth would you think that?"

Laura swallowed. "I guess it had to do with Greg's reaction," she said.

"Greg?" Julia looked astonished.

"I was afraid things might get sticky for you because of me."

"I told you, you can't take him seriously," Julia said. "All he needed was a reassuring bout in the bedroom. We finally got around to that last night. I guess he'd been feeling a little neglected."

Laura found herself picturing the two of them: locked together, rolling around on their king-size bed. The image was so vivid it made her blush, as if she'd actually been spying on them.

"At least you know he's not getting it somewhere else," she said, pushing the picture out of her mind.

"Not necessarily. No reason he couldn't be possessive of me and sleep around, too," Julia said with a twinkle in her eye. "Hey, you want to make brownies today? When the weather starts to get cold, I always want brownies. I could eat a whole pan of them by myself."

"That sounds pretty decadent," Laura said.

"That's me. Isn't that why you love me?" Julia asked.

Laura took in a sharp breath.

"Come on, let's go." Julia was already heading toward Laura's car.

"You mean right now? Just us, without the kids?"

"Well, bring Mark, of course," Julia said. "The girls are doing plenty of fun stuff at school without us; we should get to do some fun stuff without them."

An hour later, Julia's kitchen was filled with the rich odor of chocolate.

"Shall we eat them all now or save some for the girls?" Julia asked as she lifted the pan out of the oven.

"I couldn't possibly eat that many," Laura said. "But they do smell heavenly."

"Let's all come back here after school and have brownies for lunch," Julia proposed.

Laura hesitated. "Are you sure it's really OK for me to be over here so much?"

Julia set the pan of brownies on top of the stove and pulled the oven mitts off her hands. She planted herself in front of Laura and put both hands on Laura's shoulders, her face so close that Laura almost wanted to back up.

"Now listen to me," Julia said. "We are not changing anything. We are friends for good and our life is going to go on just like always, have you got that?"

Laura nodded, speechless.

"Good." Julia relaxed her grip and let go but Laura could still feel the ghost weight of her hands. She wanted more than anything to be as certain as Julia.

"OK, we'll come eat brownies," she said.

After school, the kids tore into their sandwiches and brownies and then rushed off to the playroom. Laura and Julia lingered at the table, eating more brownies, while Julia described the afternoon she'd spent with Sandy and her children. It had been a fiasco: the children didn't get along at all. At least one of them was in tears the whole time.

"We're so lucky our kids are friends," Laura said.

"Mommy, Mark's bothering us!" Jessie wailed from the playroom.

Laura rolled her eyes. "Oh well, I guess nothing's perfect, is it?"

She got up and persuaded Mark to come back to the kitchen and play with the pans. Then she sat down across from Julia and took a deep breath.

"Are you and Sandy close friends?" she asked.

"We get along all right. Better than our children, anyway—at least we weren't yelling at each other. But we don't have a lot in common. I'm not nearly as comfortable with her as I am with you."

Warmth filled Laura and she felt her face coloring. "Well, thanks," she murmured.

After awhile Mark climbed into Laura's lap and fell asleep. The girls were still in the playroom; Laura and Julia had stopped eating brownies and now they just sat and talked, while Mark snored softly in Laura's arms.

"I have to go to the bathroom," she whispered to Julia.

"Here, slide him onto my lap," Julia offered.

Laura stood up slowly, laid him in Julia's arms, and went upstairs. There was a bathroom downstairs but Laura preferred the upstairs one. She liked looking at all the bottles on the counter: Julia's collection of shampoos and moisturizers—and her rose cologne.

When Laura returned to the kitchen, Julia was gazing tenderly at the sleeping baby.

"Do you ever think of having another one?" Laura asked.

Julia looked up. "Another child, you mean? Oh no. Two is plenty for me. I don't know how people manage having more children than hands to hold onto them with. And babies are so exhausting," she went on. "I don't think I could survive that again—it's better to borrow one you can give back."

"You're always welcome to borrow mine," Laura said. "Although he is less of a baby all the time."

She heard the front door open and her stomach jumped.

"Daddy, Daddy!" Sara and Emily squealed from the playroom.

Laura looked at Julia, alarmed in spite of herself.

"I didn't know he was coming home early," Julia said, as Greg came into the kitchen.

"You look cute with a baby on your lap," he said and bent down to give her a long, lingering kiss. Laura wondered if the kiss might be exaggerated for her benefit, but she didn't know how he typically greeted his wife.

He looked at the half-empty pan of brownies on the table.

"I see you've been busy," he remarked.

"You know all I do is sit around all day and eat junk food," Julia said, lightly. "You're just lucky there are any left for you."

It was odd watching Julia in her house with her husband—like getting a glimpse behind closed curtains.

Mark slid off Julia's lap and staggered toward Laura.

"Mommy hold," he said.

She lifted him and stood up.

"We'd better be getting home," she said.

"Want to take some brownies with you?" Julia offered.

"That's OK," Laura said. "You should let your husband have them."

"Good idea," Greg said. He certainly seemed friendly now. Laura didn't feel the disturbing undertone between them that she'd felt the day before. She truly didn't know what to make of him.

Julia went with her to the playroom to get Jessie.

"See? Everything is fine," she whispered. "He just needed a night of fabulous sex." She laughed. "Don't worry, I know how to keep him happy."

"I guess you do." Again the vision entered Laura's mind, unbidden but unmistakable, of Greg and Julia naked in bed.

"I'll see you tomorrow," Julia said.

They went back to Carole's the next day and Laura bought cranberry muffins; November always made her think about cranberries. She set one in front of Mark and he started to pick it apart. He put a cranberry in his mouth, but the sour taste surprised him and he spit it back out.

"Mommy take," he said.

"OK, little bean." She tucked it into a napkin. "Would you rather have a cracker?"

He opened up the napkin to look at the cranberry and then began to pick the others out of the muffin, one by one, and put them into the napkin, too.

"What are you doing for Thanksgiving?" Laura asked Julia.

Julia looked pained. "We'll have Greg's mother here, as always."

"You don't seem thrilled," Laura observed.

"She's really hard to be around. Greg's dad left her when the kids were little . . . oh, you know all that. I think she wants the world to pay her back, somehow—including me, who married her precious, responsible son." Julia sighed. "I used to like Thanksgiving. When I was a kid, I even liked it better than Christmas. My siblings and I weren't fighting about stupid stuff like who got more presents."

Laura smiled. "Just like our children do now, right?"

"I suppose so." Julia smiled back, wryly. "What about you?" she asked. "What are you and Peter doing?"

"My sister's coming." Now it was Laura's turn to sigh.

Julia looked at her closely. "What's wrong with her?"

"I'm not too wild about her husband," Laura confided.

"She's married?"

"Yes. And trying like mad to get pregnant."

"Why don't you like her husband?"

"He's just so full of himself," Laura said. "Christine really wants to be a mother but I think Dan just wants to acquire another possession. He doesn't understand a thing about children."

Julia looked amused; she was enjoying Laura's little tirade. "You think he doesn't deserve your little sister?"

"I think she could have done better," Laura said.

"Do you think you found the perfect man for yourself?" Julia asked.

"Gosh, I don't know," Laura said, a little taken aback. "Peter was certainly the most reliable man I'd ever been with." It didn't sound very exciting when she put it that way. "What about you?"

"Greg was the best in bed of any man I'd been with," Julia declared.

"So he has the talent to back up those good looks?" Laura teased. She wouldn't have brought up Greg's appearance but she felt provoked, somehow.

"Definitely. He knows how to use it all." Julia leaned toward her. "So how is Peter in the sack?"

Laura felt herself blushing. "He's fine . . ."

"Fine?" Julia demanded. "Just 'fine'? My best friend needs to be getting better sex than just 'fine.'" She was smiling impishly and her eyes sparkled.

"OK, OK, he's good in bed," Laura amended.

"You're not just saying that to shut me up?"

"Why are you so interested in my sex life?" Laura asked.

Julia looked surprised. "I'm interested in everything about your life . . . and in everyone's sex life," she added, gaily. "Sex is fascinating, don't you think?"

"Well, yes . . . I guess so," Laura conceded.

"Laura, am I embarrassing you?" Julia asked. "Come on, I know you're fascinated, too."

"All right, I admit it." Laura put up her hands in mock surrender.

"That's my girl." Julia beamed. "You don't ever have to be embarrassed with me. After all, we're bosom buddies, right?" She threw back her shoulders, thrusting her breasts out in front of her, and batted her eyes comically.

Laura cracked up, just as Julia intended.

CHAPTER 7

Laura stood in the kitchen, trying to decide what to do first. Mark was upstairs, napping, and Peter and Jessie had left for the airport to pick up Christine. Laura rinsed a bowl of cranberries and set them to boil and burst in a pot on the stove. She was chopping onions, tears running down her face, when the telephone rang. She wiped her hands on her apron and answered it.

"Laura, she's driving me nuts!" Julia wailed.

"What's going on?" Laura tucked the phone against her shoulder. She'd pay the price with a stiff neck later but she wanted to keep working while the coast was clear.

"It's just the way she puts things," Julia said. "I feel like I'm under a microscope. I bought a fresh turkey and organic vegetables—like I always do—and she says, 'Oh, organic? You must be feeling rich.'"

"Well, organic food is more expensive," Laura pointed out.

"She just resents the choices I have. She's critical of everything I buy. I think she's proud of Greg for being a good provider but also jealous because her husband wasn't."

"Don't let her get under your skin," Laura advised. "She'll only be there for a few days."

Julia groaned. "It feels like forever."

"Maybe we should trade houses," Laura suggested. "You take my brother-in-law and I'll take your mother-in-law."

"The brother-in-law and the mother-in-law . . . give us a rest from both those pests," Julia sang. "That sounds like a country song, Loretta."

Laura laughed.

"Let's ship them both off to a desert island," Julia said. "Better yet: let's book a getaway for the two of us and we'll just leave it all behind."

Laura stood still, her knife poised over a stalk of celery. "That sounds lovely," she murmured. "But I think I hear Mark waking up."

"OK, I'll let you go," Julia said. "Thanks for letting me vent."

Laura was sitting at the kitchen table with Mark on her lap, both of them eating graham crackers, when the others arrived. She got up and went to the front door; Christine and Dan were taking off their coats and Peter was hanging them in the closet.

"Welcome to New England," Laura said.

"At least it's a short flight from New York," Dan said. "The airports are just insane."

"It's so good to see you," Christine said. "The kids look so much older."

"Jessie's whole shape has changed," Dan put in. "She doesn't have that big diaper butt anymore."

Laura couldn't imagine what to say to that.

"My kid'll be toilet trained by the time he can walk," Dan boasted.

Christine shot him a look, her lips pressed together, and shook her head sharply.

"We'll remember you said that," Peter said jovially. Laura couldn't possibly have sounded so friendly.

"Can I have a tour of the house?" Christine was trying to change the subject.

"Of course."

They left the men downstairs with the children and Laura led

Christine upstairs.

"You look all moved in," Christine said.

"Think of all the practice we've had," Laura said. "But I hope we won't be moving again for a long time."

"Do you think you'll ever live in New York?" Christine asked.

"I hope not!" Laura said. "It's a great city," she added hastily. "It just doesn't seem like a great place to raise children."

"An awful lot of people do," Christine pointed out. "I was thinking it would be fun to have cousins growing up together."

Laura peered into her face, afraid to ask. Christine had been trying for so long.

Christine met her eyes and burst out, "Laura, I'm pregnant!"

"That's wonderful!"

"It's still very early," Christine said. "I'm a little afraid to even say it out loud."

"But you couldn't hold out on your own sister!"

That felt a little forced; it wasn't as if they had been terribly close. But Laura was truly happy for her. Christine wanted so much to have a child and Laura was confident that she would be a good mother—though she had doubts about Dan's potential as a father.

"Have you told Mom and Dad?" she asked.

"I'm not ready to announce it yet. Except for Dan, you're the only person who knows."

"I'm honored," Laura said.

She bent down to pick up a toy car in the doorway of Mark's room; when she stood up again, Christine was standing by the crib, gazing into it.

"Mark will probably be out of that crib by the time your baby is born," Laura said. "Would you like to have it?"

"Thank you," Christine whispered, her eyes shining.

The guest room in Laura's last house had been downstairs, apart from the other bedrooms, but in this house it was right next to Mark's room. Laura made her ritual round of the children's rooms before going to bed and as she stood beside the crib, her hand resting on the rail, she could hear Dan and Christine moving around.

Mark stirred and reached for Laura; she picked him up and sat down in the rocking chair. He fell asleep again almost immediately but she stayed there for a while, feeling his weight in her arms, looking down into his peaceful face. She didn't register the new noises from the guest room until they became unmistakably the sounds of lovemaking: her sister's soft little gasps and the deeper groans of her husband.

Laura stopped rocking and froze, simultaneously horrified and fascinated—and grateful that Mark was asleep. She remembered Julia giggling as she described her daughter knocking at the bedroom door after she and Greg had locked it. She'd probably get a kick out of this: eavesdropping on someone else's sex life.

Laura put Mark in the crib, and tiptoed out of his room and back to hers. Peter was sitting in bed, reading. He looked up when she came in, holding his place in the book with his finger.

"They're having sex," she reported, though she hadn't intended to tell him. "I could hear them from Mark's room."

"That sounds like a good idea." Peter grinned at her.

"I wasn't trying to listen," she said, then added, "Christine is pregnant."

"That's great," he said. "They should have as much sex as they can before the baby gets in the way."

Laura climbed into bed beside him.

"How do you think they'll be as parents?" she asked.

"I expect they'll do the best they can, just like the rest of us," he said. He was so reasonable; sometimes Laura wished he would be a little catty, so she wouldn't feel like she was the only one.

Peter closed his book and set it aside.

"Did you feel inspired?" he asked.

"Oh gosh, no," she said. "I'd be much too self-conscious with guests in the house."

"Too bad." He picked up his book again.

Laura lay down and closed her eyes, thinking of Christine lying under her husband. It was strange to think of her little sister having sex. She tried to put the picture out of her mind but it was replaced abruptly by the image of Julia, astride her husband in the middle of their huge bed, her hair swinging across her mouth. Laura opened her eyes and glanced over at Peter, calmly reading beside her.

Thanksgiving Day was cold and gray. The children watched the Macy's Parade on television, with its huge, airborne balloons. Mark seemed a little daunted by the cartoon figures, lumbering weirdly at the ends of their tethers, dwarfing the people below them. He climbed into the safety of Laura's lap.

"Have you ever gone to that parade?" she asked Christine.

"Sure, we checked it out," Dan answered.

"It's easier to see it on TV than in person," Christine added.

"Do the balloons seem scary up close—are there lots of frightened children?" Laura asked.

"Nah, kids in New York are tougher than that," Dan said.

Once again, Laura didn't know how to respond to him.

After the parade, she went to the kitchen to work on dinner while the men watched football. As she stood at the sink, washing lettuce, Christine came in to join her.

"The turkey smells fantastic," she remarked. "Do you need any help?"

"No, just keep me company," Laura said. "When will you tell Mom about the baby?"

"Not until after the amnio," Christine said.

Laura turned around, her hands dripping. "You're going to have amnio? You're only 31."

"My doctor said our insurance would cover it as long as I'm over 30. We want to be sure everything's OK."

"What if it's not?" Laura asked, before she could stop herself. She suspected it was Dan who wanted the test, to make sure he didn't wind up with a defective product.

Christine's eyes filled. "I don't know," she whispered. "We've been trying for so long . . ."

Laura remembered a woman she'd known at work, years ago, who found out her baby had Down's syndrome and ended the pregnancy. It wasn't until Laura was pregnant herself that she began to fathom the heartbreak of that decision. The thought of facing such a choice was so appalling that she had decided not to have the test at all.

"Heaven will send us the child we're supposed to have," she'd said to Peter, in an uncharacteristic declaration of faith, and the ever-optimistic Peter had agreed.

She dried her hands and hugged Christine.

"I'm sure everything will be fine," she said.

By dinnertime, the table was loaded with food. Laura thought about the way animals eat as much as they can in November, before going into hibernation.

"Everything is delicious," Christine said.

"Truly a dinner to be thankful for," Dan proclaimed, pompously. "And just think: next year we'll have another mouth to feed."

Laura glanced at Christine; she was pressing her finger hard against her pursed lips but Dan didn't seem to notice.

"You're going to have a little cousin—what do you think about that?" he asked Jessie.

"What?" Jessie's mouth was stained with cranberries, her lips as pink as if she were wearing lipstick.

"Auntie Chris is going to have a baby," he told her.

"I thought we weren't going to announce this yet," Christine protested.

"Oops—I guess I'm in the doghouse now!" he said.

Laura could never tell if Christine found Dan as annoying as she did. It would be awful to be that irritated with your own spouse all the time. She wondered if Dan's child would idolize him, the way Jessie and Mark seemed to idolize their father. Mothers like Laura stayed home, tending to scrapes and bruises and hurt feelings, but daddies came into the house from out in the wide world like heroes.

"Let's talk about something else," Christine suggested. "Jessie, what's your favorite thing about school?"

"I'm in preschool," Jessie corrected, primly.

"OK, then, what do you like best about preschool?"

"Arts and crafts," Jessie said. "And dress-ups. And all my friends."

"Do you have a best friend?" Christine asked.

Jessie paused, savoring the adult attention focused on her.

"My best friend is Emily," she announced.

Laura smiled. She was pleased to hear that, although she knew it might have been just the first name that popped into Jessie's mind.

"You certainly see a lot of her," Peter remarked. He turned to Christine. "Emily's mom and Laura are practically joined at the hip these days."

Laura looked at him, startled, her smile fading. Was that meant as a crack? His face revealed nothing; he looked unruffled as ever.

"When I was your age, my best friend was Ellen," Christine said to Jessie.

Jessie gazed at her solemnly. The thought of a grown up person ever having been her age didn't seem to be quite credible to her. Lately she'd taken to asking Laura for stories of her childhood, as she wrestled with the exotic notion that her mother had actually had a childhood.

She turned to Laura. "Who was your best friend, Mommy?"

Laura hesitated. She didn't even like to think about Michelle.

"I know—it was Michelle Dooley, right?" Christine volunteered.

"I guess so," Laura mumbled. "It was a long time ago."

"Is there any more of that stuffing left?" Dan asked.

Dan and Christine left the next day; Dan was planning to go to work on Saturday.

"It's the best time to get things done," he said. "The office is empty and I can concentrate."

Peter nodded in agreement. No doubt he'd be working over the weekend, too.

"Can you all come to the airport to say goodbye?" Christine asked.

It dawned on Laura that Christine just wanted a little more of her time.

"Sure," she said. She and Christine climbed into the back of the van, behind the children.

"We're going to Mom and Dad's for Christmas this year," Christine said. "Why don't you come too?"

"Oh, I don't know . . . that house is so small . . ."

"Will you at least think about it?" Christine coaxed. "Pretty please? It will be much more fun if you're there." She hadn't pursued Laura's company like this since they were children.

"I'll talk to Peter," Laura promised.

At the airport, Laura got out of the car to give her sister a hug.

"I'm so happy for you," she whispered. "You're going to love being a mom."

Dan walked up to them, his arms opened wide. "How about a hug for me?"

Christine stepped back and Laura winced as Dan squeezed her in a stiff embrace.

As soon as she got home, Laura put Mark down for a nap and went to her bedroom to call Julia.

Greg answered the phone. "Oh, hi, Laura," he said. "Did you have a nice holiday with your family?"

"Yes. How about you?" Laura responded dutifully.

"It was great," he said. "My wife is a fabulous cook." He paused. "Did you want to speak to her?"

"Yes, please, if she's not too busy." Laura waited, the phone pressed tightly against her ear.

"Hello?"

At the sound of Julia's voice, Laura felt the muscles in her body relax.

"How are you doing?' she asked.

"Surviving, I guess." Julia sighed. "At least she's leaving on Saturday—she wants to avoid the Sunday traffic."

"Christine and Dan already left," Laura said.

"Aren't you lucky! How did it go?"

"Well, it was nice to see Christine. Guess what? She's finally pregnant!"

"Really? Does she know how good she's had it up to now?" Julia asked. "Footloose and fancy free . . ."

"Oh, come on, Julia, you adore your girls."

"I suppose I do. I'm sure your sister will be an adoring mom, too. Is her husband just as proud as a peacock?"

"That's just about exactly what he's like," Laura said. "He's completely clueless about kids."

"Weren't we all that way once?" Julia asked.

"Not like he is," Laura declared. "I just hope Christine won't feel like she's in this all alone."

"And where is your husband? Will he be home all weekend?" Julia asked.

"I doubt it. Probably just for the rest of today. Right now he's playing Candyland with Jessie."

"Be sure to enjoy him, now that your guests are gone," Julia instructed. "Greg's mother takes him over when she's here—the only time I can get his attention is in the bedroom after she finally goes to bed."

"Can you make love when she's in the house?" Laura asked. "I get too self-conscious when we have company."

"Oh, not me. I like knowing she's down the hall imagining what I'm doing with her son—and knowing she's not too happy about it, either."

"My, my, how passive aggressive." Laura laughed.

"More aggressive than passive, if you want the truth."

A picture of Julia, naked and sweaty on top of Greg's big body, flashed into Laura's mind. Embarrassed, she tried to push the image away.

"Well, I should let you go," she said. "If you feel like escaping, you know you can always come here."

"Oh sure, and inhibit your sex life? Besides, I wouldn't want to leave my girls in her clutches—I just hope they don't turn out like her."

"They won't," Laura said. "They'll be wonderful strong women, just like their mother."

"You always say the right thing," Julia said.

CHAPTER 8

Sunday afternoon, Laura went out to pick up a few groceries. It was already dark; the sky was like deep-blue velvet, pierced with a few early stars. On her way home she drove past Julia's house, propelled by an impulse to see lights on behind the curtains and know that Julia was inside.

The entire house was festooned with colored Christmas lights: outlining the windows, draped over the shrubs, hanging in clusters from the roof of the porch. It was a gaudier display than she ever would have imagined of Julia.

The next morning, at the nursery school, Laura remarked on the lights.

Julia snorted. "That's one of Greg's little passions, decorating for Christmas. One of these years he's going to fall out a window stringing all those lights I think it's his way of letting off steam after his mother's visit."

"What's your way?" Laura asked.

"I left him home with the kids and went shopping."

"For Christmas?"

"Goodness, no, for me! I'm not one of those people who takes care of Christmas this far in advance."

"It's only a month away," Laura reminded her.

Julia stuck out her tongue. "I also scheduled a massage for this morning," she said. "But I can cancel it, if you want."

"No, you should go," Laura told her. "I'm sure you can use one."

"I knew you'd understand," Julia said. "Bring the kids over later and I'll show you what I bought."

That afternoon, Laura followed Julia up to her bedroom. A shopping bag stood open on the floor; Julia pulled a green chenille sweater out of it.

"Isn't it gorgeous? It was on sale, too."

"It's a great color for you," Laura said.

"Feel how soft it is." Julia held the sweater up against herself. Laura hesitated, then stroked the fluffy, kitten-soft chenille over Julia's belly.

"There's something else in the bag that I'm not going to show you," Julia teased.

Laura pictured Julia's long legs emerging from a black lace teddy as Greg looked on appreciatively.

"I know I said I don't shop early for Christmas but I found something perfect for you," Julia said, looking immensely pleased with herself.

"For me?"

"We'll see if I can wait until Christmas to give it to you. Whenever I get a present for someone I want to give it to them right away," Julia confessed.

"Some people do their Christmas shopping all through the year and just hold onto it until December," Laura pointed out.

"Oh, that's sick," Julia declared. "I could never be that patient. Hey, what are you doing for Christmas?"

"We're going to Indiana to see my parents," Laura said. "Christine talked me into it—she'll be there, too." When she'd mentioned the idea to Peter, he'd been all for it.

"Christmas in the heartland," Julia mused. "Will that be fun?"

"I doubt it," Laura answered truthfully. "We're really not a close family."

"Now you get to spend two holidays in a row with your favorite brother-in-law." Julia grinned.

"Can we have a snack?" Emily hollered up the stairs.

"Sure. We'll be right there."

Mark was at the bottom of the stairs, considering whether to tackle them, when Laura and Julia came down.

"I keep meaning to dig out our stairway gate," Julia remarked.

"You guys are done with baby gates and stuff," Laura protested. "You don't have to modify your house for us."

"But you're practically part of the family," Julia said.

In the kitchen the girls bickered with each other, arguing about whether to have pretzels or graham crackers.

"Here's the deal," Julia announced. "We're all having popsicles."

"Popsicles!" The girls were so pleased they stopped quarreling.

Laura looked at Julia with admiration. Who else had popsicles in the freezer at the end of November?

"What flavor would you like?" Julia asked her.

"Me? Oh . . . grape, I guess."

"That's my favorite, too," Julia said.

One December morning Julia's girls didn't come to school. Laura waited, but when they still hadn't arrived after half an hour she went home and called.

"Both the girls are sick," Julia said. Her voice sounded gravelly and tired.

"Oh, Julia. Do you need anything?"

"No, we're OK. But thanks . . . you're sweet," Julia said.

Emily and Sara were out of school all week. Laura called Julia again to offer help but she declined.

"I don't want you to come near the house," she said. "I don't want you to get this."

When the girls finally recovered and returned to school, Laura and Julia went back to Carole's. Julia looked exhausted.

"Were you sick, too?" Laura asked. "You should have let me

help you."

"Greg took care of us. I wasn't really sick, anyway, just tired." Julia pushed her cup away. "It's odd, I seem to have lost my taste for coffee."

"That is weird," Laura agreed.

"It's so good to see you again," Julia said. "I wish you weren't going away for Christmas. We could have had you over for Christmas dinner."

"Really?" Laura couldn't quite picture that.

"Can we at least get together for New Year's? I already called Mrs. Nixon to babysit—let's see if she'll take all the kids so all the grown-ups can go have some fun."

"Do you think it's a good idea, getting the four of us together?" Laura asked. "I think your husband might prefer to have you all to himself."

"He'll have me the rest of the year, for heaven's sake," Julia said blithely. "New Year's Eve is supposed to be a party." She winked at Laura. "Maybe we can get our husbands to be friends with each other."

Laura tried to think of someone Peter would consider a friend. He got along with everyone but, now that she thought about it, he didn't seem to actually have friends.

"I'll talk to Mrs. Nixon," Julia said, as if everything were decided. "We won't stay out late, just long enough to have a glass of champagne at midnight."

Julia had planned a frantic rush of Christmas shopping the next morning so Laura decided to stay home and make cookies. She gave Mark his own bowl and a spoon; he was happily stirring up little white clouds of flour when the phone rang. It was the nursery school.

"Jessie's feeling sick," the secretary said. "Her teacher thinks you should come and get her."

Laura's stomach lurched. Of all the challenges of motherhood so far, sickness was the worst. She couldn't help remembering Sammy Langford, her classmate in second grade, who went home sick from school one day and never came back. What had looked like a harmless virus turned out to be a raging staph infection and by the time he got to the hospital it was too late. Rationally, Laura knew that tragedy was a rare, terrible stroke of fate, but she found herself fighting panic whenever one of her own children got sick.

She put the eggs back in the refrigerator, gathered up Mark— his overalls covered with flour—and drove quickly to the nursery school.

Jessie was slumped in a chair in the office. When she saw Laura she feebly opened her arms; Laura picked her up and Jessie's head drooped onto her shoulder.

"What's wrong with her?" Laura asked, her heart pounding with alarm.

"She's probably getting this flu that's been going around," the secretary said.

"She was fine this morning," Laura said.

"I believe it. This seems to come on very quickly."

Through the shoulder of her coat, Laura could feel the heat of Jessie's forehead. She took Mark's hand and he walked beside her as she carried Jessie to the car.

She called the pediatrician's office as soon as they got home and a nurse came to the phone, her voice calm and reassuring.

"We've been seeing a lot of this," she said. "The flu seems to be getting an early start this year."

"What should I do?" Laura asked. She felt a brief, wild desire to abdicate from motherhood, to put all the anxiety and responsibility into someone else's hands. Then she looked at Jessie, flopped down across the couch, and knew she would never give her up or let someone else take over. No one could love her child as deeply, as irrevocably, as she did.

"Give her Tylenol to reduce the fever," the nurse advised. "Make sure she drinks plenty of liquids, let her rest as much as she wants. There's not much else you can do except wait for it to run its course. If you have any concerns, call us any time."

"Thank you," Laura said. She hung up the phone, regretful to give up that comforting, confident voice in her ear.

"Mommy, my head hurts," Jessie moaned.

Laura kissed her. "Let's try some Tylenol."

She took the bottle from the bathroom cabinet and poured the medicine into a spoon. It was thick, with a sweet, grapey smell.

"It hurts my throat," Jessie said, crying.

Laura fought back tears of her own. "Just finish it, sweet pea. It's good for you."

As soon as that was over she called Julia.

"Jessie's sick," she reported.

"I'm sorry." Julia's voice was so full of sympathy it brought a lump to Laura's throat.

"I hate it when they're sick," she whispered.

"Me too," Julia said. "Is it the same thing my girls had? I hope they didn't give it to her."

"The doctor's office said there was a lot of it going around."

Jessie stirred and tried to sit up. "Mommy, I'm thirsty," she said, weakly.

"I have to go," Laura said to Julia.

"Give her a kiss for me," Julia answered.

Laura poured a little water into Jessie's favorite cup and carried it into the living room. Jessie took a sip and handed the cup back to Laura.

"It hurts," she said.

"Would you like to watch TV?" Laura offered.

Jessie nodded. It was strange to see her so subdued. She lay back on the couch, her face turned toward the television. Laura spread an afghan over her.

Mark came in and sat on the floor, watching the TV, as Jessie fell asleep behind him. Her curled legs under the afghan looked small and vulnerable and her cheeks were flushed; her lashes lay against them, fluttering occasionally. Laura sat beside her, holding her hot, limp hand. She looked down at Mark's tousled head and wondered if he was next.

They stayed there all afternoon. Laura completely lost track of time until the front door opened and Peter walked in.

"Da!" Mark exclaimed.

"What's going on?" Peter asked.

"Jessie's sick," Laura told him. "I had to pick her up early from school."

"Why didn't you call me?" Peter crossed the room and laid his palm on Jessie's forehead. She stirred and drew a ragged breath.

"Did you call the doctor?" Peter asked.

"They said to give her Tylenol and keep an eye on her."

"I can't believe you didn't call me," he said again.

"I guess I didn't think there was anything you could do."

It hadn't even occurred to her to call Peter. If Jessie had been in a real crisis, of course she would have called him, but just looking after a sick child was part of being a mother at home. It seemed more natural to call Julia—another mother at home—than Peter, Jessie's father, off in his faraway workplace.

"How is she doing?" Peter asked.

"Mostly she's been sleeping. I tried to get her to drink some juice."

"I guess she won't be very hungry," Peter said. "Feed a cold, starve a fever, isn't that what they say? Well, how about some food for the rest of us?"

Laura had forgotten about dinner; her stomach was so roiled with anxiety it made her queasy even to think about eating.

"I'm sorry, I didn't make anything," she said.

"How about Chinese takeout?" Peter suggested.

"I'm really not hungry," Laura said. "Just order what you want. Mark likes the scallion pancake."

Laura stayed by Jessie, watching her sleep, while Peter and Mark ate dinner. She finally roused herself from the couch to put Mark to bed; once he was settled, she came downstairs and heated up some plain rice in the microwave.

Peter sat down with her as she tried to eat.

"Looks like we'll have to cancel the trip to Indiana," he said. "Christine will be disappointed."

Laura looked up. "I know. But we couldn't risk making her sick," she said.

"No. Or your father, either," Peter added.

Jessie's sleep that night was fitful and even when she was sleeping Laura would jerk awake, compelled to go check on her. Peter, on the other hand, slept straight through the night. His lack of concern was reassuring in a way, but Laura was also a little annoyed that he could rest so peacefully while she was on high alert.

She called her mother the next day.

"We can't come for Christmas after all," she told her. "Jessie's sick."

"Oh, honey, I'm so sorry," her mother said. "We were sure looking forward to it. We never get to see your kids."

"Maybe you should come visit us once in a while," Laura said. She thought she'd given up suggesting that, but she was worn down by exhaustion.

"Your father can't travel, honey. And I can't leave him here alone."

"I know." Laura said. After she hung up the phone, she kissed Jessie's hot forehead and called Christine.

"The flu . . . how awful," Christine said. "That would be all I need—I already feel like throwing up half the time. Did you have morning sickness when you were pregnant?"

"I guess I did," Laura said. "I remember I couldn't stand the smell of broccoli."

"Don't even mention the word." Christine groaned.

There were some things about pregnancy that you really couldn't talk about with anyone who hadn't been there, too. Even the most understanding man couldn't imagine how it felt to watch your own body swell into a whole new shape and to know that your organs were literally moving around inside you to make room for another person.

"Did your doctor tell you to eat something before you get up?" she asked Christine.

"I don't think I could."

"Try it," Laura urged. "Keep a box of crackers next to your bed."

"Thanks," Christine said. "I'll miss you at Christmas."

Jessie's fever was up again that evening. She called out from her bed and Laura could tell her temperature was high before she even touched her, by the dull look in her eyes, the restlessness in her limbs.

Peter appeared in the bedroom doorway, outlined in the light from the hall.

"Her fever's higher," Laura told him. "It's too soon for more Tylenol . . . I hate this," she said, close to tears.

"Remember, the fever is a sign her body's fighting back," Peter said.

"I still hate it. I don't want her to have to be fighting at all."

"Children do get sick," he said. "That's part of the package."

He was trying to comfort her but Laura felt suddenly furious. He was always on such an even keel—sometimes it made her feel crazy.

"Whatever," she muttered, stepping past him to get a bowl of lukewarm water and a washcloth.

She held the damp cloth against Jessie's hot skin and sang to her in the dark room until she fell asleep. Then she brought the couch cushions upstairs and made herself a little bed on the floor next to Jessie. It wasn't very comfortable but she wasn't likely to sleep well anyway.

The week dragged on, with Jessie's fever rising at night and falling in the morning. Each day Laura moved her downstairs to the couch and each night she carried her back up to her bed. For several days, Jessie never even got dressed; Laura helped her change into fresh pajamas every morning. Laura was bone tired, in a way she hadn't been since having a newborn in the house. She moved through the days in a blur of laundry, glasses of juice, doses of Tylenol, reading stories until her voice gave out. Julia called often to check on her and Laura clung to the sound of her voice, describing the ordinary events of the day. Peter came and went, as always, but Julia had become Laura's link to the outside world.

At last one night Laura bent over Jessie to feel her forehead and it was not warm. She looked at her watch and counted back: the last dose of Tylenol was seven hours ago. She went back to her own room and lay down next to Peter.

"Jessie's fever broke," she told him, and then fell asleep in a real bed for the first time in days. The next morning Jessie climbed into bed beside her. Laura kissed her forehead; it was still cool.

"Can I have breakfast, Mommy?" Jessie asked.

Laura struggled to sit up. She felt as if she could sleep for a week.

"Of course, sweet pea."

Peter got out of bed. "I'll get her breakfast," he said. "You go back to sleep."

"You have to go to work," Laura protested.

"No, I don't. It's Saturday."

"It is?"

Laura flopped back onto the mattress and lay there, calculating: if this was Saturday there were only a few days left until Christmas and she still hadn't found a present for Julia.

She got dressed and went downstairs. Peter and Jessie were sitting at the table. Jessie's face was pale, with deep shadows under her eyes, and her hair was a tangle around her head—it hadn't been brushed all week. But she was eating without having to be coaxed.

"Couldn't sleep?" Peter asked.

"No. Where's Mark?"

"I guess he's still asleep. Smart kid."

Laura felt an intuitive twinge of misgiving but she made herself dismiss it.

"I have a little more shopping to do," she said. "Can you stay with the kids while I go out?"

"Don't you want some breakfast?"

"I'll pick up a coffee somewhere," Laura said. She kissed Jessie, savoring the sensation of the smooth, cool cheek under her lips.

"Take it easy, sweet pea," she said. "I'll be back soon."

Carole's was doing a brisk Saturday morning business. All the tables were full; Laura bought coffee and a scone and ate them standing up. Lots of people were already out and about this morning, each one attending to his or her own particular mission. Laura recalled riding through the Indiana countryside in the back seat of her parents' car, looking out at the farmhouses standing alone in the fields and thinking about how each house was home to someone whose life spun around them in a web that was supremely important to them, but had nothing to do with her.

She left the cafe and walked down the block to a little shop which had beautiful, fragile things in the window: hand-painted china, stained glass, delicate filigree jewelry. She'd always wanted to look inside but she had never dared to take a child into such a place. Now she wandered slowly through the store, laying her hands on a woven silk placemat, lifting a hand-etched wine glass to admire the way the light shone through it.

Suddenly she heard a sound, like distant fairy bells. A set of wind chimes hung above the cashier's counter and the cashier had just reached up to run her finger across them. The chimes were silver, with ceramic beads and tiny seashells strung among them. They were lovely to look at but their sound was downright magical. Laura bought them without even asking the price, imagining the pleasure in Julia's face when she heard them.

She drove back home and as soon as she opened the door Jessie ran to her. It was thrilling to see her move so fast after days of lying motionless.

"Hi, sweet pea. How are you feeling?"

"Fine. Mommy, Mark threw up."

"What?" Dread twisted in Laura's stomach.

"Mark threw up. In his high chair," Jessie elaborated.

Laura flung her package onto the couch. "Peter? Mark?" she called.

"They're in the bathroom," Jessie told her.

Mark was lying on the bathroom rug and Peter was bent over him with a wet cloth, cleaning his face.

Mark looked up at her. "Mama," he said sadly.

"Oh, sweet boy." She knelt beside him and kissed his forehead. He was unmistakably hot. Laura's eyes filled with tears.

"Looks like it's his turn now," Peter said.

"I was hoping he would escape," Laura said, struggling past the lump in her throat.

Mark's belly contracted and he started to cry. "Mama," he wailed, beginning to throw up again. Laura turned him quickly so he wouldn't choke.

"Jesus," Peter said. "I thought he was done."

Jessie came to the doorway and stood there, watching, as Mark threw up on the rug. Laura pulled a towel off one of the racks and covered her clothes with it, then cuddled him close in her lap as he cried.

"It's OK, baby," she murmured, smoothing his hair against his sweaty head. His face looked like Jessie's a few days ago: eyes glazed and sunken, cheeks flushed with fever.

"I'll take the rug down to the washer," Peter said.

Jessie followed him out of the bathroom and Laura sat alone on the floor with Mark. His crying subsided and he lay against her, heavy and hot. The smell of vomit surrounded them. Tears stung Laura's eyes as she tried to remember how it felt to be outside in the fresh air, lighthearted, the gift for Julia tucked under her arm. That had only been a few minutes ago but already it seemed like someone else's life.

CHAPTER 9

Laura moved like a zombie through the days before Christmas. She took Mark to the doctor only to hear what she knew already: he had the flu and she would just have to wait it out.

During the day, she held him most of the time. At night she couldn't get close enough to him in his crib so she brought him to bed with her. His feverish body heated up the bed; Peter camped out in the guest room while Laura lay facing the baby all night, her arm stretched out above his head, and woke up stiff and sore.

Julia kept up her daily calls, a constant, dependable source of sympathy.

"You poor thing. At least both of mine were down at once. You have to go through it all again."

"Will this ever be over?" Laura groaned.

"Oh yes. Trust me. You will come out the other side."

Now that she was well, Jessie was starting to get bored. School was closed for vacation so she had neither that diversion nor the attention of her distracted mother.

"Why are you always holding Mark?" she asked Laura petulantly. "Why can't you play with me?"

"Mark is sick, honey. He feels just as bad as you did last week."

"I feel fine, Mommy." It was as if she had no memory; she experienced life only in the present.

"I feel sorry for her," Laura told Julia. "But right now Mark needs me more."

"How about if I bring her here to play with my girls?" Julia offered.

Laura hesitated. "I don't want her to bring any of our germs to your house."

"Don't worry about it—we've already had those germs. I'll come and pick her up."

As soon as she saw Julia standing on the porch, Laura felt envious of Jessie for getting to leave with her.

"Have fun, sweet pea," she said. "Come back soon." She could as well have been saying it to Julia.

"We'll be back in a few hours," Julia assured her, stroking Mark's hair as he lay cradled in Laura's arms.

"Maybe you should take a nap with him," she suggested. "Take advantage of the peace and quiet."

Laura peered at her; Julia looked a little tired herself.

"Are you really up to having all three girls?" Laura asked.

"It'll be easy," Julia assured her. "They entertain each other."

When she brought Jessie home, Julia offered to bring over Christmas dinner the next day but Laura had already asked Peter to pick up a chicken to roast—and a pie, if he wanted one. Her own appetite had disappeared again as soon as Mark got sick.

Except for the stockings hanging from the mantel, Christmas Eve seemed like just another evening with a sick child; there was nothing festive about the way Laura was feeling. She didn't remember her own mother being so paralyzed when she or Christine got sick. She'd kept up her usual routines and didn't seem overly anxious—but Laura didn't really know how she'd felt inside. Her mother never spoke about little Sammy's death: had it not affected her as much as Laura? Did she just handle anxiety differently? Or was that tragedy too upsetting even to mention?

"Did your mother worry when you got sick?" she asked Peter,

as he spread the presents under the tree.

"Oh yes," he said. "I was her only child, her prized possession. She was terrified something would happen to me."

On Christmas morning, Jessie tore through her packages, merrily flinging paper and ribbons everywhere as Mark watched her from Laura's lap. He didn't seem interested in participating; perhaps he thought the holiday was just for Jessie.

Laura finally handed him to Peter and went to the kitchen to stuff the chicken and put it in the oven. She didn't attempt anything elaborate, but an appealing odor of roasting meat began to fill the house.

Julia stopped by in the middle of the morning.

"I brought you some cookies," she said. "I don't usually do much baking—except for brownies, because they're so easy. But I always make Christmas cookies."

Julia's face was rosy with cold. Laura drank in the sight of her; it seemed like forever since they'd sat down together and talked.

"Won't you come in?" she asked.

"I can't. I promised I'd only be gone for a few minutes," Julia said.

She turned to leave. "Oh, shoot!" she burst out. "I forgot to bring your present. See—that's what happens when I don't give presents right away."

"I have one for you but it's not wrapped yet," Laura said.

"Let's get together after Christmas, as soon as all the sickness is over."

After seeing Julia, Laura's mood lifted, as if she had taken in some of Julia's good cheer. Mark rallied to eat a little roast chicken, which was so encouraging to Laura that she ate some, too. Then she tried one of Julia's cookies—a jolly gingerbread man with M&M buttons and a frosting smile. It was delicious.

Christine called that evening.

"How was Christmas? How's Jessie?" she asked.

"Jessie's fine. Now Mark is sick," Laura said.

"You're kidding!"

"I wish. That's the trouble with having more than one child."

"I'm the one who's feeling sick around here," Christine said, her voice low. "I could barely eat Christmas dinner."

"I'm sorry."

Mark sighed and shifted in Laura's lap. He didn't seem quite as warm as other evenings.

"I heard news about someone you know," Christine went on.

"Oh? Who?"

"Michelle Dooley."

"Really? What about her?" Michelle's family had moved away after eighth grade; by then the friendship had been over for some time and Laura had never heard from her again.

"I heard she was a total tramp in her new high school," Christine reported.

It had seemed as if Michelle might be headed down that road, even in junior high. Laura remembered watching her sashay down the hall at school with her friends, tossing her hair and wiggling her newly-rounded hips. It was funny, in a way, to be talking about her now as if it still mattered, as if the whole friendship weren't in the distant past. Back then Christine had been too young to be included but now she was enjoying having some juicy gossip, after all these years.

"She got pregnant, too. Twice. Two different guys."

"Who did you hear this from?" Laura asked.

"Donna Crimmins. She knows everything about everybody."

Laura searched her memory but she couldn't remember Donna. She must have been one of Christine's friends.

"Did she have the babies?" Laura asked. If Michelle had a baby in high school, that child would already be grown up.

"No, she had abortions."

"Two of them?"

"That's right. Amazing, huh?"

"Did she ever have children?"

"I don't know," Christine said. "Donna didn't mention it."

Laura looked down at Mark's sleeping face. She and Michelle

used to talk about growing up and being mothers. They'd discussed how many children they would have, whether they'd rather have boys or girls, which names they liked or hated. It was strange to think they might have motherhood in common now—and that Laura didn't actually know, one way or the other.

"Well, thanks for the report, Christine," she said. "How was Christmas with the family?" She couldn't imagine Dan and her parents having anything in common.

"It would have been more fun with some kids around," Christine said. "Christmas really is for kids, don't you think?"

"By next Christmas, you'll have one of your own," Laura reminded her.

Mark was definitely recovering. When Julia called the next evening, Laura told her that both children were finally sleeping, fever-free, in their own beds.

"I'd like to just forget about this Christmas," she confessed.

"There'll be happier ones in the future," Julia said. "Now you can look forward to New Year's Eve."

"How was your Christmas?" Laura asked.

"Emily got the My Little Pony that Sara wanted, so they had to have a fight about that."

"Didn't Sara get one?"

"Of course she did—how dumb do you think I am?" Julia snorted. "But it was the wrong color."

"I guess that's one advantage to having a girl and a boy," Laura remarked. "They like different toys."

"Just be grateful you didn't get a truck-loving girl," Julia said.

The next day Julia and her girls came over and spent the whole afternoon. It was so good to be able to sit across from Julia at the kitchen table again, talking and munching on Julia's gingerbread cookies. Laura felt as if her life had been suspended for the last few weeks and now at last it was back in motion.

That evening she ordered a pizza for the kids and cooked pork chops—Peter's favorite—in a wine and mushroom sauce the children would have hated. By the time Peter got home, the children had finished eating and a delicious fragrance of simmering pork and basmati rice was wafting through the house.

"That smells wonderful," he said, coming into the kitchen.

Laura turned to greet him. She'd put on a frilly apron, like a perfect TV wife. It felt a bit like a performance, costume and all, but she was enjoying it; it was such a relief to be out from under the weight of all the illness in the house.

"Would you like a drink, dear?" she asked.

Peter looked amused. "What are you offering?"

"How about a Scotch and soda?"

"Sure."

Laura hunted in the cupboard for the bottle, dusted it off and poured Scotch into a tumbler full of ice, admiring the way it flowed over the ice cubes. She poured in soda water and watched it foam invitingly, then carried the drink to Peter in the living room.

"Won't you join me?" he asked.

"I thought I'd put the children to bed first."

"Great idea," he agreed.

After going through the bedtime routine, Laura turned on the baby monitor in Mark's room and came downstairs, feeling more cheerful than she had in a long time.

Peter was on the telephone; he looked tense—his brow furrowed, his jaw clenched in a hard line.

"I'll go right away," he was saying. "Tomorrow morning."

"Who was that?" Laura asked, when he hung up.

"Work," he said. "The VP in Chicago just collapsed and died. Massive heart attack."

"How awful!" Laura said.

"He was only in his forties," Peter went on. "He'd just started working in that office—he hadn't even been there a week. I need to get out there—I'm sure everything is in complete chaos."

"Oh, Peter, do you have to?"

His blue eyes held hers with their steady, honest gaze.

"They're counting on me," he said.

Laura sighed inwardly. Would things ever settle down in her own household?

Peter went into his study to call the airlines; by the time he came back, the rice was cold and the pork was overdone. Laura had thought they might have wine with dinner, but the mood was disrupted now. Peter sat across the table, brooding and preoccupied, and she felt deserted, alone, as if he were already gone to Chicago.

Standing in the children's rooms that night, Laura laid her hand gratefully on each cool forehead. At least they were well before Peter had to leave town. She hadn't realized how much she'd counted on his reliable presence throughout the recent siege.

Peter left very early in the morning; it was just like so many other times he'd gone away on business, except for his somber mood. When he called from his hotel that night, he sounded drained.

"It's just tragic," he said. "There are photos of his family all over his desk. The man had five children, Laura."

"Oh my God."

"His wife is a basket case—I don't know how she's going to cope with this."

"You met his wife?"

"She came to collect his stuff." Peter's voice was so subdued she could barely hear him.

Laura had never seen him at a loss, without a smooth answer or a quick solution. Perhaps he'd felt this way when his parents died, but that was before Laura knew him; all she'd ever seen was confidence and self-control.

He heaved a long, sorrowful sigh.

"I should still make it back for New Year's," he said. "There's only so much I can do here now. And I have to get back to Boston—we're starting a big new project in January."

"The kids are eager to see their Daddy again," Laura said.

"I'll be home soon."

The morning of New Year's Eve, Laura woke feeling leaden,

as if her body were heavier than usual. She could barely move her limbs and it felt as if a giant vise were crushing her skull.

Jessie was sitting on the edge of the bed.

"Time to get up, Mommy," she announced.

Laura looked at the clock, struggling to keep her eyelids open. It was past 7:30—Jessie had probably been awake for a while.

"Mama!" Mark was calling from his crib.

Laura hauled herself upright in bed. The thought of actually standing up was appalling and a groan escaped her.

"Mommy, what's wrong?" Jessie stared at her.

"It's OK, honey," Laura said. It was an effort even to speak.

She put her feet on the floor and stood up slowly. Taking one careful step at a time, she made her way along the hallway to Mark's room, bracing herself against the wall.

Jessie followed, wide-eyed, and Laura tried to keep talking, to reassure her. She knew she must look like a stranger, moving in that weird way. But it was hard to think of things to say and when Laura talked she realized how sore her throat was. How could this be happening?

"Mama?" Mark's tone changed when he saw her and his eyes grew round.

She concentrated fiercely on lifting him out of the crib without dropping him. The muscles in her arms felt weak, atrophied, as she sank into the rocking chair. Mark climbed out of her lap and started walking around; it looked so effortless for him. Laura slumped in the chair and stared at her children. How was she going to take care of them? Thank God Peter would be home in a few hours.

Somehow she mustered strength she didn't think she had and got Mark's diaper changed and the children downstairs. Once they were settled at the breakfast table, with their cereal in front of them, Laura sat too, and put her head down on her folded arms.

The telephone rang. Wasn't it too early for anyone to be calling?

"Hi, honey." It was Peter.

"Where are you?" Laura asked, alarmed. He was supposed to be on a flight back to Boston.

"I'm still in my hotel," he said. "I think I have the flu."

Tears started running silently down Laura's cheeks. She turned toward the window, away from the children, so they wouldn't see that she was crying.

"I hope I didn't expose anyone here," Peter said. "I'd feel terrible if that poor widow came down with the flu."

"I know." Laura couldn't manage to say more.

"I couldn't bear to get on a plane," he said. "I just have to sleep."

Laura felt adrift, abandoned.

"Let me know when you'll be coming home," she said, numbly.

She hung up the phone and wiped her eyes. When she turned around, Mark was dropping Cheerios over the side of his high chair tray and watching each one hit the floor, completely absorbed. She heard the unmistakable sound of his diaper filling again.

Laura sat there thinking about picking up all the Cheerios before they got stepped on, wiping off Mark's hands and face, changing his diaper again. It seemed like a staggering amount of labor.

She put her hands on the table to push herself up out of her chair and then the phone rang again. She grabbed it desperately.

"Peter?"

"No, it's me," Julia said, her voice full of energy. "I'm calling about tonight—it's New Year's Eve, remember? I have something amazing to tell you when I see you."

"Peter isn't coming back today," Laura said..

"Why not? Did his flight get cancelled?"

"No. He got sick."

"Laura, are you OK?"

"No." It was a relief to admit it. "I'm sick, too. I feel awful."

"Oh, Laura." Julia paused a moment, thinking. "I'm coming over there."

"What about the girls?"

"Greg took the day off. He can stay with them. I'll be right over," Julia said again.

When she hung up, Laura's heart felt lighter, but her body was still weighed down, moving in slow motion. She was just lifting Mark out of the high chair when the doorbell rang.

And then Julia was coming into the house, taking off her coat, greeting the children, and hurrying into the kitchen.

"I want you to go back to bed this minute," she said. "I'll take care of everything."

"Mark needs a diaper . . ." Laura protested.

"I can change a diaper," Julia assured her. "Go back to bed."

"They're on the changing table in his room," Laura said. "But don't change him up there, he's too wiggly . . ."

"Go to bed," Julia said again, and flashed her incredible smile. "We'll be fine."

"Thank you," Laura whispered. She made her way cautiously up the stairs and fell back into bed.

Sometime in the afternoon, Jessie tiptoed in to check on her. Laura woke to see her standing next to the bed.

"How are you doing, sweet pea?" she asked.

"Julia made soup for lunch."

"Did you like it?" Jessie had never eaten soup.

"The noodles were slippery," Jessie said.

Laura closed her eyes again as Jessie padded back out of the room.

Later, Julia peeked in from the doorway.

"Would you like something to eat?" she asked, softly. "I could heat up some chicken soup and bring it to you."

Laura shook her head; she hadn't the slightest desire to eat anything. Her stomach felt shut down, her muscles ached, her throat hurt, her eyelids felt tight and hot over her eyes.

Julia came closer. "How about just a drink of something?" she suggested. "You look like you're running a fever."

Laura's mouth was dry. She lifted a hand to her forehead; both her hand and her face were hot.

Julia brought her Tylenol and a glass of water, then sat on the edge of the bed while Laura sipped. It hurt to swallow but the water was cool and Laura was thirsty.

Julia took the empty glass.

"Would you like to change your shirt?" she asked. "That one is pretty sweaty."

"OK," Laura said, obedient as a child.

Julia went to the dresser and found a drawer full of tee shirts. She brought one back to the bed. Laura tugged weakly at the sleeve of the shirt she was wearing.

"Let me help you," Julia said.

Laura lifted her arms and Julia pulled the shirt off. Laura vaguely became aware that Julia was looking at her—that she was sitting there, bare-breasted, in front of Julia. Julia's glance flickered downward and she took a breath as if she were going to say something, but she didn't. She looked at Laura's face and smiled at her, then pulled the fresh tee shirt over her head.

In the evening, Julia brought the children in to say goodnight. They were both snugly dressed in their flannel pajamas.

"I'll just stay the night," Julia said. "I can sleep in the guest room."

"But . . ."

"Hush. You rest," Julia said. "Sweet dreams."

She guided the children back out of the bedroom and closed the door.

In the middle of the night, Laura woke. Someone was standing beside the bed, in the dark. Laura could smell roses and she felt a cool hand laid gently across her feverish forehead. She kept her eyes closed.

"Happy New Year," Julia whispered.

CHAPTER 10

In the morning, Laura opened her eyes, disoriented, and then remembered that Julia was in the house. When she got up to go to the bathroom she could hear Jessie's voice down the hall. She peeked into her room; Jessie was sitting on her bed, having a lively conversation with Julia. They both looked up.

"How's the patient?" Julia asked.

"I think she's going to live," Laura replied. She still felt weak but standing up didn't seem impossible anymore.

"Would you like coffee?" she offered, eager to be a host now, not a burden.

"Are you going to have some?" Julia asked.

"I don't feel quite ready for coffee yet," Laura admitted. "I'd better start with something easier on the tummy. But I'll be happy to make some for you."

"How about herbal tea for both of us?" Julia suggested.

"Mama!" Mark called and they both went to his room.

"Yesterday I could hardly lift him out of his crib," Laura said.

"Let me get him." Julia picked him up and handed him to Laura, then sat down abruptly on the rocking chair.

"Are you all right?" Laura asked.

"I'm fine." Julia seemed annoyed with herself. "Listen, I should call home and check in. Will you be OK for a few minutes?"

"We'll go start breakfast," Laura said. "You can use the phone in my bedroom."

She steered the kids to the kitchen and poured Cheerios for them. As she reached for the milk, she heard Julia's voice upstairs rising sharply. Was she having an argument with Greg? Maybe he was mad about missing New Year's Eve with his wife.

Julia came downstairs a few minutes later, glowering.

"That man: he's trying to order me to come home," she fumed.

"He probably misses you," Laura said.

"No, he just wants to tell me what to do," Julia insisted. "He thinks he's the boss or something. I don't know if I can stand his protectiveness getting even worse."

"Why would it get worse?" Laura asked, recalling her encounter with Greg after he heard that she and Julia had been in a gay bar.

"Just because I'm pregnant," Julia burst out, furiously.

"You're what?!"

"You see? This isn't the way I was going to tell you," Julia stormed. "This is all his fault."

Laura pointed to a chair. "Sit down," she said.

Julia sat and Laura did, too. The children watched with great interest.

"Are you really pregnant?" Laura asked her.

Julia sighed. "Yes, I really am."

"Why didn't you tell me?"

"I was going to tell you at our New Year's Eve party. I just found out for sure yesterday."

Laura shook her head. She was still weak and she hadn't eaten anything yesterday—could she be hearing things?

Julia reached across the table and put her hand over Laura's.

"I really was going to tell you," she said. "But you were so sick when I got here it didn't seem like the right time."

"You shouldn't even be around me," Laura said. "I was worried about my sister catching this and here I am, exposing you . . ."

"Stop it," Julia ordered. "You're as bad as he is."

"Well, maybe he's right, Julia."

"I'm fine! My girls had the flu, remember? I didn't get sick then."

"But you never know. I thought I was safe and then it got me."

"Laura, stop. I'm fine. You needed help."

Laura's eyes filled with tears. "But you're pregnant," she whispered, acutely aware of the pressure of Julia's hand on top of hers.

"Mommy, what's pregnant?" Jessie asked. "Is it bad?"

"No, honey. It means that Julia has a new baby growing inside her." Saying it gave Laura a strange fluttery feeling in the pit of her stomach.

"You really should go home," she said to Julia. "I know you don't want to hear this, but I think your husband is right. You need to protect yourself and your baby."

Julia stuck out her tongue at Laura and the children giggled.

"I feel much better today," Laura assured her. I can manage—really. Now go home."

It was hard to watch Julia go but Laura found she was able to make it through the day without her, as long as she moved slowly. She planted Jessie in front of a nice long video and took a nap when Mark did. All day, the thought floated in and out of her consciousness: Julia is pregnant.

Peter called to say he'd be flying home the next day. He was feeling better too, after sleeping for two days straight in his hotel room.

"How are you doing?" he asked. "How was New Year's Eve?"

"I slept through it," she said.

"You didn't go out with Greg and Julia?"

"No. I wasn't feeling too great myself." That had to be the understatement of the year.

"I bet you just didn't want to go without me," Peter teased.

"Well, actually I had the flu, too," Laura admitted.

"You're kidding!" Peter exclaimed. "I'm sorry I wasn't there for you."

"You couldn't have done anything. You were sick, too. Julia came over to help me."

There was just the slightest pause on the other end of the line—or had she imagined it?

"That's good," Peter said. "Well, I'll be back tomorrow."

"Have a safe trip," she said.

School finally started again on Monday. It felt like forever since Laura had driven there.

Julia arrived late, as usual; Laura waited in the car with Mark while Julia took her girls into the building. When she came back out, she walked straight to Laura's van, and climbed into the passenger seat.

"What a relief," she said.

Laura laughed.

"What are you waiting for?" Julia asked her. "Aren't we going to our old hangout?"

"Carole's?"

"Where else? That place with the purple door?" Julia grinned mischievously.

"Do you really want coffee?" Laura asked.

"No, I'll probably have mint tea. But I love sitting in there with you."

When they arrived, Laura persuaded Julia to sit down with Mark.

"I'll get the drinks," she said. "Would you like a scone, too?"

"I'm not really hungry," Julia said.

Laura bought tea and coffee, and a scone for Mark. She sat down and took a sip of coffee, feeling the warmth of it slide down through her body.

"How are you doing?" she asked Julia.

"Mornings aren't great but as long as I stay away from coffee, I'm OK," Julia said.

"It's probably just as well. Caffeine isn't good for the baby,"

Laura pointed out.

"I should have known something was up when I stopped wanting coffee. I just never imagined I could be pregnant again."

"How far along are you?" Laura asked.

"A couple of months."

Laura leaned forward. She knew the answer but she had to ask. "Julia, were you trying?"

"Are you joking? I told you: two is enough—sometimes two is more than enough. I was just incredibly stupid and careless."

"Did you forget your Pill?" Laura asked.

"I don't take the Pill. I tried it once and it made me feel horrible. I have a diaphragm."

"You forgot to use it?" Laura was incredulous.

"Well, sometimes. Don't you ever get carried away?"

"That's why I take the Pill," Laura replied, but the truth was that she'd never been so swept up by passion that she could have forgotten about birth control. She'd started using the Pill because men liked it better—then they didn't have to think about anything.

"You're lucky," Julia said. "You won't get yourself knocked up like some foolish teenager." She let out a long, low sigh.

"I thought I was done with this," she said. "I don't want to do it all again."

Laura looked up; Julia's eyes were swimming with tears. Laura had never seen her cry.

"It'll be OK," she said, leaning across the table to take Julia's hand. "You just have to get used to the idea."

Julia brushed her other hand across her eyes.

"Let's not talk about it right now," she said. "All I need is to embarrass myself in public. How are you doing? All recovered now?"

"All recovered, thanks to my angel of mercy," Laura said.

"How is Peter? Did you have a romantic reunion, with great sex?"

Laura covered Mark's ears in mock horror.

"Actually, we were both still worn out from the flu," she said, truthfully.

Julia looked disappointed. "Well . . . soon, I hope."

Sometimes it seemed as if Julia were more interested in Laura's sex life than Laura was.

Laura wanted to talk about the pregnancy, to ask a hundred questions. But she held herself back; she had to let Julia control that subject.

There was a burst of cold air as the door opened.

"Docky!" Mark shouted. Jim Darling and his guide dog were coming in.

"He's with a new woman this time," Julia whispered. "The guy sure gets around."

"Maybe he just has a lot of female friends," Laura suggested.

"Come on—have you forgotten the shared biscotti? That looked awfully intimate to me."

Jim Darling's new companion ordered two coffees to go. Mark slid off his chair and headed after them.

"Mark, wait," Laura cried, but he was already out of reach.

"Docky," he said, making a beeline for the dog.

"I'm sorry, Mr. Darling," Laura said. "My son is crazy about your dog."

He smiled into the space ahead of him. "I remember," he said. "Is your daughter with you, too?"

"Not this time." Laura said, touched that he would ask.

"You know what, Mark? I'm crazy about this dog, too," he said.

Mark was already petting the dog. Laura glanced back at Julia; she was watching with amusement.

"Thank you, Mr. Darling," Laura said. "Come on, Mark, Mr. Darling has to leave."

When she returned to the table, Julia remarked, "That one didn't look too thrilled, either. You and your adorable little boy just scare them to death."

"You have an overactive imagination," Laura chided, affectionately.

"Guess what? Now I'm hungry," Julia said. "I'm going to get a muffin—do you want anything?"

"No, thanks." Laura picked up a piece of Mark's crumbled scone and popped it into her mouth. "I'll just share with Mark."

She watched Julia walk to the counter and back again. She couldn't imagine that slim body swollen with pregnancy.

"I only lose my appetite in the morning," Julia said, as she unwrapped the muffin. "I guess some people feel sick all day."

"My sister felt terrible all through Christmas," Laura said. "She had a hard time hiding her pregnancy from my parents because she felt so queasy all the time."

"Why was she hiding it?"

"She doesn't want to tell them until she gets her amnio results."

"You mean, in case she decides to get rid of it?"

Laura drew back, startled to hear it said so bluntly.

"Something like that," she conceded.

"Would she really do it?" Julia asked.

"I don't think she knows. I just hope her husband doesn't try to push her into it."

Julia gave a bitter little laugh. "I wish my husband would do that to me," she said.

"Julia!"

"I don't want another baby. You know that. Greg knows that. I'm done with babyhood."

Laura was speechless. She stared at Julia, who was looking down at the table, folding her muffin paper over and over until it was a tiny wad under her fingers. When she looked up her eyes were wet again.

"Do you think I'm awful?" she whispered.

"No, of course not." Laura glanced at Mark. "But could you really . . . ?"

"Have an abortion?" Julia mouthed the word without a sound.

Laura nodded.

"Before I had children, I think I could have," Julia said. "But after going through childbirth—seeing an actual baby come out of your body—it's like a miracle. Didn't you think so?" A single tear spilled over and rolled down her cheek.

Laura smiled at her. "Yes, I did," she said. "Now let's get out of here."

Outside, in the crisp winter air, Julia took Mark's hand and turned to Laura.

"Let's go to my house and I'll give you your Christmas present," she suggested.

"OK. But we have to stop at my house on the way." Fortunately, Laura had finally managed to wrap Julia's present during the weekend. She dashed inside and retrieved it from her underwear drawer, then came back and set the package in Julia's lap.

"No peeking," she said. Julia shook the box, but Laura had padded the chimes with tissue paper so they made no sound.

Mark toddled off to the playroom in Julia's house; he seemed to feel perfectly at home.

Julia disappeared upstairs and returned a moment later, holding a package covered with ornate bows and long curls of ribbon.

"You go first," Laura urged. "I want to admire mine a little longer."

Julia sat down on the couch with her present and tore off the wrapping paper. Inside was a children's shoe box.

"I don't think these are my size," she joked, lifting the lid.

She pulled away the tissue paper and took out the wind chimes. As she held them, Laura reached out and ran her finger across them. There was that magical sound, right here in Julia's living room.

Julia drew in her breath. "Oh, Laura, they're beautiful!"

Mark came back from the playroom to investigate. Julia lowered the chimes so he could ring them.

"What a peaceful sound," Julia said. "That's a good sound for the little one to hear, from inside."

She and Laura looked at each other, wordless, for a long moment.

"Now open yours," Julia said.

Laura took a last look at the beautiful package before she opened it. Inside was a long, wide scarf, woven of the softest imaginable chenille, in shades of blue, turquoise and lavender.

"You are so sweet," she said, lifting it to hold against her cheek.

"It was made by a local weaver," Julia said. "Isn't it just softer than a bunny's bottom?"

Laura laughed. "It's wonderful," she said. "I love it."

She held out the scarf, admiring the colors, then laid it in her lap and stroked it. She would never have bought something so lovely for herself.

Jessie's birthday was in the middle of January and for the first time Laura planned a real birthday party for her, with other children her age. They invited a few friends from school, including Emily and Sara. Jessie wanted all the girls to wear dress-up clothes; she pulled out the collection of used cocktail dresses Laura had bought for her at thrift stores. Laura helped her spread them all out in the living room.

"It's looking mighty girly in here," Peter remarked. "Maybe I should rescue my son; we can go to the playground and toss a ball around or something." He grinned.

"That's a great idea," Laura said. Julia had already offered to stay and help with the party.

"We'll be back for cake," Peter assured her.

Jessie's friends were delighted to put on the fancy dresses. Laura played a CD of "The Nutcracker Suite" and she and Julia sat on the couch and watched the little girls dance around the living room. They were starting to look like five-year-olds now: their legs were stretching out, their hands were losing their pudginess, their heads no longer seemed too big for their bodies. They were already moving toward the bloom of young womanhood.

Laura sighed and Julia turned to look at her.

"I was just thinking: in less than ten years all these girls are going to have their periods," Laura said.

"I suppose you're right," Julia said. "Unless they're already pregnant."

"Don't even say it." Laura thought of Michelle, pregnant twice as a teenager.

"What about the girls who get anorexic in junior high and can't gain enough weight to have periods?" Julia went on.

"You're in quite the mood," Laura said.

"All I'm saying is you never know," Julia insisted. "Life is full of unexpected turns."

Laura looked into her face. "You're still not really reconciled to this, are you?" she asked, quietly.

Julia didn't answer but her eyes filled. She let out a long sigh and leaned her head on Laura's shoulder. Laura closed her eyes, feeling the weight of it there.

The front door opened and both women sat up straight as Peter came in, carrying Mark and a big bunch of balloons.

"Is it time for cake yet?" he asked.

The little girls followed him into the dining room where he proceeded to tie a balloon to each chair, letting the rest of them bump up gently against the ceiling.

"That looks like a real party," Julia declared approvingly.

Laura went to the kitchen to put candles on the cake while Peter and Julia kept the children amused in the dining room. She couldn't imagine being left alone with Julia's husband to entertain a group of kids but it didn't seem to be awkward for Peter and Julia.

She carried the cake into the dining room and Jessie's face glowed with pleasure.

"Don't forget to make a wish," Julia said.

After devouring cake and ice cream, the children went back to the living room and Jessie opened her presents, which included two new Barbie dolls. She was busily taking off their clothes as the other mothers arrived to pick up their children.

"We should go home, too," Julia said. "But first I need to get something out of the car."

She came back carrying a huge package.

"Oh, Julia, what have you done?" Laura reproached her.

Julia gave the package to Jessie who ripped off the paper as fast as she could. Inside was a full-scale Barbie Dream House.

Jessie's mouth dropped open, like a cartoon of surprise. "Thank you, thank you!" she said, clasping her hands in grateful joy.

"You certainly had her number," Laura said to Julia. "She'll be your friend for life."

"I hope so," Julia said. "Come on, girls, it's time to go home."

Laura opened the door and stepped onto the porch with them.

"Thank you for helping with the party," she said. "The Barbie house really was too much, though."

"I can't help it—it must be the surging hormones," Julia said.

"Well, you made Jessie's day. Mine, too."

Julia started down the steps.

"Look, it's snowing!" she exclaimed.

Laura opened the door and called inside, "Hey, kids, it's snowing!"

Peter came out with Mark and then Jessie appeared behind them, a naked Barbie doll clutched in each hand.

"Better hurry home," Peter said teasingly to Julia. "You might get snowbound."

She smiled at him and Laura felt an odd pang of something like jealousy. Julia opened the door of her van for the girls to climb in, then turned around.

"You two go put your feet up and have a drink," she instructed. "That's the best part of the birthday party, you know."

Peter laughed and took the children inside. Laura stood on the porch, shivering.

"Thanks again," she said.

"You're welcome. And don't forget about that drink. I'll be enjoying it vicariously."

The reality hit Laura again: Julia was pregnant. She hugged herself in the cold and watched Julia get in her van and drive away through the falling snow.

Julia called the next morning.

"Let's go to the beach," she proposed. The snowfall had ended during the night, leaving just enough to whiten the ground and soften the bare tree branches. School was closed for Martin Luther King Day, but Peter and Greg had both gone to work.

Laura laughed. "The beach in January? Well, why not?"

"It'll be too cold for a picnic this time," Julia admitted.

"Why don't you come here for lunch first?" Laura suggested. "We can go to the beach in the afternoon."

The next day, after peanut butter and jelly sandwiches, the six of them climbed into Laura's van.

"Bring your new scarf," Julia advised. "It will probably be windy."

Laura hesitated.

"Come to think of it," Julia went on, "I haven't seen you wearing it. Don't you like it?"

"I love it," Laura said earnestly. "It's so beautiful I feel like I should save it for a special occasion."

"Don't be silly. You're supposed to wear it. Besides, what's more special than a trip to the beach with your best friend?"

The parking lot at the beach was completely deserted.

"People don't realize how beautiful the beach is in the winter," Julia remarked.

They walked along the path through the dunes; Laura carried Mark and Julia walked beside her, carrying a beach blanket and the diaper bag. As the path opened onto the beach, the wind grew stronger, blowing in from the sea and whipping up whitecaps.

"If we lie down flat on the blanket, we might get out of the wind," Julia said.

They wrestled the billowing beach blanket onto the sand and then they all sat down, huddled together like a party of pioneers braving the elements. Laura fingered the soft cloth of her scarf and stared out over the ocean. It looked angry and powerful to-day—and unbearably cold. She tried to imagine crossing it in a wooden boat.

"I would never have survived," she said aloud.

"What?" Julia asked.

"Crossing the ocean in a little boat like the Mayflower. I'd have been one of the people who died during the voyage."

Julia gazed at her. "I'll bet you'd have been stronger than you think. I can picture you as a midwife, helping some poor mother give birth at sea while the boat pitched through the waves."

"You have to be kidding," Laura said.

"No, I mean it."

Laura never had this kind of conversation with Peter. If she said something out of the blue like that to him he'd probably just let it go unanswered. He wouldn't jump in and continue the train of thought like Julia. Men were so practical; Laura didn't believe they allowed themselves such flights of imagination, wondering about things that would never happen.

"Mommy, I'm cold," Sara said plaintively.

"Shall we take a fast walk along the beach to warm up?" Julia suggested.

They got up and started down the beach, moving clumsily through the sand in their shoes and socks.

"My nose is freezing," Jessie declared.

"Mine too," said Emily.

Sara was shivering, Mark was all hunched over—they were a miserable little troop of waifs, like something out of a Dickens novel.

Laura stopped. "Julia, look at them," she said. "I think we should give up and take these children home to some hot choco-late, don't you?"

"You're right. I'm freezing too," Julia admitted.

The car was still alone in the parking lot.

"I'm glad you're driving," Julia said. "I'm sleepy all the time now."

She leaned back in her seat and before they were back to the highway her eyes were closed. Laura glanced over at her; she had a strand of hair across her face, her mouth slightly open. Laura felt tender and protective, like when she watched her children sleeping.

The car began drifting toward the side of the road and Laura forced herself to stop looking at Julia. She focused on the road ahead, listening to the children's conversation behind her.

"We're going to get a baby," Emily declared.

"I know that," Jessie replied confidently

"My mommy is growing a baby in her tummy," Emily went on. "When it's all done I'll get a new sister."

"Or a brother," Jessie said. "You'll find out when it pops out of her tummy."

"How?"

"You have to see if it has a peanuts," Jessie asserted. "If it has a peanuts then it's a brother."

Laura smiled out the windshield, sorry that Julia wasn't hearing this, too. Of course, if Julia were awake, she and Laura would be talking to each other and then they both would have missed it.

Back in her driveway, Laura turned off the motor and Julia's eyes flew open.

"Was I asleep?" she said. "I'm sorry."

"Don't apologize, it's perfectly OK," Laura assured her. "Let's go inside and have hot chocolate."

Mark was sound asleep in his car seat. Laura eased him out and carried him to the house. The telephone was ringing; she ran inside to answer it.

"Hello?" she said, a little breathless.

There was a sound like a strangled sob. "Laura?"

"Who is it?" Laura said, warily.

"It's Chris . . ." Another sob.

It didn't sound like her—but who would pretend to be Christine?

"What's the matter?" Laura asked, but as soon as she asked, she knew. Her stomach clenched with apprehension.

"I . . . lost . . . it," Christine pushed each word out. Then, all in a rush, "I-lost-the-baby."

"Oh, Chris, I'm so sorry." Laura's eyes pricked with tears.

"It happened so fast. Yesterday I was pregnant and now I'm not." Christine's voice broke.

"I'm sorry," Laura said again. What else was there to say? So much of what happened in a person's life was just luck—or fate if you thought of it that way. Getting pregnant in the first place, carrying a child to term, delivering a healthy baby: in the end, so much of it was really just luck. She was lucky and her sister wasn't.

She shifted Mark against her hip as tears coursed silently down her cheeks. Julia walked into the kitchen, then stopped and looked at her, alarmed.

"Peter?" she mouthed.

Laura shook her head. "Christine," she mouthed back.

Julia came over and lifted Mark into her arms.

"I'll take him," she whispered.

The little girls trooped into the kitchen and Laura turned away to hide her tears.

"Can we have hot chocolate now?" Jessie demanded.

"Your mom's on the phone right now but I'll put Mark down on the couch and then I'll make some for you, OK?" Julia said smoothly.

Laura threw her a grateful glance and headed upstairs with the telephone.

"Do you want to talk about it?" she asked Christine.

Christine gulped and sniffed.

"It's OK if you don't," Laura assured her. She wasn't sure she wanted to hear the details.

"I just started having cramps yesterday, all of a sudden," Christine said. "I called Dan at work . . ."

"He was at work?" Laura interrupted. "On a Sunday?" She felt irrationally critical, convinced that he had let her sister down.

"He came home as soon as I called," Christine went on. "We went straight to the hospital but there was nothing they could do." She stopped, overcome with weeping.

"Christine, I'm so sorry," Laura said helplessly, tears of sympathy streaming down her face.

"Why did this happen to us?" Christine wailed.

It really wasn't fair: Christine had been sick for weeks and then she lost the baby anyway.

"Dan is devastated," Christine said. "He was even more excited about this baby than I was. If that was possible."

"You really wanted this, I know," Laura said.

"Dan did, too. He's totally heartbroken."

That was a startling thought; Laura couldn't quite imagine it.

"You're so lucky," Christine said. "You and Peter." She didn't sound resentful, just terribly sad.

"I wish I could fix this for you," Laura said. "I would if I could, Christine."

"I know." Christine's sobs were subsiding. "Would you consider coming to see me?"

"You mean, come to New York?"

"I guess you can't leave your kids, can you?"

Christine hardly ever asked for anything—not since they were children and she'd given up on getting Laura's attention.

"Well . . . I could talk to Peter . . ." Laura said, uncertainly.

"I don't think I'm up to traveling but I'd love to see you," Christine said. "If you think you could get away. If it's OK with Peter."

Julia wouldn't feel she had to ask Greg for permission, Laura thought. Julia would just do it if she wanted to, and Greg would just have to accept it.

"I'll try to come this weekend," she promised. "I'll call you back tonight."

She hung up the phone and sat for a moment, motionless. She could hear Julia and the children downstairs: Jessie asking for more hot chocolate, Emily and Sara arguing about something, Julia's adult voice answering, intervening, soothing. Laura felt immersed both in her own good fortune—having them all in her life—and in sorrow for her sister's loss of all this rich possibility.

Julia was standing at the sink, rinsing out the cups; she turned around when Laura came into the kitchen.

"What is it?" she asked, quickly drying her hands.

"Christine had a miscarriage," Laura reported.

"What a disappointment," Julia said.

"She's heartsick. She tried for so long to get pregnant."

"It's ironic, isn't it, when you think about it? Someone like your sister, trying so hard, and then someone like me, not trying at all."

"She asked if I would come and visit her," Laura said. "Just me, without the kids."

"You should go. It'll be fun to spend some time in New York City," Julia said.

"I don't quite picture it as fun," Laura said. For perhaps the first time, she and Julia didn't seem to be on the same wavelength. It was disorienting; she'd grown so used to their constant, implicit understanding.

"Christine is awfully sad," she added.

"I know she is. It's too bad I didn't have the miscarriage instead," Julia said. "Then you and I could have gone to New York together and had a good time."

"Julia!"

"What? Oh, I feel bad for your sister. It's just weird that what's a disappointment for her would be a relief to me."

"Stop it!" Laura pleaded. She looked Julia full in the face. "How dare you say that?"

Julia took a step backward. "What do you mean?"

"You have to stop wishing away that baby," Laura said, with ferocious intensity. "It isn't just yours, you know."

"I know . . . Greg wanted another . . ."

"I feel as if it's mine, too," Laura went on, as if Julia hadn't spoken.

Julia's eyes widened and Laura's filled with tears.

"I already feel attached to that baby inside you and you keep talking about it like it's just a big mistake . . . I love that baby!" Laura broke down. She put her hands over her face, and sank into a chair.

Julia knelt beside her, putting her arms around Laura awkwardly as she sat crumpled in the chair.

"I'm sorry . . . don't be sad . . . I didn't mean to upset you," she murmured.

Laura struggled to stop crying, but when she looked up at Julia the tears started anew.

"I'm sorry," she said. "I'm just so sad for Chris and . . . I don't know . . . it's like I feel guilty or something."

"You haven't done anything wrong," Julia said tenderly. "You are the dearest friend, and the sweetest sister. I wish I had a sister like you and I'm jealous that you're going to New York and leaving me behind."

"You are?"

"Of course. I want you with me always—you're my rock, you keep me steady. You're my model for motherhood, Laura."

"I am?" Laura was astonished.

"I'm not as good as you. You're such a natural. I don't believe I'll do a good job with another baby."

"Of course you will." Now Laura was doing the comforting as tears appeared in Julia's eyes.

"I'm no good with babies. When Sara was a baby, do you know what I did?"

"What?"

"I left them. Both of them. Sara was colicky; she was crying nonstop, then Emily started in and I just got up and walked out the door."

"But you went back . . . ?"

"Not for almost an hour. I just left them wailing and walked away. Anything could have happened. I felt like I didn't even care—I was numb and heartless."

"It happens to all of us," Laura said, a little uncertainly.

"You would never do that. Never," Julia asserted and now she really was crying. "I'm just an awful mother."

"No, you're not," Laura insisted.

"Yes, I am."

"No, you're not."

"I am."

"You're not," Laura repeated and the absurdity of their childish exchange suddenly struck her. "So there!" she added, sticking out her tongue.

Julia started laughing through her tears. They reached for each other and embraced, shaking and laughing and crying all at the same time.

Laura opened her eyes and looked over Julia's shoulder. The children were crowded together in the doorway, staring.

"Why are you crying?" Sara asked fearfully.

"It's OK. Mommies cry sometimes," Julia reassured her. She held out her arms, gathering in her daughters.

"How will I do this with three?" she whispered to Laura, a look of anguish on her face.

"I'll help you, I promise," Laura said, hugging Jessie and reaching out a hand to Mark, who was staggering, half-awake, into the kitchen, his hair plastered to the side of his head.

Jessie looked up at her. "Why do Mommies cry?"

"Lots of reasons, sweet pea," Laura said. "Just like children, I guess."

"Do Mommies ever fight?"

The two women looked at each other.

"Sometimes," Julia said. "But they try to make friends again right away."

"Especially when they're best friends," Laura added.

CHAPTER 11

The plane circled over Boston Harbor and started down the coast toward New York. Laura stared out the window, watching the harbor islands pass by, far below. A huge tanker, looking tiny as a toy, its long wake trailing, headed out toward the open sea.

Laura felt as if she, too, were sailing into unknown territory. The last time she'd been alone on an airplane was before she had children—a lifetime ago. Peter was the one who did this, who boarded a plane with only a carry-on bag and no one else to account for.

She had half-hoped Peter would refuse to let her go, but he had encouraged her.

"Of course you should go," he said. "You and Christine are lucky to have each other."

"What about the kids?" Laura asked, feebly.

"What about them? We'll be fine," he declared, with his usual confidence. "We'll have fun," he added. "I never get them to myself."

It had never occurred to Laura that Peter might want to have what she had: long stretches of time with the children, enough time so that every single minute didn't have to be significant. She'd always thought that "quality time" was a sorrowful phrase; what she wanted with her children was quantity, as much time as possible. But she hadn't considered that Peter might feel that way; he'd always seemed the cheerful, dutiful breadwinner.

She called Christine to say she'd be on the shuttle Saturday morning.

"I can only stay one night," she added. "I have to come home on Sunday."

"I'm just so glad you're coming," Christine said.

Peter and the children came to the airport to see her off. Laura had thought about taking a cab, the way Peter did, but she wanted those final hugs before embarking, the sweet smell of her children still fresh in her nostrils. The children dashed through the airport as if it were a playground. Jessie remembered coming with her daddy at Thanksgiving—Christine had been newly pregnant then, and so happy.

"Be good and help Daddy," Laura said to her. "I'll call you tonight." She pressed her lips against her daughter's hair. "I love you, sweet pea," she murmured.

She lifted Mark and held him close, speaking over his shoulder to Peter. "Don't forget to dilute their juice with water," she reminded him. "And don't forget Jessie's vitamins—she knows which cupboard they're in."

Peter smiled at her. "We'll be fine," he said. "You'll only be gone for a couple of days . . . we can muddle through."

Laura stopped herself from saying "Are you sure?" but Peter saw the doubt in her face.

"I'm really not incompetent," he said. "I can take care of my own children."

"I know, I know," she said, hastily.

She kissed them all and started walking down the long corridor toward the gate. When she paused to look back they had already turned away; Peter had promised to take the children to the big window to watch her plane take off. It's only one night, she told herself firmly, and stepped onto the plane.

Now that it was airborne, she began to feel lighter, her mundane responsibilities dropping away. The flight attendant stopped by her seat to offer something to drink. Laura selected plain orange juice and leaned back in her seat, sipping slowly. It felt odd to be all by herself, alone on a plane full of strangers.

After a surprisingly short time the plane began to descend and Laura could see the sheer vastness of New York City spread out below her. As the wheels of the plane touched down, she let out her breath.

Christine was waiting for her in the terminal.

"It's so good to see you," she said. "Thanks for coming."

She picked up Laura's bag and led the way to the taxi stand. As they waited for a taxi, Laura realized that she was unconsciously feeling around her for her children, as if she expected to find them right at her knees.

Christine gave the driver her address and sat back in the seat. Laura had never seen her on her own turf, making her way around the city.

"You look good, Christine," she said, cautiously.

"That's nice to hear. I still feel pretty terrible."

"It's only been a week. It will take a while to get over this."

"I don't know if I'll ever be over it," Christine said. "Dan, either."

Laura still couldn't picture Dan as anything but his usual jocular self.

"Where is Dan?" she asked.

"He's home . . . he's having a tough time getting out of the house. He's barely even going to work."

"That must be hard for you."

"I'm hoping you can help me cheer him up," Christine said.

"Me?!"

"I'm so glad to have you here," Christine said.

The taxi proceeded impatiently through the streets of Manhattan and stopped at last in front of a tall building with an immaculate, marble facade. Christine opened her purse to pay the driver.

"I can pay for the cab," Laura offered, but Christine shook her head.

"I'm the hostess this time," she said firmly.

They got out and Laura stared up at the building.

"Is this where you live?"

"This is it. Home, sweet home," Christine replied. "Quite a contrast to that dinky little house we grew up in, isn't it?"

They rode the elevator to the fifth floor; Christine unlocked her apartment door and ushered Laura in.

The place was spotless, full of antique furniture and Oriental rugs. Laura was taken aback; she was suddenly seeing a different side of her sister.

"This is beautiful," she said.

"I can't believe you've never seen it," Christine said. "We've been living here since before we got married."

"It's beautiful," Laura said again.

"Dan?" Christine called. "Laura's here."

He emerged from the bedroom, unshaven, dressed in sweat-pants.

"Hi, Laura," he said. His voice sounded dull and hollow.

"I was just telling Chris I think you guys have a great apartment."

He waved his hand dismissively. "It's OK for Manhattan."

"Some people would kill to have a place like this," Christine pointed out.

"I know. We're so lucky," he said, his voice heavy with sarcasm.

Laura glanced at her sister. Christine shrugged, almost imperceptibly.

"Let me show you to your room," she said.

The guest room was small and cozy. Two of the walls were papered with a Beatrix Potter print, the other two were bare.

"You can guess what room this was going to be," Christine said quietly. "Dan was spending every spare moment getting it ready."

"Oh, Christine," Laura whispered.

Christine put the suitcase on the bed. "I'll let you get settled," she said. "The closet is empty—you can hang things in there if you like. The bathroom is at the end of the hall."

Laura sat down on the bed beside her suitcase. She opened her purse and took out the photographs of Mark and Jessie that she had brought with her. She stared at them for a few minutes, then set them on the table next to the bed.

When she went back to the living room, Christine was flipping through a stack of mail and Dan was slouching glumly on the couch. They weren't talking to each other; they might as well have been in different rooms.

Laura took a deep breath. "How about if we all go out and you can show me around?" she suggested.

Christine looked up. "OK." She turned to her husband. "Are you coming?"

"No, you girls go ahead," he said, drawing his feet up onto the couch. "I'll stay here where it's warm."

Laura wasn't really sorry. She and Christine put on their coats and headed for the elevator.

"Ever since it happened, he's been stuck in a deep black hole," Christine said. "I'm almost afraid to leave him alone."

"Do you think he'd actually harm himself?"

"I don't know what to think."

"We don't have to go out if you'd rather not," Laura said.

"No, we might as well," Christine replied.

Outside, the winter sun was bright but the air was cold. Laura tucked the scarf from Julia snugly into the front of her coat.

"The city looked better a month ago," Christine remarked. "It's so festive with all the Christmas decorations and corny Christmas music blaring out of the stores."

Laura looked at her. "You really like New York, don't you?"

"I love it. There's always something happening here."

Laura was struck by how little she knew about her sister. Apart from the dream of motherhood, she didn't really know how Christine felt about anything.

"I wish I could get Dan to come out," Christine said. "I think the hustle and bustle would be good for him."

"Maybe he's just not ready yet?"

"Well, I'm the one who had the miscarriage." Christine's voice was full of pain and she stopped to wipe her eyes.

"It's OK to be sad, Chris," Laura said softly.

Suddenly Christine was sobbing, her hands covering her face. Laura stepped in front of her, to shield her from curious stares, but nobody even seemed to notice. The two of them were just part of the mass of humanity sweeping through the city.

"I'm sorry," Christine said, struggling for control.

Laura laid her hand on Christine's arm. "We don't have to be out in public, you know, if it's too hard."

"No, I'd rather be out of the apartment. Would you like to go to a museum or up the Empire State Building or something?"

"Really, Chris, I came to see you. I don't have to be a tourist. The only thing I have to do while I'm here is buy presents for Jessie and Mark." Laura wondered too late if mentioning the children would make her sister feel worse.

"Would you just like to go shopping?" Christine asked, her face brightening.

The only time in years that Laura had been shopping without a child in tow was when she found Julia's Christmas present.

"Sure," she said. "That sounds like fun."

Christine's sorrow seemed to lift as she took Laura into all her favorite boutiques. They egged each other on, trying absurdly expensive dresses and summer hats—the spring fashions had already arrived in the stores. They giggled like schoolgirls, the way Laura used to do with Michelle when they were young: still flat-chested and ponytailed and innocent. She couldn't remember ever enjoying her sister this way, as if she were a friend.

They stood outside a vintage jewelry store, admiring the sparkling gems in the window.

"Let's go in," Christine urged. "That emerald necklace would look stunning on you."

Laura tried it on; it was gorgeous and she couldn't help thinking how nice it would look with her birthday earrings. But she wasn't really going to spend that kind of money, especially on a present for herself.

Christine slipped on a set of silver bangles. They jingled merrily and reflected the sunlight coming through the window.

"Oh, Chris, I love those," Laura exclaimed. She picked up a bracelet of garnets set in a lacy filigree of gold.

"That's beautiful. Try it on," Christine encouraged.

Laura let her sister clasp the bracelet around her wrist. It was delicate and lovely against her skin, but she was thinking of Julia. She wanted to see the bracelet on her.

"Are you going to buy it?" Christine asked.

"Yes," Laura said, to her surprise.

"Oh, good. Then I'll buy these," Christine said. She thought Laura was buying the garnet bracelet for herself but Laura didn't correct her.

When they left the store, their purchases tucked in their handbags, Christine suggested they stop somewhere for lunch. There were so many little restaurants and coffee shops to choose from; Laura wondered if she and Julia would have settled on a favorite if they lived here.

She followed Christine into a deli. It was loud and crowded and warm inside. They slipped out of their coats and ordered sandwiches, then sat down to eat, listening to the clamor of conversations all around them.

"I suppose I should call Dan," Christine said. She excused herself but came back almost immediately.

"He isn't answering the phone," she reported.

"Maybe he went out?"

"No, he's been holed up in the apartment all week." Christine sighed. "I know he's suffering, but after a while, don't you think it's time to pick up and go on?"

The reactions of Christine and her husband to their bereavement were almost exactly the opposite of what Laura would have predicted. Sometimes it seemed that when it really counted, women were stronger than men.

Christine pulled on her coat.

"You wanted to buy presents for your kids, didn't you?" she said. "My favorite children's store is right near here."

The cold air was a shock after the warm humidity of the restaurant. They walked quickly, their breath emerging visibly in front of them. It had been a long time since Laura walked around in a city; she'd forgotten how the spaces between tall buildings could become bitter canyons of wind.

"This is it." Christine stopped. "I haven't been in here since Christmas . . ."

"We don't have to go inside," Laura said.

"No, life goes on," Christine said stubbornly, and pulled open the door. Warm air rushed to meet them as they stepped inside.

"We were looking at that high chair and that crib." Christine pointed them out.

"I thought you were going to use Mark's crib," Laura said.

"Dan wanted to get everything brand new." That sounded more like the Dan Laura knew.

"He wanted to feel like a good provider, I guess," Christine added.

A woman walked in with a newborn in her arms, its eyes tightly shut, hands curled in tiny fists against its chest.

Laura felt a burst of nostalgia for the utter newness of a baby just after it arrives, still partly in some other world, not quite yet all of this one. She thought about Julia's baby: there would be another new baby in Laura's life in a few months. Christine had lost her pregnancy but Laura was still expecting.

"Can you believe she brought her baby out in weather like this?" Christine whispered, her eyes filling.

Laura took her arm. "Come on," she said, guiding her away.

In the toy section, Laura caught herself feeling around her legs for her children again. She could almost hear their voices, as if they were phantoms hovering nearby. It might have been difficult to actually have them there, wheedling for some toy or another, but Laura had a sudden craving to hold them close. How was she going to get through a whole night without touching them?

She'd intended to buy simple token gifts but, overcome with missing them, she picked out a Barbie speedboat for Jessie and a fire truck with a revolving light and siren sound effects for Mark.

"Are you going to get something for Peter?" Christine asked.

The thought hadn't crossed Laura's mind. "I don't know what to get him," she admitted. "Do you have any ideas?"

"I bought Dan some nice cashmere socks at Macy's for Christmas," Christine said.

They walked there and Laura was struck again by how comfortable Christine seemed in the city, how natural it was for her to stride along the sidewalks amidst the crowd. Laura tried to imagine living in Manhattan with little children—navigating through the sea of people with a stroller.

"Shall we pick up some takeout for dinner?" Christine suggested. "There's a great little Jamaican place on the way home—Dan and I love their food. Does that sound OK?"

"Sure," Laura said.

Dan was sitting on the couch in the apartment, still in his sweatpants. There was a football game on TV, but he didn't really seem to be watching it.

"We brought food from Jimmy the Jamaican," Christine said.

"Uh-huh," he grunted.

Laura wanted to shake him. Christine was trying so hard to be upbeat and he wasn't making any effort at all.

Christine took all the food out of the Styrofoam containers and arranged it artfully on platters. Then she leaned into the living room. "Dan, come and eat while the food's still hot."

There was no answer.

"What would you like to drink?" Christine asked Laura. "Beer goes well with this food but we also have wine or milk or sparkling water . . . whatever you want."

"What are you having?"

Christine thought a moment, then declared, "I'm going to have a beer. I'm sick to death of milk and there's no reason not to drink beer now, is there? You want one, too?"

"Sure." The last time Laura drank beer was with Julia at the gay bar.

The food was spicy and delicious. The children would have hated it and Peter wasn't a fan of spicy food either, but Laura enjoyed it; this felt like a rare treat.

After a while, Dan came in, loaded up a plate, and carried it back to the living room.

"Aren't you going to be sociable?" Christine asked as he walked away. "I'm sorry," she whispered to Laura.

"You don't need to apologize for anything," Laura said.

After dinner, Laura called home. She had to think for a moment to remember her own phone number; she hardly ever dialed it herself. Peter answered after the first ring.

"How's everything going?" she asked.

"It's going just fine. How's New York?"

"It's cold."

"How's your sister?"

"She's doing OK. But Dan is a basket case. He hardly talks."

"That's hard to imagine," Peter said.

"How are the children?" Laura asked. "Can I talk to them?"

"Sure, hang on."

"We had hot dogs," Jessie informed her.

"Did Daddy cut them up nice and small?" Laura asked, thinking anxiously about the choking potential of hot dogs.

"Yeah. I had ketchup and mustard, too," Jessie continued.

"Mustard, wow—that's new for you."

"We're watching *Cinderella*," Jessie said. She was probably eager to get back to it.

"I miss you. I'll be home tomorrow." Laura closed her eyes, wishing she were there now.

Peter put Mark on the phone; Laura could hear him breathing but he didn't say anything.

"He looks confused," Peter reported. "He knows it's your voice but he can't figure out where you are."

"Give them both giant hugs for me," Laura begged. "And don't forget to read *Goodnight, Moon*."

"Don't worry. Jessie's giving me explicit instructions about everything," Peter said. "I miss you, honey."

Almost to her surprise, Laura realized she missed him, too. She was so accustomed to his familiar, dependable presence.

"I'll be home tomorrow," she said.

Going to bed was difficult, just as Laura had expected. It was unsettling not to be able to look at her sleeping children—that was as much a part of her bedtime routine as brushing her teeth. She lay awake in the half-finished nursery for a long time, listening to the traffic far down on the street outside the window.

When she finally fell asleep, she dreamed that she went home and found out Julia had miscarried while she was gone. She woke abruptly, trembling, and sat up, staring into the unfamiliar room. She wanted to call Julia, to hear the sound of her voice, to be reassured that everything was OK . . . but it was the middle of the night. She threw back the covers and got out of bed.

Her mouth was dry; she felt her way along the hallway toward the kitchen to get a drink of water. Someone was sitting on the couch in the living room, a big silent lump in the darkness. Dan's voice came out of the shadow: "Chris? Is that you?"

"No, it's Laura," she said.

"Couldn't sleep, either?"

"I had a nightmare," she said.

"I'm sorry. Do you want to talk about it?"

Laura was taken aback. Dan had always seemed so completely wrapped up in himself—now more than ever.

"It was . . ." she hesitated. "It was about a miscarriage."

"That is definitely a nightmare," he agreed.

Laura stood at the edge of the room, uncertain what to do next, and then she heard it: a muffled, heartbroken sob. Without deciding to, she found herself moving toward him and then suddenly she was sitting next to him.

"I'm so sorry about what happened," she said. She had not yet expressed that to him directly.

He kept on crying: a wrenching, terrible sound.

"You and Christine can try again," she offered.

"You know how long we tried," he said.

Laura sat beside him, silent, full of unexpected sympathy.

"I just feel so helpless," he went on, after a minute. "I couldn't do anything to save my own child."

Laura tried to think of something comforting to say. She'd never attempted to really talk to Dan before but sitting here in the dark with him, listening to him cry, was so intimate somehow. It made everything feel different.

"You know that a miscarriage usually means something wasn't going right," she said. "The fetus probably wasn't developing properly."

"It wasn't a fetus to me," he said. "That was my son, little Christopher. I wanted to name him after your sister."

"You knew it was a boy?" Laura asked, thoughtlessly.

"No, I just thought so. Christine thought it was a girl; we had a bet going. We were going to find out in two weeks."

"Two weeks?"

"After the amnio." He let out a long shuddering sigh.

"I really wanted that kid," he said. "I wanted to take him to Yankees games and teach him to ride a bike. Or teach her . . . whichever."

They sat there quietly for a while. Dan's sniffling gradually subsided.

"You know, you smell like Christine," he said. It was a characteristically weird remark, but for some reason it didn't irritate Laura this time.

"Maybe you should go to bed and smell the real thing," she suggested. "I'll bet Christine would like the company."

"Maybe you're right," he agreed. He sat still for another minute and then stood up. "Thanks, Laura."

"There's nothing to thank me for."

"I hope you have only good dreams for the rest of the night," he said.

"You, too."

She got up and suddenly he turned and hugged her. Startled, she hugged him back, and they stood like that for a moment, holding on to each other. Then he pulled away and walked toward the bedroom, leaving Laura alone to marvel at her own change of heart.

CHAPTER 12

"So he turns out not to be an insensitive jerk after all," Julia said.

She and Laura were sitting in her kitchen on Monday morning, drinking tea.

"No. I was surprised," Laura admitted. "His grief was just as deep as Christine's." She paused, recalling the sound of Dan's ragged sobs in the darkness.

"I guess I never thought a man would have the same feelings as a woman," she added.

Julia took a sip of her tea and looked at Laura for a long moment.

"I think they have the same feelings we do," she said. "It's just that most men are so bad at expressing them."

"It's easier for me to talk to you than to anyone else," Laura observed. "We always understand each other."

"Well, of course." Julia beamed at her. "That's because I'm a woman. And besides, you and I are soul mates."

Laura's heart soared. It was so good to be in the light of Julia's gaze again. They had rushed joyfully into each other's arms at school that morning, as if they'd been separated for weeks. Laura had been relieved to get back to her family but not until she saw Julia did she feel completely at home.

"I'll bet your husband was happy to have you back," Julia said.

"Oh yes. He was exhausted after dealing with the kids all weekend."

"Not too exhausted to give you a proper welcome, I hope." Julia batted her eyelashes comically, then poked a finger slowly in and out of her closed fist, her sparkling eyes fixed on Laura.

"Stop that," Laura scolded, laughing.

In fact, Peter had come to get Laura out of Mark's room the night before, as she stood there reveling in the nearness of her baby. He'd been eager to make love and once he managed to coax her away from the sight of her sleeping child, Laura was quite amenable. Knowing her children were just down the hall again made her feel grateful, relaxed, ready to satisfy his desire.

"Tell me how you're doing," she said to Julia. "Is everything OK?"

"I'm fine. I feel huge already, though . . . and I still have such a long way to go."

"Two years ago I was so pregnant with Mark I thought I would burst," Laura mused.

"That's right, he has a birthday coming. What are you doing for him?" Julia asked.

"I don't know. I already gave him a fire truck I bought in New York—with a siren and everything."

Julia laughed "You'll regret that," she predicted.

"I also got a Barbie boat for Jessie," Laura confessed.

"Oh, Laura, shame on you," Julia teased. "They'll be S-P-O-I-L-E-D," she sang, to the tune of Tammy Wynette's song, "D-I-V-O-R-C-E."

"I got a present for you, too," Laura said.

"You did? Really?"

Laura took the garnet bracelet, nestled in its box, out of her purse and gave it to her. Julia opened the box and looked inside.

"Oh!" she said. "It's beautiful. You are so sweet."

She laid the bracelet across her palm, admiring it, then handed it back to Laura.

"Put it on me," she directed, pushing up her shirt sleeve.

Laura fumbled with the clasp, her fingertips brushing against Julia's skin. Julia held out her arm and surveyed the glittering stones.

"I love the color," she said. "It'll be perfect for Valentine's Day."

"Red looks good on you," Laura said, trying to ignore the competitive tug she felt as she thought of Greg and Julia doing something romantic together. Greg probably made a big deal out of Valentine's Day.

"Do you have special plans?" she asked.

Julia looked surprised. "Didn't Peter tell you? We're going out together."

"You and Peter?!"

Julia burst out laughing. "No, silly!"

For a wild moment Laura pictured herself and Julia going out, dancing together, wearing their sparkling jewelry.

"All four of us," Julia said. "I called Peter while you were gone and suggested it."

Laura remembered the first Valentine's Day she and Peter had spent together: he'd sent two dozen perfect red roses to her office and all her co-workers had been impressed and envious. That evening, he'd cooked dinner for her at his apartment and they had made love half the night. But since the children came along they just bought each other cards and left it at that.

"We never got to have our New Year's Eve party so I thought we should have one now," Julia added.

"It sounds like fun," Laura said, a little uncertainly. "Where are we going?"

"To a romantic little restaurant on the harbor," Julia said. "Greg and I went there last year. They have a live band and dancing right in the dining room; it's very old-fashioned. You'll love it."

Her enthusiasm was irresistible. Laura's doubts about going out as a foursome—let alone to a restaurant where Julia and Greg had already had a romantic evening—faded as she smiled back at

Julia.

"I had an idea for Mark's birthday," Peter said that evening, after the kids were in bed.

"You did?"

Since when did Peter come up with ideas for the children? It was true that he'd pushed Laura to enroll Jessie in nursery school, but Laura still thought of herself as the one who planned the children's lives, just as Peter was the one who did the traveling. Things were getting a little topsy-turvy now.

"I heard you can get a tour of the firehouse. Don't you think that would be fun for Mark?" Peter suggested.

Laura stared at him. It was perfect, and she never would have thought of it.

The next Saturday, Peter drove the whole family to the fire station in the center of town. Fortunately, it was a slow day; all the trucks were in the station, along with several bored firefighters who were delighted to show the children around. Laura took pictures of Mark in a fireman's helmet and Jessie sitting behind the wheel of the hook-and-ladder. Peter slipped his arm around Laura's waist as they watched the children talking to the fire chief, who knelt to shake Mark's hand and wish him a happy birthday.

"What a nice family you have," he said to Peter.

"I'm a lucky guy," Peter said. He swung Mark onto his shoulders, Laura took Jessie's hand, and they all walked back to the car.

Peter offered to drive both couples into Boston on Valentine's Day. Mrs. Nixon was going to stay with Laura's children again; Julia had hired a high school student whose name was posted on the bulletin board at the nursery school.

"It would be fun if we could get ready together," Julia said, wistfully.

"Well, let's do it," Laura replied. "My house or yours?"

Julia brightened. "Could you come to mine? I have to be home with the girls while Greg picks up the babysitter. Then Peter can drive over and get all of us."

Peter was baffled when he heard the plan.

"Why do you want to get dressed together?" he asked.

"It's kind of a girl thing, I guess . . . it's hard to explain," Laura floundered. "It's just fun."

He shrugged. "If you say so. Take the minivan—I'll pick you up in my car." Peter had a new Mercedes, which Laura hardly ever rode in; the children's car seats were always in the van.

She packed her carry-on flight bag with clothes, shoes, makeup. The children eyed it suspiciously as she put on her coat.

"Are you going away again?" Jessie asked.

"No, Daddy and I are just going out for dinner," Laura said. "Mrs. Nixon will be here to babysit—you remember her?"

"Why do you have your suitcase?" Jessie persisted.

"That's to carry my dress in. I'm going to change at Julia's house."

"Why?" Jessie didn't understand it either.

"Just for fun, honey," Laura said. "Julia's coming to dinner, too."

"Oh." Jessie still looked confused.

"Mommies like to play dress-ups, too, remember?" Peter put in. "They're a lot like little girls."

Laura looked at him, unsure what to think. Was he making fun of her? She kissed the children and picked up her bag.

"See you soon," Peter called after her. "Don't get so dolled up I don't recognize you."

Greg answered the door at Julia's house, looking splendid in a charcoal gray suit.

"Come on upstairs," he said. "Julia's picking out a tie for me."

Laura followed him into the bedroom. Julia was standing there in a bathrobe, her hair still wet, looking over an array of ties spread across the big bed. She picked up a pink-striped one and handed it to Greg.

"Wear this one. Pink is a good valentine color," she advised.

"Whatever you say, boss." Greg put it on, standing in front of the full-length mirror, then turned back to Julia.

"How do I look?" he asked. Laura suspected he knew perfectly well how good he looked.

"Handsome, of course, as always," Julia replied. He pulled her into an embrace and she looked over at Laura and rolled her eyes.

"Not so tight—you'll squash the kid," she said.

Greg bent down and kissed her belly.

"Sorry about that," he said.

Laura watched them, wondering if she should have come. To her relief, Emily and Sara appeared in the bedroom doorway.

"Hi, girls," she greeted them. "Happy Valentine's Day."

"Where's Jessie?" Emily asked.

"She's home with Mark. I came by myself this time."

"Mommy and Laura are going to get dressed up together," Julia said. "We're going on a double date."

"Can I come?"

"No, it's just for grown-ups. Claire is coming to babysit."

Emily looked pleased; Julia must have hired Claire before. She and Greg had probably gone on a date by themselves, Laura thought with a twinge of jealousy.

Julia turned to Greg. "You need to go pick her up," she said. "Why don't you take the kids with you? Let us primp in peace."

"Oh, all right," he said. He leaned down to kiss Julia and Laura watched his hand briefly graze her breast. Then he and the girls clattered down the stairs.

"Sometimes I'm just so eager to see them all go," Julia said. "Is that dreadful of me?"

"Of course not," Laura assured her.

"I think I feel that way more often since being pregnant," Julia observed. "I'm just such a mass of hormones. It's like having PMS all the time."

"I remember," Laura said. "But that won't last. Soon you'll be a serene and placid mother-to-be."

"Serene and placid?" Julia snorted. "I don't think those words could ever apply to me." She untied the belt of her bathrobe, shrugged it off her shoulders, and tossed it onto the bed. There she stood, unselfconsciously naked.

Laura looked at her and then looked away, feeling a little giddy. Julia's belly was gently rounded, her breasts a little fuller now than they had been under the tank top she was wearing at the beach back in October.

"You're not wearing those clothes, are you?" Julia asked. "I thought we were getting dressed up."

"Oh yes, I brought clothes with me," Laura said. She felt exposed, even though it was Julia who was naked. "They're in my bag."

"Well, let's see them," Julia said. She put on a bra and underpants and then started to pull on a pair of pantyhose.

"Who am I kidding?" she exclaimed. "I can't wear pantyhose—they're way too tight." She pulled them back off her feet. Her toenails were covered with bright pink polish; Laura wondered if Greg had painted them for her but she didn't want to ask.

She unpacked her dress, a clingy rayon in shades of blue and green.

"That's beautiful," Julia said.

Laura shook it out. "I'm afraid it got all wrinkled on the way here."

"I'll hang it in the bathroom and steam it," Julia suggested. "We can put on our makeup while we're waiting."

They stood side by side in front of the bedroom mirror. Julia, still in her underwear, blew her fine hair dry, while Laura put on mascara and opened her lipstick.

"That color is way too subtle for tonight," Julia declared. "This is Valentine's Day, remember? Try this one."

She picked up one of the lipsticks on her dresser and handed it to Laura. It was a deep red, almost maroon. Laura leaned toward the mirror and put it on.

"That's much better," Julia said. "Look at you—you're so sexy. Peter will love it."

Laura stared at her reflection. The dark color called attention to her full lips; there was something unmistakably erotic about it.

"That would look great with the black wig," Julia said. "Do you still have that?"

"Oh yes." Laura had retrieved it from the floor of the coat closet, packed it into a shoebox, and put it under her bed. She couldn't imagine ever wearing it again; it seemed inextricably linked to the night out with Julia.

Julia flung open her closet door.

"I have absolutely nothing to wear!" she cried. "Help me, Loretta!"

Laura peered in. "That closet is packed with clothes."

"I can't fit into most of them anymore," Julia wailed. "Will you help me find something?"

They settled on a stretchy lace blouse and a black jersey jumper. The jumper hugged the little mound of Julia's belly and flared prettily around her calves. She had great legs; a skirt really showed them off.

"Do I look OK?" she asked.

"You look wonderful," Laura told her.

"You better take off your clothes and get changed, too," Julia advised. "Greg will be back any minute."

Laura stood in her underwear, shivering, while Julia went to the bathroom to get her dress. Laura lifted it over her head and Julia zipped up the back.

"Very pretty," Julia murmured. "Now what about jewelry?"

"I'm wearing my emerald earrings," Laura pointed out.

"I have the perfect necklace to go with them," Julia said.

She pawed through her jewelry box. "Here we go."

She pulled out an emerald pendant on a silver chain. Laura turned around and Julia fastened the clasp at the back of her neck. The emerald nestled in the hollow of her throat.

"Look in the mirror. Don't you love it? Go ahead, borrow it," Julia urged.

She put on a pair of dangling gold earrings that swung beside her face, reflecting the light. Then she picked up the garnet bracelet.

"Will you put this on me?" she asked. As she held out her arm, Laura heard the front door open and the excited voices of Julia's little girls. She quickly fastened the bracelet and pulled her hand away.

"Thank you." Julia fluffed her hair with her fingers and smiled at Laura.

They stepped out of the bedroom just as Greg was coming up the stairs.

"Are you ready?" he asked.

"Don't we look fabulous?" Julia demanded.

"Of course." Greg was looking at her as if he wanted to eat her.

"I'll call Peter and tell him it's time to come over," Laura said.

A few minutes later, Peter was at the door. He was wearing the leather jacket Laura had given him.

"You look great," Julia told him. "And doesn't your wife look gorgeous?"

Peter looked at Laura. "Yes, she does," he said.

Sara and Emily were showing the babysitter the valentines they'd made in nursery school. They looked a lot like the one on the refrigerator at Laura's house.

Julia kissed her girls goodbye and the four adults left the house.

"Claire looks so young," Laura remarked to Julia.

"I know. But the kids think it's much more fun to have a teen-age babysitter than dear old Mrs. Nixon," Julia said. "Someday our girls will probably be babysitting," she added.

"It's hard to imagine," Laura said.

"Maybe they could do it together at first, like a team," Julia suggested.

Laura smiled and then it hit her that they probably wouldn't be living in the same town by then. She pushed the thought into the back of her mind.

"Hey, nice wheels," Greg exclaimed when he saw Peter's car.

"Thanks." Peter grinned. It occurred to Laura that he might

have suggested driving so he could show off his car. She'd never thought of Peter as competitive.

"You have the longest legs—you sit up front," Julia said to Greg. "We girls can sit in back together."

Laura settled contentedly in the back seat, breathing in the smell of Julia's rose cologne, mixed with the leather of Peter's jacket. In the front seat, Peter and Greg were discussing the various features of the car.

Peter drove faster than usual, taking corners sharply; after a few blocks Julia started to look distressed. She reached for Laura's hand.

"Are you OK?" Laura whispered.

"I just feel a little queasy," Julia said. Her face was pale.

Laura leaned forward. "Peter, can you pull over?" she asked.

He guided the car to the curb as Greg turned around to look at Julia. She sat very still, taking slow, steady breaths.

"Let's switch places," Greg proposed.

He got out and opened Julia's door. They both stood outside in the fresh air for a few minutes and then he ushered her into the front seat.

"I'll be fine as soon as I eat," she said.

"Do you want to stop and pick up some crackers or something?" Laura suggested.

"No, I'll be OK now. The front seat is always better for some reason."

Greg got into the back beside Laura. She felt kind of crowded; he took up a lot more space than Julia.

As soon as they were seated at the restaurant, Julia seized her menu. "Let's order appetizers right away," she said. "I'm getting the bruschetta."

"Shall we have some wine?" Peter suggested.

Laura looked at Julia. "Do you mind?"

"No, go ahead, enjoy yourselves," she said.

"You don't want any?" Peter asked.

Before she could respond, Greg said, "She can't drink. She's pregnant."

"Oh! Well, congratulations," Peter said.

He ordered a bottle of cabernet with three glasses. The waitress poured a little for him to taste but he deferred to Greg, who
looked flattered. It was just that sort of gesture that made Peter so
good at his job.

When the appetizers arrived, Julia devoured hers, then sat back
in her chair with a sigh.

"That's a relief," she said. "I was starving."

"You want some of my salad?" Laura offered.

"No, no, I'm fine now." Julia looked longingly at Laura's glass
of wine. "That looks so good—can I have a taste?"

Without waiting for an answer she picked up Laura's glass and
took a sip. The red wine was the same rich color as the garnet
bracelet on her wrist.

"What do you think you're doing?" Greg demanded.

Julia set the glass back down. "Oh, relax," she said. "One sip
isn't going to do any harm." She turned to Laura. "Men have no
idea what we go through to perpetuate their precious genes."

"We're very grateful to you ladies," Peter said, smoothly. "How
about a dance?"

He stood up and held out his hand to Laura.

She felt rusty, out of practice, dancing in his arms. Most of the
other couples were older and more polished; the atmosphere of
the whole place had a certain bygone elegance.

Laura looked over at Greg and Julia, still sitting at the table.

"Maybe we should go back," she whispered to Peter. "I'm
afraid they're fighting."

"They're entitled," he said. "It's not really our business, is it?"
He tightened his arm around her.

"I'm afraid they'll have a bad time," Laura said. "I think we
should go break it up."

"I think we should leave them alone," Peter replied, spinning
Laura out and back. When she looked again, Julia and Greg were
coming toward the dance floor.

"I'm way too heavy to dance," Julia said as they settled into a spot next to Peter and Laura.

"Don't be silly," Greg said affectionately. They seemed to be completely at ease with each other.

It was more fun dancing now that Julia was doing it, too. Laura watched the skirt of her jumper swirl as she turned under Greg's arm.

After a few numbers, Julia leaned toward Greg and whispered something. He hesitated, then came over to Peter and Laura.

"Would you care to change partners?" he asked. Peter looked as surprised as Laura felt.

"I guess so," he said. "Is that OK with you, honey?"

Laura looked at Julia, still swaying to the music.

"Sure," she said.

In a moment she was dancing with Greg, her hand buried in his big one. She glanced up at him; he was looking past her at Peter approaching Julia. Laura watched, too, as they began to dance together, Julia looking into Peter's face, smiling her bright smile.

When she stepped back, Greg and Laura pulled apart and the four of them returned to the table. Their entrees arrived; Julia ate hers and then nibbled off Greg's plate while the others made their way through a second bottle of wine.

After dessert, Julia excused herself to go to the ladies' room.

"Are you coming?" she asked Laura.

"Oh yes." Laura stood up quickly.

"Isn't it nice that women get to go the restroom together?" Julia remarked, as they stood side by side in front of the mirror, renewing their lipstick.

Laura turned to face her. "What was the idea, getting Greg to dance with me?" she asked.

"I just thought it would be more interesting to mix things up," Julia said. "Didn't you think so?"

"I doubt your husband was all that thrilled about it," Laura said.

"How could he not be?" Julia said. "I just wish I had the nerve to dance with you myself."

She rubbed a stray smudge of lipstick off the corner of Laura's mouth with her finger. Laura felt her heart pounding inside her chest. A woman emerged from one of the toilet stalls and stared at the two of them, then hurried out the door.

Julia snickered. "Do you think she was afraid of us?" she said. "You never know what you might encounter in the Ladies' room."

"You're so bad, "Laura said.

The check arrived just as they came back to the table. Peter took it from the waitress.

"Hold on a minute," Greg objected.

"I told you we'd treat you the next time," Peter reminded him. "Now we're even."

Laura remembered how she used to keep track of how many lunches she or Julia had served the other's children. It had long since ceased to matter; the give and take was implicit and spontaneous now, something they could rely on with confidence.

"I'll be fine in the back seat now," Julia said when they got back to the car.

"I'll sit there with you," Greg offered quickly.

Laura got into the front seat next to Peter. As he drove, he reached over to put his hand on her knee and Laura glanced at his profile, his eyes focused on the road ahead. He really was a good man, she thought, caring and responsible . . .

She heard rustling in the back seat and a giggle from Julia. Laura pictured the scene behind her: Greg's arm around Julia, one hand slipping over her breast or creeping up her thigh under her skirt. Laura turned to look out the window, watching the houses go by, each one containing the hidden lives of the people inside.

Peter pulled up in front of Julia's house and Greg and Julia opened their doors.

"Thanks for dinner," Greg said. "Now it's time to get this expectant mother into bed."

Laura had a feeling Julia wouldn't be going right to sleep. She thought of the baby, deep inside Julia, a tiny presence between her body and Greg's.

Julia knocked on the outside of her window. Laura opened it and Julia leaned in to put her arms around Laura's shoulders in an awkward embrace.

"Happy Valentine's Day," she said.

Greg came around to Laura's side of the car.

"Good night," he said, drawing Julia away. Laura watched them go into the house.

"He's quite the hunk, as you women say, isn't he?" Peter remarked.

Laura turned to him, startled. "What?"

"Greg is a pretty good-looking guy," he said. It wasn't like him to make such an observation. Could he be jealous? Of Greg?

"He's not a very good dancer," she said truthfully, thinking about dancing with Julia in the gay bar.

Peter sat still, with his hands on the steering wheel.

"Well?" he said, finally.

"Well, what?"

"Aren't you going to drive the van home?"

She had forgotten all about it. She got out, glancing again at the closed door of Julia's house, then climbed into the van and drove home.

She went upstairs to look in on the children; when she came back down, Mrs. Nixon was gone. Peter had taken off his jacket and tossed it onto the couch. Laura picked it up and pressed her face into it, then put it on and closed her eyes, stroking the smooth leather over her arms

Peter came up behind her and put his hands on top of hers.

"You really like this jacket, don't you?" he said softly.

Laura turned to face him. "I guess I do," she admitted.

"You look sexy in it," he said. Laura thought of Greg, looking at Julia with hungry eyes, taking off her clothes and then his own.

She reached toward Peter. "Let's go upstairs." Her voice sounded strangely husky and she felt the weight of Julia's necklace against her throat.

"Make love to me," she whispered.

Peter stared at her; sex between them was always his idea. He slipped his hands inside the open jacket and wrapped them tightly around her.

CHAPTER 13

Snow began falling late at night and by the time Laura woke up the ground was covered. Peter and the children went outside to build a snowman while Laura attempted to put the house in order—a never ending task. She paused in Jessie's room to look down at the children in their snowsuits and mittens; they seemed very small in the vast whiteness. Mark lifted his feet, in their tiny red boots, high up out of the snow like a short-legged puppy. Through the closed window, Laura could see their mouths moving, but it was like watching a silent movie.

Peter worked diligently on the snowman, pushing a ball of snow around the yard. He was wearing gloves—dark brown against the huge white snowball—but he had taken off his hat and from above, Laura could see the bald spot beginning on the crown of his head. Over the six years they'd been together, there were already visible signs of aging: Peter's thinning hair, Laura's widened waistline. What would it be like, she wondered, to grow old with someone you had known your whole life, from as far back as she had known, say, Michelle? Or to be together for as long as her parents had: they'd been sweethearts in high school. Would that kind of history make a person more loyal, or more likely to wonder what they might have missed?

She watched Peter throw a snowball at Jessie. The snow was soft and fluffy and the snowball exploded against her bright blue jacket. Jessie laughed and threw a handful of snow toward her daddy; it fluttered down in front of her in a sparkling shower. Peter went over and showed her how to make a proper snowball, patting it into shape between her mittened hands. Then he stood close and let her throw it at him. Laura smiled and turned from the window.

By the next morning the streets were clear. Laura drove Jessie to school and there was Greg, delivering his daughters.

"Is Julia OK?" she asked.

"She's fine—just tired. I let her sleep late," he replied. "I had a good time on Saturday—did you?"

An image flashed into Laura's mind of Greg and Julia in bed together, naked. But of course that wasn't what he meant.

"It was a nice restaurant," she said.

"Did you know you left your clothes at my house?" he asked.

"What?" She felt herself coloring and looked away.

"The other night, when you changed your clothes at our house. I'm sure Julia will bring them to school for you sometime."

Laura dawdled inside the school with Mark, waiting until Greg left so she wouldn't have to walk back to the car with him. He still made her feel a little edgy.

She drove to Carole's, bought scones, and took them to Julia's house. Julia, her hair uncombed, was padding around in sweatpants and a big tee shirt that was probably Greg's.

"I know, I look terrible," she said as she opened the door.

"No, you don't," Laura protested.

"I wouldn't let just anyone see me looking like this," Julia said.

"Well, I hope I'm not just anyone," Laura replied. "Look, I brought scones."

She held out the bag; Julia took it with one hand and flung the other arm around Laura.

"You're an angel!" she exclaimed.

They sat down at the kitchen table. "I should make some tea,"

Julia said, not moving.

"Let me," Laura said. "Stay right where you are."

She set the kettle on to boil, measured tea leaves into the pot, and took two mugs out of Julia's cupboard. While she waited for the tea to steep, she pulled a jar of juice out of the refrigerator, and filled a sippy cup for Mark. He picked it up and headed off to the playroom.

"So . . . did you and Greg have a hot and steamy Valentine's night?" Laura asked as she carried the mugs to the table.

"Laura!" Julia feigned shock. "Did I really hear you say that?"

Laura grinned. "Life is full of surprises, isn't it?"

"Well, to answer your question, yes, we did," Julia said. "How about you and Peter?"

"Sure," Laura answered, sorry now that she'd asked.

"It's lucky that Greg is so good in bed; it redeems his more irritating qualities," Julia said. "My first husband wasn't even a decent lover—I don't know why my stupid ex-friend even wanted to have an affair with him."

Julia rarely spoke about her first marriage but when she did, Laura could hear the residual bitterness in her voice. She found herself thinking about Michelle: Julia had been betrayed by her best friend, too.

Julia picked up her mug of tea and blew across the surface to cool it.

"The truth is . . ." she paused to take a sip. "What I really would have liked would be for him to clean the house. Now that would be a truly romantic gift."

Laura scrambled to follow her train of thought.

"Clean the house?" she repeated. "You mean Greg?"

"I know, it's a ridiculous idea," Julia said. "He would never in a million years think of such a thing."

"I'll clean your house for you," Laura offered.

Julia set down her mug.

"You don't have to do that. I'm just letting off steam. I could hire a cleaning service or something; it's just that I always feel like if I don't have a job, I should at least keep house. Isn't that silly?"

"Julia," Laura said firmly. "I'd like to do this for you. If you'll keep an eye on Mark, I can clean your house while the girls are at school."

"Laura, that is just so sweet of you." Julia seemed awestruck. "But only do the downstairs, OK? I'll feel bad if you work too hard."

"OK," Laura agreed. "You're not supposed to feel bad, only happy. I could even get a babysitter for Mark—then you could just relax all morning."

"Don't you dare," Julia said. "I love hanging out with Mark—and if you won't let me do anything useful, I can't possibly let you do my housework."

"It's a deal, then," Laura declared. "Leave your car at school tomorrow and I'll drive you and Mark back to my house. Then I'll come here and clean and pick you up again to go get the girls."

Driving to Julia's house the next day, with Julia's house key in her pocket, Laura felt an odd pulse of excitement. Maybe this was a way to make those boring chores more interesting: women could trade routine tasks with each other and get a change of scene. Or was it just because she was so fond of Julia that the thought of doing something for her felt so exhilarating?

She turned the key in the lock, pushed open the front door, and stepped inside, breathing in the distinctive, familiar smell of Julia's house. Julia—or maybe Greg—had hauled out the vacuum cleaner and it waited silently in the living room. Sunlight streamed through the windows, lighting up the hardwood floors.

Laura picked up the books and toys and turned on the vacuum cleaner. A small stray sock lay halfway under the couch; she put it on the bottom stair to take up later. The rug in the dining room was littered with cookie crumbs, desiccated peas, and dried up macaroni elbows. Julia had said once that the only reason she could think of to have a dog was to eat all the food that landed on the floor. Laura thought about Jim Darling's elegant dog; she couldn't imagine him cleaning up under the table.

The kitchen sink was full of breakfast dishes. Laura loaded the dishwasher and washed out the coffeepot; evidently Greg was still drinking coffee. She wiped the counter and the kitchen table and paused to survey the top of the stove, covered with greasy spatters of soup and spaghetti sauce. Laura's mother had always been fanatical about the state of her stove; before she even set fried chicken on the table, her stove would already be spotless. Laura's own stove wasn't up to that standard but Julia's was worse. Wouldn't it be a surprise for her to see it really shining? Laura took out a sponge and went to work.

She cleaned more efficiently here than she did at home; it was fun pretending to be a maid. As she finished up the downstairs bathroom, she folded the first sheet of the toilet paper into a triangular point, like in a hotel. She could imagine Julia chuckling when she saw it.

Then she went back through the house, picked up the little sock on the stair, and carried it up to the laundry hamper in the bathroom. The bathroom was warm; Laura pictured Julia taking a hot shower while Greg shaved over the sink.

She opened the window a crack. It was a cold crisp day, the snow on the leafless trees glistening in the morning sun. Winter sunlight in New England seemed richer somehow than the wan light Laura remembered from the Midwest, straining to make its way through the clouds. Here the winter sky was a pure shade of cobalt, with brilliant sunshine slanting down at an angle that flattered the landscape.

She looked at her watch. There was still plenty of time before she had to pick up Mark and Julia. She was savoring the experience of being alone in Julia's house; she had the inexplicable sensation of getting away with something.

She wandered into Julia's bedroom. After glancing back toward the doorway, as if she expected someone to appear, she opened the closet and looked in. On one side were Greg's suits, lined up soberly in a row, and next to them a section of shirts, professionally cleaned and pressed. On Julia's side was the hodgepodge of clothes Laura had gone through with her on Valentine's Day: fancy dresses mixed with casual skirts, a beaded blouse crammed in beside a threadbare sweatshirt.

Laura closed the closet and crossed the room to the big armoire opposite the bed. She turned the knob and pulled it open; inside was a large television set. All the times Laura had imagined Greg and Julia in bed, she'd never pictured them watching TV. Did they really lie there side by side, watching late night talk shows?

Uncertain what was driving her, Laura kept exploring. She opened the drawers of the dresser and looked at Julia's underwear, her tee shirts, her socks and sweaters. In the bottom drawer, not quite hidden under a pair of flannel pajamas, the edge of a book peeped out.

Laura pulled it out carefully. It wasn't a book after all, it was a videotape. Who had videotapes anymore? She stared at the picture on the front of the box: it was unmistakably pornographic. There was an X-rated video in Julia's dresser.

Laura glanced at her watch again—she still had time for a peek. She slipped the tape into the VCR underneath the television and turned it on.

It started in the middle of a scene. Two women, dressed in garter belts with black lace stockings and high heels, stood beside a long couch, as a thumping, tuneless soundtrack played in the background. Then one of them fell back onto the couch and lay sprawled, legs apart, displaying a tiny triangle of hair. The long blonde mane of the other woman fell forward as she bent down and the woman on the couch opened her mouth wide. Her eyes rolled back in her head, she moaned and thrashed, her big breasts heaved impressively.

Laura stared at the screen, transfixed. Who was this for, she wondered: Greg or Julia? Did they watch it together?

She kept on watching, aroused in spite of herself, until a wave of shame swept over her and she forced herself to look away. Her hands shook and her heart pounded as she rewound the tape to exactly the same place it had been. She wouldn't want anyone to know she'd seen it, or to guess that she had been poking around in Julia's dresser drawers like a common thief. She felt as if she hardly knew herself.

She put the tape in its box and tucked it back into the drawer where she had found it. Then she closed the doors of the armoire over the empty television screen and backed out of the bedroom, checking to make sure she had left no trace of her presence.

When she got home, Mark and Julia were sitting on the couch and Julia was reading *Winnie the Pooh*, using a different voice for each of the characters. Mark leaned against her, looking down at the book, then up at Julia's face in rapt wonder when she changed voices.

"I wouldn't have thought he'd sit still for a story that long," Laura said. "Jessie never had that kind of patience."

"He's been a terrific listener," Julia said.

Mark wriggled down off the couch and ran to Laura. She picked him up and hugged him. "How was your morning?" Julia asked, getting up slowly. It took a little more effort now to move her body around.

"It was fine," Laura said. She was finding it hard to meet Julia's eyes.

"Really?" Julia sounded skeptical. "Have you decided house-cleaning is just the most fun a girl can have with her clothes on?"

"What makes you think I had my clothes on?" Laura retorted.

Julia laughed. "You mean I had a naked maid in my house? What would the neighbors think? What if Greg had forgotten something this morning and had to come back?"

A shudder ran through Laura. She'd never thought of that possibility.

"Don't worry—I was fully dressed the whole time," she said, primly.

"Well, either way, I am humbly grateful to you," Julia said. "I can't possibly thank you enough."

"You haven't even seen it yet," Laura protested. "You don't

even know if I did a good job."

"I don't even care," Julia said gaily. "You were incredibly sweet to do it at all."

"We should get the girls," Laura said.

She picked up Mark's snowsuit from the top of the radiator where it had been drying out and started to load him into it. He resisted at first, until Julia came and helped to slip it over his arms.

"Thanks for letting me borrow your boy," she said to Laura, zipping up the snowsuit. "We had a great time."

Laura drove to the school, her eyes fixed on the road, her mind racing, thinking about the women in the video. There was a tingling restlessness in her thighs and a kind of tightening deep in her abdomen. She tried to shut off her thoughts but the truth was inescapable: she had been aroused by that video. Could it be that Michelle's accusation, all those years ago, had been legitimate? Was she really "a lez"?

Julia was sitting right beside her but Laura could barely hear her voice through the torrent of her own confusion. She felt as if she were standing alone in a rushing, swirling river and Julia was far away on the bank. Out of the corner of her eye, she saw Julia's hands flitting around as she talked, running her fingers through her hair, loosening a strand which had pasted itself to her lip.

Laura remembered how Julia's hair swung around her mouth when she was dancing in the gay bar. Had she known that was a gay bar, really, even though she denied it? Could she have a secret parallel life that Laura had never guessed? But no: Julia had told her husband about that night; Laura was the one who'd wanted to keep it secret. Her hands felt clammy, gripping the steering wheel.

The children were already outside in the schoolyard; the girls ran up to them and Laura stood there in a daze as they chattered around her. Gradually she became aware of Julia waving a gloved hand back and forth in front of her face.

"Earth to Laura," she was saying. "Where are you? You look a million miles away."

"I'm sorry," Laura replied automatically.

"It must be the fumes from all those cleaning products," Julia teased.

Laura didn't respond and Julia's face grew serious.

"Laura, are you OK?" she asked. "Did I do something wrong?"

"No." Laura shook her head vehemently.

"I sure hope you'd tell me if you were ever mad at me," Julia said. "About anything," she added.

"I'm not mad at you," Laura said. "Honest."

She took her children home and made grilled cheese sandwiches for lunch. Her mother used to make those for Laura and her sister on cold winter days like this one. The children ate, but Laura just sat and stared at her sandwich.

Julia had told her husband but Laura hadn't. What did that mean? Julia had thought Greg might find the notion of his wife dancing in a gay bar amusing—even sexy, she'd said. Maybe the video was just part of their spicy love life. When Jim Darling first came into Carole's Coffee Shop Julia had talked about making love blindfolded. Maybe she and Greg had a whole repertoire of erotic games and tricks.

Laura pictured Julia dressed in black lace stockings like the women in the video, laughing as her husband tied a blindfold over her eyes. She imagined Greg's big hands traveling down Julia's body, his handsome face poised over hers, teasing her with his nearness as his lips descended slowly . . .

The phone rang and Laura jumped.

"Hello?"

"It's fabulous!" Julia said. "I hardly recognized my own house. The stove is unbelievable. You're a miracle worker, Laura."

"I'm glad you like it."

"I love it. You made my day—no, my week—no, my life!" Julia gushed. "I am so grateful to you."

"It really wasn't that big a deal . . ."

"It means the world to me," Julia insisted. "You are such a sweet friend."

"Thanks," Laura murmured.

"I'll see you at school tomorrow," Julia said. "Maybe we can go to Carole's again?"

It sounded so normal: just their usual routine. In fact, nothing had really changed, Laura reminded herself.

"Right now I'm going to walk around my wonderful clean house in my stocking feet," Julia declared

"Whatever turns you on," Laura said without thinking.

After Julia hung up, Laura sat for a moment, the dial tone humming in her ear. That was the thing about Julia: she did whatever turned her on. She was unabashed and unapologetic about what she thought was sexy. But did the images in that video excite her; did she have the same unbidden response as Laura had?

Laura carried her plate to the sink and stuffed the sandwich into the disposal. She turned around just as Mark careened headlong into the kitchen, stumbled in the drunken way of an exhausted toddler, and crashed onto the floor. He burst into furious sobs and Laura gathered him up.

"Poor guy, you're so tired. You had a big exciting morning with Julia," she said soothingly. "It's time for a nap."

"No nap," Mark whimpered but his body was already relaxing, growing heavier in her arms, as she carried him upstairs.

She laid him on her bed to change his diaper. Eyes half-closed, he reached unconsciously for his penis.

Laura watched him, pondering his future. What kind of man would he grow up to be? Whom would he love, what would he find arousing?

She slid a new diaper under him, gently lifting his hand out of the way. Was it weird to be thinking about her son's sex life? she wondered. But she couldn't help it: she wanted her children to be happy, fulfilled.

She lifted him into her arms again and sat down in the rocking chair, rocking slowly back and forth until his breathing was deep and regular, then stood up and put him in his crib. He let out a sigh and his fingers curled into the soft fur of the stuffed monkey Julia had given him for his birthday.

His needs were still so simple, Laura thought. It was so much easier to care for a little child than to navigate the intricacies of adult relationships. Loving a baby was effortless, instinctive.

That evening, after feeding her family, loading the dishwasher, bathing the children and tucking them in, Laura stood alone in her bedroom, thinking. She had intended to slip on her pajamas and settle into bed with a book. Peter was downstairs watching TV, trying to unwind; his job was in an especially intense phase lately.

Laura thought about Greg and Julia and the giant TV in their bedroom. She pictured them lying naked in bed, propped up against piles of pillows, the door locked, watching that video together.

She looked around her own bedroom. Peter's bathrobe hung from a hook on the back of the door; his deodorant sat on his dresser, next to his hairbrush and his nail clippers. His dirty clothes were in the hamper, his shoes lined up under his side of the bed, a bed she had shared with him for six years. The details of their lives were intimately entwined, but Laura realized that she had no idea how he would react to a video like that.

She remembered Julia claiming that good sex would calm her husband, gleefully claiming to have seduced him while his mother was in the house. Julia maintained that Greg was good in bed, but some of the credit for that surely belonged to her and to her own exuberant, unfettered sexuality. If Julia was aroused by that video, Greg reaped the benefit of her excitement.

Laura opened a drawer of her dresser and rummaged inside until she felt the smooth fabric of a satin nightgown. She pulled it out and held it up in front of her. It was bright red, deeply cut in front, with skimpy little shoulder straps. Peter had given it to her when the doctor said they could have sex again after Jessie's birth, but Laura had only worn it a couple of times before it was relegated to the back of the drawer; she'd felt funny trying to nurse a baby in such a thing.

She took off her clothes and pulled the nightgown over her

head, wondering whether it would still fit. It was tight now, hugging her body closely. Laura looked in the mirror; she didn't look like herself at all. The last time she had looked so different was when she wore Julia's curly black wig.

Laura pushed aside the memory of that evening. Tonight she was going to focus on Peter: she was going to seduce her own husband.

She headed downstairs, the slippery satin nightgown clinging to her, feeling as if she were in costume, playing a role. But then, who was she anyway? Who was the real Laura?

She sashayed into the living room.

"Hey, big boy," she said in a low, throaty voice.

Peter turned around and his eyes widened at the sight of her.

"Oh wow," he said. "I'd forgotten all about that little number."

Laura licked her lips suggestively, then sauntered over and sat down on his lap. Peter turned off the TV and spread his hands against her back; she began to unbutton his shirt—slowly, teasingly, one button at a time—as she imagined being filmed in her own erotic movie.

"What has come over you?" Peter asked.

Laura burrowed her fingers under the hair on his chest. "I'm just hot for my man."

She pressed her mouth to his and he responded eagerly. Some part of her that seemed to be watching from a distance observed that kissing him felt pleasurable. It was as if she were conducting some kind of experiment, trying to prove something, though she wasn't sure exactly what.

She unbuckled his belt and Peter stood up to pull off his pants. He sat back on the couch and Laura pulled the nightgown up over her thighs and straddled him. He slipped his hands under the satin onto her bare skin and closed his eyes.

"Oh, my God," he groaned softly.

She looked down into his face, his eyes squeezed shut, and listened to his breathing getting faster, feeling him growing harder underneath her. She felt as powerful as a priestess, celebrating some ancient rite. This was how she imagined Julia with Greg.

Julia, Julia, why did she keep thinking about Julia? Laura closed her eyes and bent to kiss Peter again.

The telephone rang and they both froze.

"Jesus," Peter muttered.

"Let's ignore it," Laura said, in her new, sexy voice. "They'll leave a message."

She licked her lips and kissed him as the answering machine clicked on and off, but a moment later the phone started ringing again. Peter pulled away, distracted; Laura could feel his arousal disappearing.

"I guess we should answer it," he sighed.

Laura climbed off him and walked to the phone.

"Hello," she said in her normal voice.

"Laura, honey . . . you're home? Laura, it's Mama."

"Hello, Mom." Laura glanced at Peter, who was watching her intently.

"I have some real bad news, honey."

Laura felt a jolt of anxiety in her stomach. The phone seemed almost unbearably heavy in her hand.

"What is it?"

"Your daddy . . . it's your daddy . . ." her mother's voice broke.

"What, Mom?"

"He passed away this afternoon."

Laura's legs went watery; she wasn't sure they would hold her up. She opened her mouth to speak but nothing came out.

"Are you there, Laura?"

"Yes, I'm here," she whispered.

"He took a real bad turn this morning. He couldn't breathe; the oxygen wasn't helping. We went to the hospital but he just got worse and worse. And then he died. It happened so fast, I didn't even have a chance to call you or Christine."

"Oh, Mama."

Peter had pulled his pants back on; he came and stood quietly next to Laura.

"The funeral is on Sunday," her mother said. "Can you be here?"

"Of course I'll be there," Laura said.

"If only you could have come at Christmas, before it was too late," her mother said mournfully.

"I couldn't, Mama. Jessie was sick, remember?" Laura felt a little defensive—it wasn't as if she'd had a choice then. Still, it had been a very long time since she'd visited; the truth was that mostly she'd avoided it.

"I just can't believe he's gone," her mother said.

"I know, Mom, I know." Laura's throat felt constricted.

"I have to call your sister," her mother said.

"OK, I'll talk to you soon, I promise."

Laura stood there, stunned, holding the disconnected phone.

"Laura?" Peter said softly.

She turned toward him.

"My father is dead," she said hollowly. For the second time that evening, she felt like an actor speaking someone else's lines.

"Oh, honey, I'm sorry." Peter opened his arms but Laura stood still, immobilized. He lifted the telephone gently out of her hand.

"I knew he was sick," she said. "He's been sick for years. I just somehow never thought he would die."

She looked up at Peter.

"You were the one whose parents died," she said thoughtlessly.

"Well, eventually it happens to everyone," he replied. "I'm sorry, honey."

Laura shivered. Her arms and legs were covered with goose bumps and her cold nipples pushed out against the tight smooth fabric of the nightgown.

"Go put on something warmer," Peter urged.

Laura went upstairs, took off the red satin, and put on wool ski socks, sweatpants, and her warmest sweater. She went into Jessie's room, pulled the blankets over her, and stroked her hair, listening to the soft regular exhalation of her breath.

She crossed the hall: Mark was curled on his belly, his breathing full of tiny snorts and snuffles, like a baby animal. Laura put her hand on his back and felt the comforting rise and fall of his small lungs filling and emptying.

Far away, downstairs, the phone rang again. Laura heard the low murmur of Peter's voice and then his footsteps on the stairs. She left Mark's room and met him in the hallway.

"It's your sister," he whispered, handing her the phone.

"Oh, Laura, Daddy's gone," Christine's voice was choked with anguish.

"I know. I heard," Laura said, numbly.

"Poor Mom. Can you imagine losing your husband after all those years?"

Laura couldn't even imagine being married for so long, let alone how such a loss would feel.

"At least Mom has friends . . ." she faltered.

"I already called Mrs. White. She's going to stay with Mom until we get there."

The Whites had lived across the street for as long as Laura could remember. They had no children of their own, but Mrs. White had often looked after Laura and Christine when they were growing up. It was Mrs. White who'd been in the house the morning Laura, at five years old, woke up to find her parents gone.

"Your mama has gone to the hospital to get you a new little brother or sister," she'd told Laura cheerfully, and proceeded to make a delicious batch of blueberry pancakes.

"Dan and I are flying out tomorrow," Christine went on. "How soon can you leave?"

Laura was still dazed, disoriented; she marveled that Christine could see so clearly what needed to be done.

"I haven't figured it out yet," she said.

"Well, come as soon as you can, OK? Mom needs you. And so do I."

"I need you, too," Laura admitted.

She hung up, full of appreciation for her sister. It was strange to recall that she used to think of her as a pest.

All at once, Laura's mind was flooded with a detailed vision of her childhood home. She pictured herself and Christine, playing on the porch on a summer afternoon as a storm approached, listening to the thunder growing louder, smelling the charged air that preceded the rain. She could see her father mowing the back yard, his ever-present cigarette held loosely between his lips, and her mother standing at the kitchen counter peeling carrots, sweat beading on her face as an electric fan oscillated in front of her, barely stirring the heavy air. They all seemed fixed, arrested in a certain time, like figures in a diorama—not real people, who changed and grew older and died. She felt herself looking back as if from a great distance, unsure exactly where she was now.

Suddenly, unexpectedly, the numbness gave way. Laura stood on the stairs, her shoulders shaking, tears running down her face. Then, as abruptly as it had come, the spasm passed, like a Midwestern storm, and she felt drained, realizing that more than anything she wanted to talk to Julia.

She called her, hoping Greg wouldn't be the one to answer, and went weak with relief at the sound of her voice.

"It's Laura," she said. "I know it's late . . ."

"Are you OK?" Julia asked. "What's going on?"

"I just heard from my mother. My father died this afternoon."

"Oh, Laura, I'm so sorry," Julia said.

"He'd been sick . . . I mean, he had lung cancer and everything. But it's still a shock, you know?"

"I sure do. I've been through this, too: my father died when I was pregnant with Sara. I know how you feel—there isn't anything that feels quite like it. When is the funeral?"

"Sunday. But Christine thinks I should go right away. She's leaving tomorrow."

"Could you?" Julia asked. "Do you want to?"

"I don't know. I don't know what to do. I feel so unprepared."

"No one is ever prepared," Julia said.

Laura and Julia hardly ever talked about their parents. The friendship was focused on their own children, their own experiences as mothers. Now, all at once, it felt as if the frame had shifted outward and the view had widened.

"I should go, I should be there," Laura said. "But Peter is so busy at work right now. I don't know if he can get away."

"He can get away," Julia said confidently. "It isn't every day your father-in-law dies. But I have a question: do you need a little time out there without your kids or your husband—some time just with your mom and with yourself?"

Laura was startled. She wouldn't have thought of it but now that Julia had asked, she realized there was a part of her that wanted to be alone with this for a while.

"I couldn't leave the children," she said, hesitantly.

"You did it before—just last month when you went to New York. Peter took good care of them. They were fine, and so were you, remember?"

"But Peter wasn't quite so swamped at work then. Besides, it was a weekend . . ."

"Here's an idea," Julia said. "I'll take care of the kids during the day until Peter gets home. I can take all the girls to school and bring them back to my house afterwards. And Mark and I always have a good time together."

It was only this morning that Julia had looked after Mark while Laura cleaned her house and snooped in her bedroom. It felt as if an eternity had gone by. Only a few hours ago, all Laura could think about was Julia's sex life; that seemed so trivial now.

"Laura? What do you think?" Julia prompted. "Would that be helpful?"

She was being a little pushy but that was probably deliberate. Julia had an uncanny way of knowing what Laura needed.

"Are you sure it wouldn't be too much for you?" Laura asked. "In your condition?"

"My condition? Pregnancy, you mean? Come on, Laura, don't start sounding like Greg. One of him is more than enough. Anyway, this will be easy: the girls amuse each other and Mark amuses me."

"It's awfully generous of you . . ."

"Not as generous as you cleaning my dirty house," Julia replied. "Look, I know how strange and hard this time can be. If you need a little space to yourself—a little breathing room—I understand. And I will be happy to help you, any way I can."

Tears filled Laura's eyes. Her heart was full to overflowing, brimming with so many emotions at once: grief, shock, confusion, and a powerful feeling of love, as strong as any love she'd ever known.

"Thank you," she whispered. "You are such a friend."

CHAPTER 14

The next day, still in a haze of disbelief, Laura managed to buy herself a plane ticket, pull together some clothes, and call her mother and Christine with her flight information.

"Dan and I rented a car at the airport," Christine told her. "We'll come pick you up."

"I can rent a car myself," Laura protested.

"I'd really like to come and meet you," Christine said. "Living in New York, we hardly ever get to drive anywhere."

"All right." It was easier to let someone else make decisions.

Peter looked perplexed when Laura told him about Julia taking care of the children.

"Shouldn't we all be going to Indiana?" he asked. "Wouldn't your mother like to see her grandchildren?"

"You should all be there for the funeral," Laura said. "But I know you're in the middle of something at work."

"I'm always in the middle of something," Peter said. "It's that kind of job." He paused. "I suppose it could be useful to have a couple more days to try to wrap up this project," he admitted.

""That's what we thought."

"We?"

"Me and Julia."

"Oh. Well . . . at least let me drive you to the airport," he said.

When they went to bed, Peter turned toward her and Laura wondered if he was hoping to have sex; after all, just yesterday she'd been straddling his lap, deliberately trying to turn him on. But he said simply, "Try to sleep," and kissed her goodnight.

Julia arrived early to pick up the children. As soon as Laura opened the door, Julia stepped inside and embraced her. The comfort of being in her arms brought tears to Laura's eyes but she fought to stay in control.

"Thank you," she whispered into Julia's neck.

"We really appreciate this," Peter said, coming up behind her. "It's a big help."

"I'm happy to help," Julia said. "Mark and Jessie are welcome to stay with me for as long as you like."

"We're in your debt," he said.

"Nonsense," Julia answered. "It's my pleasure."

Laura watched them discussing schedules and exchanging phone numbers; they both seemed grounded and steady, while she felt as if she were untethered, floating outside her life. She turned to her children and gathered them close, trying to soak in everything about them. It was hard to believe she was leaving them again.

Peter loaded the car seats into Julia's van, Laura buckled the children in, and then Julia drove away. Laura's tears spilled over, running down her cheeks, as Peter put his arm around her.

They drove to the airport in Peter's Mercedes.

"You can just drop me off at the terminal," Laura suggested. "It takes so long to find parking."

For a moment she thought he was going to argue but he didn't. He pulled up to the curb, took her suitcase out of the trunk, and set it down beside her.

"We'll see you on Saturday," he said. He laid his hands on her shoulders and looked into her face. "I'll make reservations as soon as I get to the office."

Laura thought briefly about how expensive all these last minute airline tickets would be. But money really wasn't an issue, she reminded herself. Peter had plenty of frequent flier miles; besides, he earned far more money than her father ever had. She glanced over at the Mercedes, its motor still running. What would her father have thought about that car?

Her eyes filled unexpectedly.

"Will you be OK?" Peter asked.

She nodded. "You and the children have a safe flight," she said.

"You too, sweetheart." He bent and kissed her tenderly on the mouth.

The trip went smoothly, all things considered. Only the change in Chicago was difficult—Laura had to run from one concourse to another to make her connection. That would be even harder for Peter when he came with the children. He was so used to traveling by himself; Laura hoped he would be patient with them.

Christine and Dan were waiting for her by the luggage carousel. Dan looked better than when she saw him in New York, although there was a gravity in his expression now. Christine threw her arms around Laura; as they hugged each other, Laura's carry-on bag slid down from her shoulder.

"Let me take that," Dan said.

Laura handed it to him and their eyes met.

"I'm sorry about your dad," he said.

"Thanks. I'm glad you're here," she said, startled to realize it was true.

"How are the kids?" he asked.

"They don't understand. They don't know what death is."

"My first encounter with death was when my dog got hit by a car," Dan said. "I was coming home from school and he was running across the street to meet me. The poor mutt went spinning like a top, straight into the gutter."

"Right in front of you?" Laura exclaimed, horrified. "How old were you?"

"Oh, nine or ten, I guess."

"How awful! I'm so sorry!"

"It's not your fault. Dumb dog should have known better—it's just natural selection."

That was exactly the sort of flippant comment Dan was liable to make, but Laura heard it differently now.

Her suitcase was coming around on the luggage belt. She reached for it but Dan stepped up quickly beside her and grabbed it. The three of them walked toward the parking lot.

"I don't know what my children will make of a funeral," Laura said. "But I think they should be there. Even though they didn't really know Dad."

"At least they had a chance to meet their grandfather," Christine said.

It might have been a comfort to Christine to be looking forward to a baby now. It would have been cheering news for their mother, too.

"How's Mom?" Laura asked.

"She's exhausted. I don't think she's really slept for two days," Christine said. "She isn't eating, either."

"You should see all the food she has in the house," Dan put in. "Her fridge is ready to explode."

"The neighbors have been bringing stuff," Christine said. "You know how it is when someone dies."

Dan put the suitcase in the trunk and they all got into the car. Christine twisted around to talk to Laura.

"I'm so relieved you're here," she said. "The house feels strange and different now, without Dad."

Laura wondered how different it would feel to her. Even when he was alive, her father had seemed like only a vague presence in the house. He used to work long hours as a roofer and come home at the end of the day, exhausted and taciturn, an outsider to the life of the family.

"Chris, I need your help," Dan said abruptly. "These little country roads all look alike." He was definitely sounding more like his old self.

Christine turned around to navigate and Laura settled back in her seat and looked out the window. The landscape stretched as far as you could see; the car was a tiny vessel in the middle of the vast, flat plain. The cornstalks had been cut down months ago and their winter stubble was dark and barren-looking, poking up out of a thin layer of snow. The late afternoon sky was gray and heavy and everything seemed melancholy.

Christine switched on the radio and Dwight Yoakum's heart-broken voice emerged from the static.

"Oh, leave that on!" Laura begged.

Christine turned around again.

"That's right, you used to like country music, didn't you?"

"I still do," Laura confessed.

Christine had been scornful when Laura listened to country music back in high school. By then she'd pretty much given up on imitating Laura or seeking her attention. But now, indulgent, she left the radio tuned to the country station and Laura listened, watching the empty fields go by and thinking about Julia dancing to Hank Williams in her living room.

Her parents' house looked even smaller than she'd remembered. Laura walked up the front steps and hesitated, then Christine opened the door and they stepped into the living room.

It still smelled of cigarette smoke. How long would it take for that smell to disappear—from the sofa, the curtains, the easy chair her father used to sit in to watch football on TV?

Mrs. White emerged from the kitchen, a dish towel in her hand, and hurried across the room with small, shuffling steps. She moved like an old person now, but her embrace was warm and hearty as she pressed Laura against her generous bosom.

"Laura, honey!" she exclaimed. "It's so good to see you. How was your flight?"

"It was fine," Laura said. "Except for Chicago—that airport is always a challenge."

"Is that right? I really don't ever fly," Mrs. White said. Laura wondered if she ever traveled at all. She could only remember the Whites being at home, in their house right across the street.

"I'm so sorry about your daddy," Mrs. White said. "We never thought he would go so fast. I'm sorry you didn't get to say goodbye."

"Where's my mom?" Laura asked.

"She's lying down to rest. She'll be so happy to see you."

"Thank you for helping her," Christine said. "It's good to know she has friends who care about her."

"I think the world of your mother," Mrs. White said earnestly. "She's awfully special to me."

Laura looked at Mrs. White's plump face: her double chin, the soft wrinkles in her cheeks, the kind eyes behind her glasses. Could she and Laura's mother have the same kind of friendship— the same feelings for each other—that Laura had with Julia? Mrs. White had always just been part of the landscape of Laura's childhood, a presence she took for granted.

"Well, I'll be going now." Mrs. White was untying her apron. "I'm sure you want some time with your mother. Tell her I'll call her later."

Laura's mother appeared on the stairs, descending cautiously, one hand gripping the banister.

"Oh good, you're up." Mrs. White smiled at her. "I spoke to Mr. Fields at the funeral home—we're all set for the viewing tomorrow."

"Thank you, Janice. Thank you for everything," Laura's mother said.

"I'm going to go now so you can visit with your daughters," Mrs. White said, opening the front door.

"Don't you have a coat?" Laura's mother asked. "It's cold out there."

"I'm just running across the street," Mrs. White said. "I'll call you tonight." She pulled the door shut behind her.

Laura looked at her mother. Like the house, she seemed smaller than Laura remembered, and she seemed older now too, vulnerable in a way that Laura had never seen. Laura was struck with the thought that someday her mother would die and then she and

Christine would be orphans.

"I'm so glad you're home," her mother said.

Laura crossed the room and hugged her. "I'm sorry about Daddy," she murmured.

"Where are the children?" her mother asked. "And your husband?"

Laura pulled back, disconcerted; she had explained the whole plan over the phone.

"They're coming on Saturday, remember?" Christine put in quickly.

"Oh, that's right . . . I can't seem to keep track of anything anymore."

"There's a lot on your mind right now," Christine said.

"Yes . . . well, you can take your stuff up to my bedroom."

"Where will you sleep?" Laura asked.

"I'm used to sleeping on the couch. Your father couldn't climb the stairs so we had a bed in the living room for him and I stayed down here to keep an eye on him."

The last time Laura was here her parents were still sleeping in their own room, in their own bed.

"You don't want to move back?" she asked.

"I'm comfortable here. You and your family can have that big bedroom."

Laura glanced at Christine. She was like a bridge between Laura's childhood and the present, a kind of reality checkpoint.

"Come on, Laura," Christine said. "I'll help you get settled."

"Don't you and Dan want Mom and Dad's bed?" Laura asked as they went upstairs.

"No, it's OK. Their bedroom is bigger—there'll be plenty of room on the floor for your kids to sleep when they get here."

They sat down, side by side, on the edge of the bed. It was covered with a smooth polyester bedspread but Laura remembered the tufted chenille spread that had been on this bed when she was little. She used to smooth down the tufts with one finger when she was sick and nestled into her parents' bed.

"How long has Mom had this new bedspread?" she asked Christine.

"New? I don't think it's very new."

"I suppose not." Laura sighed. "What happened to the bed in the living room?"

"Dan took it apart and put it in the basement. We thought it would be hard for Mom, just having it sit there, empty."

Laura sighed again. Her father's sickbed had come and gone from the living room and she'd never even known it was there. And now his body was lying in a funeral home across town.

"Are you OK?" Christine asked.

"I guess so. It just all feels so strange, you know? How is Mom doing, really?"

"I think she's mostly in shock. I'm so grateful she's had Mrs. White to look after her. Everyone should have a friend like that."

The image of Julia's face appeared in Laura's mind. She'd be at home with all the children now—it was still too early for Peter to have left work.

"I should call home and let them know I got here safely," she said.

"OK. I'll see you downstairs."

Laura called Julia, her fingers finding the numbers by heart. The phone rang several times before Julia answered.

"Hi, it's me," Laura said.

"Oh, Laura! I was just getting Mark up from his nap."

"He took a nap at your house?" Laura was filled with longing for his sleepy weight in her arms, the smell of his sweaty head after he'd slept on one spot for a couple of hours.

"He was tired. I wore him out playing this morning and then the girls ran him ragged after they got home."

"How are the girls getting along?" Laura asked.

"Just great. Playing and squabbling with each other as if they were all siblings," Julia laughed.

"You see? You're doing fine with more than two," Laura pointed out.

"Oh, well, for a couple of days I can do anything," Julia said. "It's the endlessness of caring for another baby, day in and day out, that I'm not sure I can face."

"Yes, you can," Laura assured her. "When is Peter coming?"

"I don't know, exactly. I offered to feed him and the kids so he wouldn't have to worry about dinner."

"That is awfully sweet of you." Laura was touched and a little jealous that Julia was taking such good care of her family. It made her feel even farther away.

"How is everyone there? How are you?" Julia asked.

"I guess we're all still kind of stunned."

"Well, you take care of yourself, Laura. Everything is going fine here."

"Can I talk to the children?" Laura asked.

"Of course," Julia said. "Here's Mark right now."

In a moment, Laura heard him breathing through the phone. He'd probably been sitting in Julia's lap the whole time.

"Hey, Mr. Marco. It's Mommy, sweetie."

"Mommy?" he said. Laura pictured him looking up at Julia, his eyelids droopy with sleep.

"Are you having fun with Julia?"

"Doolia," he repeated. Laura hadn't heard him use a name for her.

"I love you, honey." Laura made a kissing sound into the phone and then Julia was back.

"Hang on a minute, I'll get Jessie," she said. She put down the phone and Laura heard her say, "Come on, little buddy." No doubt Mark was trailing after her into the playroom.

Loneliness—and a profound sadness—washed over Laura. Her throat ached and warm tears began to slip down her face.

"Hi, Mommy," Jessie said gaily.

Laura pressed the receiver against her ear and wiped her cheeks with her free hand.

"Hi, sweet pea. How are you? How was school?"

"Fine," Jessie said with her usual lack of detail. "Guess what,

Mommy?"

"What, sweetheart?"

"Julia said we can have pizza for supper."

"That's great, honey. You love pizza."

There was a brief silence. Jessie was probably distracted; talking to a child on the phone was a lot more difficult than in person. This must be what it was like for Peter, trying to talk to the children when he was away on business.

"I love you, Jessie. I'll see you on Saturday," Laura said.

"Mommy, will I fly in a plane?"

"That's right—you and Mark and Daddy."

That plane trip with the children was something only Peter would experience. Laura's throat felt tight again.

"OK. Bye, Mommy," Jessie said.

"Bye, sweet pea. Can you give the phone back to Julia?"

"Hello again," Julia said, and Laura began to cry.

"I miss them so much," she said.

"I know, I know," Julia murmured.

Laura sat there, crying and sniffling over the phone. She couldn't imagine doing that with anyone but Julia.

"It's a sad time," Julia said softly.

It occurred to Laura suddenly that maybe some of her sorrow wasn't about the children. Any grief she felt about her father's death was buried under the surface, hidden even from her. But Julia probably understood that, too.

"I really appreciate you taking care of the kids," she said. "I'm so glad they're with you."

"I'm glad, too. I love having them around."

"You are such a friend."

"So are you. I love you, Laura."

Laura's breath caught in her throat. "I love you, too," she whispered.

"Uh-oh, I think I have to go break up an argument," Julia said. "Take care of yourself, Laura."

"Thank you. For everything."

"You are always welcome."

Laura hung up, blew her nose, took a deep breath, and went back downstairs. Her mother was sitting on the couch with Christine, their heads bent over a Bible.

"We're trying to find Dad's favorite Bible verse," Christine explained. Laura wouldn't have guessed her father had the slightest interest in the Bible. She couldn't remember him ever going to church.

"Mom wants Reverend Mallory to include it in the funeral service," Christine said. "It's one of the psalms but we can't seem to find it."

"The Lord is My Shepherd?" Laura suggested. "That's psalm 23, isn't it?" It was the only one she knew.

"No, it's a different one," her mother said.

Laura watched her mother slowly turn the pages, pausing periodically to lick her finger. She had the hands of an old woman: there were little wrinkles all along the backs of them and they were covered with the brown speckles that she called liver spots.

Christine leaned close to her mother, reading verse fragments out loud. Laura felt like an outsider, at a distance that was somehow of her own making.

"Here it is," her mother said at last.

"I will lift up mine eyes unto the hills, from whence cometh my help," Christine read.

"Yes, that's the one. I'm sure of it."

Laura stared at them, astonished. How was it that she had never known her father had a favorite psalm—or that he knew any psalms at all? She went to stand beside Christine, so she could read over her shoulder.

"I will lift up mine eyes unto the hills . . ."

"What did Daddy know about hills?" Laura wondered aloud. There weren't any hills in this part of the country.

"He did some training in Colorado when he was in the service," her mother said. "He thought the Rocky Mountains were the most beautiful sight in the world."

Christine was nodding, as if that were something she had already known. Laura felt as if she must have been asleep all through her childhood: her parents were strangers to her, their actual lives and feelings a mystery, something she'd never thought about.

Her mother laid the ribbon bookmark sewn into the Bible's binding over the page and closed the book.

"I'm glad we found that," she said. "I should call Reverend Mallory."

"Would you like me to call?" Christine offered.

"No, I'll do it. I need to talk to him."

"How about if Laura and I get started on dinner then?" Christine proposed. "What would you like to eat?"

"Oh, I don't know. I don't have much of an appetite. I'm afraid I haven't been to the supermarket . . ."

"Mom, the fridge is overflowing with food," Christine reminded her.

She beckoned Laura toward the kitchen. Laura had never prepared a meal in her mother's kitchen but Christine seemed right at home. She opened the refrigerator and started peeking inside the various containers.

"What are you in the mood for?" she asked Laura. "We have soup, quiche, shepherd's pie, lasagna, cold fried chicken—there's a whole church potluck supper in here."

"Anything's fine with me," Laura said.

"You're no help. You're as indecisive as Mom," Christine declared. "Maybe we should find out what Dan wants."

"Where is he?" Laura hadn't seen him since she'd gone upstairs.

"He went outside to salt the front steps. It's supposed to get really cold tonight and they might get icy."

Winter nights here could be so bitter, Laura remembered. With no ocean to moderate the extremes of weather, winters were brutally cold and summers were stiflingly hot.

"It seems like he's been out there forever," Christine remarked. "I guess the fresh air is good for him, anyway."

"How is he doing?" Laura asked.

"He's OK. He's still sad about the baby, of course . . ." Christine paused, her eyes filling. "We both are," she added. "It makes all this even harder somehow."

"I know," Laura murmured. "I'm sorry."

Christine wiped her eyes and turned back to the refrigerator.

"You want a root beer?" she asked.

Root beer was one of those things that Laura associated utterly with Indiana—not that she couldn't get it anywhere else, she just never thought of it except when she was home. Her mother kept cases of it in the basement.

Christine opened two cans and poured each one into a glass. The root beer fizzed and sparkled as she handed a glass to Laura.

"Well . . . cheers, I guess," she said.

Laura looked around the kitchen at all the familiar things: the set of matching canisters on the counter, the ancient toaster that never broke down, the dish towel hanging neatly on a rod over the sink.

"Laura, how are you doing?" Christine asked.

Laura hesitated.

"I don't really know," she said. "I don't know how to feel. Dad always seemed like . . . well, kind of a stranger."

She had never admitted that to anyone. She felt suddenly, frighteningly, exposed and tears pricked her eyelids.

Christine surveyed her thoughtfully for a moment.

"I guess it was different for me," she said. "I got to know Dad after you were gone. I was the only child at home for five years, you know."

Laura pondered that. She'd been the only child before Christine was born, but she couldn't remember now what it was like.

"Dad and I got pretty close when I was in high school," Christine said. "He kind of confided in me."

"Really?" It was an amazing thought: her father opening up. "About what?"

"Well . . ." Christine paused. "Did you know that Mom had an affair?"

"What?!"

Christine nodded and put a finger to her lips.

"Mom doesn't know I know," she said.

"Chris, you have to be joking." This was unbelievable: her devoted, long-suffering mother—who spent her life taking care of her husband—having an affair?

"I know. It's hard to imagine."

"An affair with who? When?"

"She took a painting class at the community college. He was her art teacher . . . he was quite a few years younger than Mom."

"Why would Mom take a painting class?" Laura asked stupidly.

"I suppose she wanted a hobby or something. She was probably feeling like her life was kind of boring. You'd already left home, I was busy at school, Dad was busy at work . . . I suppose she got lonely," Christine said.

"How did Dad find out?"

"He picked up the phone one night and Mom was on the extension, talking to Gary."

"Gary?"

"That was his name. Gary Trumbull."

Laura felt a little dizzy. She pulled a chair out from the kitchen table and sat down heavily.

"How come you never told me about this?" she asked.

"Dad didn't want me to tell anyone. I don't think he meant to tell me, either, but it slipped out after he'd had a few drinks. I came home late from a basketball game at school and Mom was out—she was at the class—and Dad was just sitting alone in the house, brooding and drinking and smoking cigarettes. He made me promise not to tell."

"Why are you telling me now?" Laura asked, torn between wanting and not wanting to know about any of it.

"Well, Daddy's dead now. He's gone. I don't see how he can mind anymore," Christine said. "I still don't think we should tell

Mom, though. It would just make her feel bad."

Laura gazed at her sister, impressed again by her maturity and kindness.

"You're right," she agreed. "But you have to tell me the rest. What finally happened?"

"He confronted her and she confessed. I heard them a few nights after Daddy told me. He was yelling and Mom was crying . . . I only knew what it was all about because he had told me."

"So he forgave her?"

"Yes, he did. She quit the class and somehow they put the whole thing behind them. He really loved her a lot, you know," Christine said.

Laura was quiet for a long moment.

"I guess I didn't know," she said, finally. "I always thought she totally sacrificed herself to him, taking care of him. I never dreamed she could do anything to hurt him."

"Marriages are complicated," Christine said. "You never really know what's under the surface."

Laura sat there, thinking about her mother and father, and about Christine and Dan, and Julia and Greg. For the first time, it occurred to her to wonder what her own marriage looked like from the outside or, for that matter, how it looked from inside.

"Hey," Christine said. "We're supposed to be making dinner."

She pulled a casserole out of the refrigerator and handed Laura some lettuce to wash for a salad. As Laura stood at the sink, cold water running over her hands, Dan walked into the kitchen. His hair was flattened from being under a hat and his cheeks were flushed with cold.

"There you are," Christine said fondly. "I was starting to wonder if you got lost."

"I was talking to Mr. and Mrs. White," he said. "They seem like awfully nice people."

Laura wondered if there were any hidden secrets between the Whites. She'd never given the slightest thought to their marriage before.

Dan lowered his voice. "I think your mother is crying upstairs," he said. "She is so broken up . . . it must be awful to lose someone you love so much."

He looked at Laura.

"Maybe you should talk to her," he suggested.

Laura remembered sitting with Dan as he wept in his dark living room. She glanced at Christine, who nodded.

"Yes, go," she said. "Dan and I will take care of dinner."

Not knowing what in the world she would say when she found her, Laura dried her hands and left the room in search of her grieving mother.

CHAPTER 15

Laura's mother was in her bedroom, sitting on the edge of the bed, where Laura and Christine had sat a little while earlier. She was crying, just as Dan had thought, holding a box of tissues on her lap.

Laura stepped cautiously into the room. It was disorienting to see her mother in tears; the image didn't match either the stoic, selfless woman Laura remembered or the unfaithful wife Christine had described. Right now she looked only like a bereaved widow, facing the rest of her life alone.

"Mama?"

Her mother patted a spot beside her on the bed and turned a tearful face toward Laura.

"I can't believe he's gone," she said. "Forty-six years he was my life . . . what am I supposed to do now?"

Forty-six years. Her parents were married right after high school; by the time Laura's mother was the age Laura had been when she met Peter, she'd been married to Laura's father for twelve years.

"You never know how much a person means to you until he's gone," her mother said. "It's so easy to take each other for granted, you know?"

Laura nodded.

"You're lucky . . . you have a good husband. Your father thought very highly of him," her mother declared. Laura couldn't recall her father offering any opinion about Peter.

"Uh-huh," she murmured.

"Your father was a good husband, too," her mother said. "He was very good to me . . ." Her voice dropped.

Laura sat still, trying not to think about her mother's affair.

"He really loved you," her mother said. "He loved you and your sister very much."

Did he? Laura wondered silently. What did that mean? It had been her mother who bought her birthday presents, took care of her when she was sick, drove her to swimming lessons, scolded her when she stayed out after curfew. Her father had been peripheral, a figure in the background of her childhood.

She had an image of herself as a little girl, curled in her father's lap in the big recliner, but the picture was as dim and vague as a dream. Was it an actual memory or just her imagination? There was so little she really knew about him: what was his favorite color? his favorite food? which football team did he root for?

All at once, she was overwhelmed with sadness, with a sense of having missed out. It wasn't so much her father's death she was mourning as his absence while he was alive. Tears filled her eyes and began to run down her face.

Her mother set the box of tissues on the bed between them.

"I know it's a shock," she said. "I'm so sorry you didn't get to see him again before he left us."

Laura sat there crying, trying to recall exactly what her father had looked like, or the sound of his voice. The only clear memory she had of him was how he smelled—his clothes, his hands, his hair: always of cigarette smoke.

"He was so proud of you and Christine—going off and having such adventurous lives."

"Is that what he thought?" Laura pulled a tissue from the box.

"Oh, he was proud as anything. But he sure did miss you."

Laura had never considered his feelings. She'd never thought about him having feelings.

"Mama?" she said. "Could I have a picture of Daddy?" She didn't have a photograph of her father; until now it hadn't occurred to her to want one.

"Of course." Her mother leaned over the bed and opened the drawer of her nightstand. She pulled out a stack of photographs and handed one to Laura. There was her father, smiling, in a picture taken when he was still healthy.

Laura hesitated. "Oh, Mama, I shouldn't take one of your pictures," she said.

"Don't worry about it. I have plenty," her mother said.

Laura looked at the photograph, wiping her eyes so she wouldn't drop tears on it.

"Soup's on!" Christine called up the stairs. That was what their mother used to say when dinner was ready. Laura stood up and laid the photo carefully on top of her suitcase.

"You go ahead," her mother said. "I'm not hungry."

"Just come down and sit with us, then," Laura coaxed. "We need to stick together."

Christine had spread a tablecloth over the kitchen table and set out a couple of candles, along with a steaming macaroni casserole and a big bowl of salad, garnished with cleverly cut vegetables.

"What a pretty salad. Look at those darling little radish roses," Laura's mother said.

"Dan made them," Christine declared.

"He did?" Laura and her mother spoke in unison.

"I'm a man of hidden talents," Dan said.

"It's nice to see a man who's comfortable in the kitchen," Laura's mother remarked. "Your father couldn't even boil an egg."

"Sometimes Dan gets home first and has a whole dinner ready for me when I get home from work," Christine said proudly.

"That must be nice for a working girl like you," her mother said. "Your father never could have done that. I couldn't leave him on his own in a kitchen—he was hopeless." She said it affectionately, almost dreamily, and her eyes welled up. She turned to Laura.

"Who's cooking for your husband while you're away?" she

asked. "Or is he as talented in the kitchen as Christine's husband?"

Laura felt immediately defensive. Even if Dan wasn't a complete moron after all, it was unthinkable for Peter to be compared to him.

"He can cook," she said. She was flooded unexpectedly with a memory of Peter making an omelet the morning after she'd first spent the night in his apartment: standing at the stove in his pajama bottoms, sunlight spilling in through the window. Laura had watched the muscles moving in his forearm as he whisked the eggs in a bowl, the look of concentration on his face as he turned the pepper grinder.

"Tonight my friend Julia is making dinner for him and the kids so he can stay at work longer," she added. "He has a lot to do." She knew Julia was just ordering pizza, but there was no need to mention that.

"Will your friend help him put the kids to bed?" her mother asked.

"Oh no, Peter can take care of that." It was odd to remember that she'd been doubtful of his capability herself a few weeks ago, before her trip to New York.

"He'll give them baths and change diapers and everything?"

"Well, sure," Laura said, although she suspected the children might not have baths tonight; probably they'd get home late enough that Peter would just tuck them into bed. Would he go back to their rooms during the night, she wondered, to look at their lashes lying against their cheeks, and listen to them breathing?

"Your father never gave you girls baths when you were little," Laura's mother said.

"Why not?" Christine asked.

"I don't know . . . I guess I thought it wasn't appropriate." Her mother sounded remorseful.

"Because we were girls?"

"I suppose so. It seems silly now, when I think about it. He might have really enjoyed that," she said, her eyes filling again.

Laura felt sorrow rising in her, too. She knew how sweet it was to hold her hand against a baby's wet back, to touch the delicate skin of an infant with her fingertips. She thought of Jessie and Emily, covered in bubbles, giggling in the bathtub after the trip to the beach with Julia—and of Mark, sitting upright in the warm shallow water, clutching his tiny penis.

After dinner, Christine and Laura did the dishes while Dan sat in the living room with their mother. By the time the sisters joined them, he had led her into a conversation about their father. She was describing the first dance they'd attended together in high school: how Laura's father had been almost too shy to invite her and how he'd brought flowers when he came to pick her up.

"Did he try to kiss you on the first date?" Dan asked.

"Oh my, no . . . but I would have said yes if he had."

"Aha! So were you easy or was he irresistible?" Dan teased.

Laura's mother sighed. There was the merest shadow of a smile on her lips.

"I don't know. Maybe a little of both," she said.

Laura tried to picture her parents as teenagers, overtaken with love and hormones.

"Your father was very popular," her mother said. "All the other girls thought I was lucky to get him."

The phone rang. Christine answered it, then handed it to Laura.

"I'll take it upstairs," Laura said.

She went into her parents' bedroom and picked up the extension.

"Hi, honey," Peter said.

"Hi. Where are you?"

"I'm still at Greg and Julia's. I'll be leaving soon—the kids are already asleep—but I thought I should call you before it got any later."

Had they been sitting around talking, too? Laura wondered. What did they talk about?

"How is everything?" she asked.

"Just fine. Julia gave us dinner."

"Yeah, she told me."

"You talked to Julia?" Peter asked.

"I called earlier to talk to the children."

"Oh." Peter paused. "How are things out there? How's your mother?"

"She's pretty sad but Dan's been getting her to talk."

"Dan? Really?"

"He's good at drawing her out. I'm hearing things about my dad I never knew."

"I wouldn't have guessed Dan could do that," Peter said.

"I know, me neither. How are the children?" Laura asked.

"They're fine. Julia took good care of them."

Laura sighed inwardly. It wouldn't occur to him to offer the mundane details she craved: how many slices of pizza they ate, what time they fell asleep, if they'd asked for her.

"They're exhausted, though," Peter added. "I'll have to carry them into the house."

Laura pictured him, a sleeping child in each arm, trying to get his key in the lock and open the door.

"I wish I were there," she said.

"I miss you, too."

She'd meant being there to help with the children but she didn't correct him.

"Is Julia coming again tomorrow morning?" she asked.

"Yes. She even offered to help me pack," Peter said. "I told her I could manage, though."

"Don't forget Mark's little monkey," Laura reminded him. "And Jessie likes to have her own pillow . . ." It was strange to think of Peter doing all the packing for the children.

"We'll be fine. Don't worry about us," Peter said. "I'll call you again tomorrow."

"Kiss the children for me," she said wistfully.

"I will," he promised. "Goodnight, sweetheart."

When Laura went back downstairs, Christine and her mother

were spreading sheets on the couch.

"Are you going to sleep?" Laura asked.

"I'm going to try," her mother answered. "There's so much to do tomorrow."

"Shall I sit with you for a while?" Christine offered. "I could read to you."

"No, you go on up to bed. I'll call Janice and talk to her for a bit."

It was odd to hear her call Mrs. White by her first name, an acknowledgment that Laura and Christine were adults now, too.

Laura followed Dan and Christine up the stairs. They went into the bedroom Laura and Christine used to share and closed the door. Laura wondered if they would sleep separately in the single beds or try to squeeze onto one together.

She went alone into her mother's room. She felt restless: tired but not sleepy. She missed having her children down the hall and it struck her that she was missing Peter, too—the reassuring presence of his body beside her, the solace of his unwavering devotion.

She opened the drawer of the nightstand and pulled out the pile of photos. Her mother had written on the back of each one, in her small, careful handwriting. Laura found a photo of herself in her prom dress—a peach-colored, strapless gown—her long hair tumbling over her bare shoulders. She still remembered the shoes she'd worn that night: a pair of high heels dyed to match the dress, the most glamorous, grown-up shoes she'd ever owned. She could recall those shoes more vividly than the boy who'd been her date.

Another photo showed a group of little girls dressed in Halloween costumes; it was labeled "Laura's birthday, eight years old." Laura was in the center, clasping hands tightly with Michelle, their faces shining out toward the camera. There were pictures of Laura and Christine, their hair in pigtails, playing together in a sandbox, and of five-year-old Laura sitting in a corner of the couch, holding baby Christine on her lap. Farther down in the pile were photos of her father as a young man: in his Army uniform, in a pair of swim trunks, flexing his muscles playfully for the camera, sitting on the branch of an apple tree in full bloom.

Her mother must have taken all these photographs. She used to take a camera everywhere but only now did Laura realize what good pictures her mother took. She had a real artist's eye.

At the bottom of the stack, under the pictures, lay an envelope addressed to "My darling Elizabeth." Laura picked it up warily, as if it might burn her. Was it from her mother's lover? She told herself not to open it, but her disobedient fingers lifted the flap and drew out a letter, written on plain lined paper and folded to fit inside the envelope. She unfolded it, simultaneously afraid to look and too curious not to.

"My sweet darling wife," it said, "You are the most beautiful mother in the world. Thank you for making me the proud father of a perfect daughter. All my love, your devoted Richard."

Her father. And he was writing about her. Tears filled Laura's eyes as she folded the letter carefully, tucked it into the envelope, and put it back in the drawer, covering it again with all the photos. She turned off the lamp and lay awake in the dark for a long time.

Mrs. White came over early the next morning. She and Laura's mother went through the bedroom closet, deciding which clothes to deliver to the funeral home. Laura wondered if either of them had ever discovered a secret in the other's house, the way she'd found the erotic videotape in Julia's. Did Mrs. White know about the affair with the art teacher? What did she think about it? Was it just forgotten history by now?

Other people came and went throughout the day: Reverend Mallory showed up to discuss the funeral service, neighbors dropped by, bringing more food, and the local florist made multiple deliveries.

"There are even more flowers going to the funeral home, you know," Christine remarked, as she carried another bouquet into the house.

"I didn't realize Mom knew so many people," Laura admitted.

Her mother asked them to go through the photographs of their father and choose some to take to the funeral home. Laura and Christine pored over them, selected the best ones, then went around the house collecting childhood pictures of themselves, which they took out of the frames and replaced with pictures of their father.

At the end of the afternoon, they went to the funeral home. Mr. Fields, the funeral director, took the photographs and placed them around the room. Christine was right: there were flowers everywhere; the place was redolent with the smell of lilies.

Laura walked over to the open casket and looked in at the lifeless body wearing her father's clothes. They'd been cleaned—aired of the familiar smell of smoke; they might have been the clothes of any man. She stared down at the waxen features, trying to comprehend that this was her father's face, but it looked even less real than the photographs. Laura had thought this would be a chance to bid some kind of farewell to her father but she saw now that it was too late—he was already gone. She turned away, dry-eyed and numb.

Mr. Fields opened the door and for the next two hours a steady stream of visitors arrived. Laura was impressed by the network of roots her mother had in this town: Reverend Mallory; Mrs. White; Mrs. Tully, her longtime hairdresser; Mr. Baxter, the butcher at the supermarket; the ladies from church and from her canasta club— all part of an interconnected system of support.

But they were her mother's friends; they'd known Laura only as a girl, and this town was no longer her home. Laura was suddenly awash with homesickness. She closed her eyes for a moment, trying to picture her children's faces.

"I'm sorry about your dad," said a voice beside her.

"Thank you," Laura replied automatically. She didn't want to talk to anyone.

"You look just the same," the voice continued. "Except you

cut your hair."

Disconcerted, Laura turned to see a heavyset woman, closer to her own age than to her mother's.

"You don't recognize me, do you?" the woman said.

It hit her all at once, with a jolt like an electric shock. "Michelle?"

"Yes, it's me. Your old pal."

Could it be, really? Laura stared at her, trying to find some vestige of the girl she had been. The ripe young adolescent Laura remembered, swinging her hips saucily, was gone, a ghost of the distant past. This woman was . . . well, she was fat, and her hair was cropped short, with dark roots showing under a blond that didn't suit her. If she hadn't spoken, Laura wouldn't have recognized her at all.

"You cut your hair too," she said, weakly.

"I heard you moved away," Michelle said.

"That's right. I live in Massachusetts now."

"Wow. I never got any farther than Indianapolis."

"Is that where you live?"

"Not anymore," Michelle replied. "I'm back—I couldn't stay away from this thrilling little town." She offered a sardonic smile.

Laura had dreamed for years about seeing Michelle again, but now that it was actually happening she felt completely unprepared.

"How are your parents?" she asked. "Did they move back, too?"

Michelle laughed bitterly. "No, they kicked me out."

"Oh!" Laura said, sorry to have asked.

"They got born again and now they think I'm just a hopeless sinner." Michelle shrugged as if she were trying to shake something off.

"Michelle . . ." Laura stopped, stuck; she couldn't imagine what to say.

"Those were the good old days, huh?" Michelle said.

"What?"

"Those carefree days in junior high . . . wasn't that just the best time of your life?"

Did she really feel that way? Was she totally unaware of Laura's misery—of the pain Michelle had caused her?

"My life is happier now than it was back then," Laura said.

"Really?"

Laura tried to imagine living Michelle's life. She wanted to ask her if she had any regrets—about anything.

"Oh, my gosh, is that Michelle Dooley?" Christine said, joining them. "You look so different—I hardly recognized you."

"I guess we've all grown up a little," Michelle said.

"Yes, we have," Christine replied.

There was a brief, awkward silence.

"Well . . . I'm sorry about your loss," Michelle said, backing away. "Tell your mom I said Hi."

"Mom never liked her," Christine whispered to Laura. Laura thought about how she and Michelle used to exclude her when they were all kids; apparently Christine was revisiting her own wounded feelings.

These days Laura felt a new allegiance to Christine, but there was no connection left with Michelle; all they had in common was the history of an old friendship, a friendship they didn't even re-member the same way. Laura felt again that sensation of home-sickness—of distance from her present life and from the people she loved most in the world.

As soon as she got back to her mother's house, she called home.

"I'm so glad you called," Peter said. "I'm trying to get the kids to bed early tonight—they have a long day ahead of them."

"Are they in bed already?" Laura asked anxiously.

"Not yet. I knew they'd want to talk to their Mama," Peter said.

Laura breathed out with relief. Sometimes he was wiser than she expected. She spoke with the children, drinking in the sound of their voices, and then Peter came back on the line.

"We should make this quick so I really can get them to bed," he said. "We'll be arriving around nine-thirty tomorrow . . ."

"Nine-thirty at night?" she interrupted, dismayed. "My flight got here at four o'clock."

"We couldn't get three seats together on that flight. Julia said she could take the kids again in the morning and I'll put in a few hours at work before we leave."

It seemed almost impossible to wait so long.

"I reserved a car but I'm not sure I remember how to get to your mother's house," Peter continued.

"I'll meet you at the airport," Laura said quickly.

"I can't wait to see you," Peter said, his tone shifting from businesslike to tender. "I've missed you."

"It's not easy being a single parent, is it?" she teased.

"That's not what I meant."

"I know," she said, relenting. "I miss you, too."

Saturday was spent in a flurry of cleaning, preparing the house for a reception after the funeral. Everyone pitched in: Dan vacuumed, Christine scrubbed the kitchen, Laura cleaned the bathroom. It struck her that she'd spent more time lately cleaning other people's houses than her own.

She and Christine fashioned little beds using layers of blankets on the floor of their mother's bedroom. The children would be arriving so late they'd probably go right to sleep wherever they were.

"You know, someone has to drive me back to the airport," Laura said. "Peter's renting a car for us . . . if I'd done that earlier you wouldn't have to go now."

"But wasn't it nice to be met?" Christine asked. "I don't mind driving you back to meet your family."

"I'm dying to see them," Laura confided.

"I can tell. Are you sorry that you came by yourself?"

Laura thought for a minute.

"No," she said finally. "It was good to be able to talk to you—

and to Mom—without interruptions."

Dan also offered to drive, but Christine suggested he stay home and keep their mother company.

"She's so comfortable with you," Christine said. "Besides, I'd like some time alone with my sister."

As they drove to the airport, Christine talked about her work. She was a producer at a TV station—a fast-paced, high-pressure job she clearly loved.

"It makes me feel important," she said. "Although I'd still rather be doing what you do."

"What I do?"

"You know . . . being a mom."

The plane had just landed when they arrived at the airport; Laura waited impatiently as all the other passengers walked by. When she finally saw her family coming toward her, she had a sudden giddy sense of lightness, as if something weighing on her had just been lifted.

Jessie walked along next to Peter, her eyes on the floor, weaving and staggering with sheer exhaustion. Peter was holding Mark in one arm and somehow carrying two car seats and the diaper bag as well. How had he ever managed the airport in Chicago? He looked exhausted too; he'd probably stayed up late working after he'd put the children to bed.

"There's Mommy," he said to Jessie.

She looked up and her face brightened.

"Mommy!" she cried and ran full tilt toward Laura.

Laura knelt and braced herself for the impact of Jessie's solid little body. She gathered her daughter into her arms and held her close. When she stood up again, Peter was right in front of her. Mark lay sound asleep against his shoulder, drooling onto his shirt.

Laura felt a great rush of tenderness. She kissed the back of Mark's head, then turned her face to kiss Peter on the mouth.

"I'm so glad you're here," she said. "How was the trip?"

"Well, it's not the easiest thing, traveling with two little kids.

Trying to fit all three of us into an airplane restroom was quite a challenge. But here we are."

"Here you are," Laura echoed.

"How are you holding up? Is everyone OK?"

"Yeah, we're OK. Right, Chris?" Laura turned toward her sister, who was hanging back, watching the reunion.

"That's right," Christine said. "Welcome to Indiana. Can I help you carry something?"

They walked together to baggage claim, retrieved the suitcases, then took everything out to the rental car, loaded the trunk, and buckled the children into the car seats.

"I guess I'll head back to Mom's house now," Christine said. "Do you remember how to get there?"

"Oh yes," Laura said. "We'll see you soon." She watched as Christine started her car and headed off into the night.

"I'll drive," Laura suggested and Peter handed her the keys. He sat in the passenger seat, leaning back against the headrest, his eyes half-closed. Laura wondered if he was thinking about losing his own parents.

When they arrived at the house, both children were sound asleep.

"I'll carry Jessie—she's heavier than Mark," Peter offered.

"You don't mind?"

"It's a lot easier than carrying them both," he said, wryly.

Laura's mother was sitting in the living room with Dan; her face lit up at the sight of the children. Peter was right to think they'd be a consolation in the midst of her sorrow.

Christine came down the stairs.

"I turned on a light in the bedroom," she said.

"Thank you," Laura and Peter answered at the same moment.

They carried the sleeping children upstairs. The bedside lamp cast a soft glow around the room; the children's beds looked inviting, like snug little nests.

Peter knelt and laid Jessie down on one of them. He pulled the top blanket over her and smoothed her hair gently off her face.

She opened her eyes for a second; he kissed her forehead and they fluttered closed again.

Laura stood still, watching. Peter got up, lifted Mark out of her arms, then knelt to tuck him in beside his sister.

"They won't know where they are when they wake up," Peter whispered.

"But we'll be here," Laura said. Peter slipped his arm around her waist and she turned toward him.

"Hello, sweetheart," he whispered and kissed her. She leaned into him, kissing him back.

She longed to close the door and be alone with her family, but she and Peter went back downstairs instead and she listened distractedly as he made conversation with her mother.

Finally, he said, "I think I'd better go to bed. I'll see you in the morning."

"I'll come with you," Laura said. "Goodnight, Mama."

When she came out of the bathroom a few minutes later, Peter was in bed, asleep already, the lamp still on. Laura walked over to look at the children. Mark's arm was flung around his stuffed monkey; Peter must have put it into his bed while Laura was in the bathroom. She knelt and kissed both children, then got into bed, and turned off the light. She lay there quietly as her eyes adjusted to the darkness, listening to the breathing of her children across the room.

Peter turned toward her in his sleep; Laura propped herself on one elbow and looked down at him. Here she was, beside her husband, in the bed her parents used to share. She thought of her mother, sleeping here next to the husband she'd betrayed, and of her father, lying beside his unfaithful wife—forgiving her, still loving her. There was a whole history of emotion in this bed.

She lay down again, still listening. She heard Christine and Dan come up the stairs and go into their room. Now her mother was all alone downstairs. Laura closed her eyes and sank into sleep.

She woke abruptly in the middle of the night to find Jessie standing by the bed, her face just above Laura's.

"Mama?" she whispered.

"What is it, sweet pea?"

"Can I get in your bed?"

Laura glanced at Peter, sound asleep beside her.

"Sure, honey," she said. Jessie climbed in and settled between her parents. Laura curled around her; it was indescribably sweet to have her so close again.

Early in the morning, Mark woke and whimpered in confusion across the room.

"Come here to Mama," Laura said.

He padded to the bed and she lifted him up on top of her. She wrapped her arms around him, feeling his weight against her breastbone.

Today is my father's funeral, she thought.

Peter stirred and turned over.

"Hey, where did all these kids come from?" he asked.

"Daddy, you silly, we're your kids," Jessie giggled.

"Oh, that's right. I forgot," he teased.

Laura tried to imagine herself in bed with her parents. She used to get into their bed when she was sick but never when they were in it, too.

Peter reached across Jessie and laid his hand on Laura's arm.

"How are you doing?" he asked.

"I'm glad you are all here," she answered.

They got up and made their way downstairs. Laura had assumed they'd be the first ones awake but Dan was already in the kitchen, standing over a mixing bowl.

"So the little tykes are alive after all," he said.

"Of course we're alive," Jessie retorted. "Grandpa's dead."

Laura had never heard Jessie say Grandpa; he had never been a topic of conversation. Peter must have been talking to the children about him while she was gone.

Dan, to his credit, looked embarrassed. "I just meant you were fast asleep when you got here last night," he explained.

"We were all pretty tired," Peter said. "And now we're pretty hungry, aren't we?"

"Yes!" the children exclaimed.

"You guys like pancakes?" Dan asked.

"I love pancakes! Can I help you cook?" Jessie asked.

"I'd be delighted," he replied.

Jessie climbed onto a chair and seized the mixing spoon. In a few minutes, her shirt was covered with splatters of pancake batter.

"Good thing we didn't put on her church clothes before breakfast," Peter remarked.

Laura's mother came into the kitchen, her eyes red and swollen, and sat down across from the portable highchair Peter had set up for Mark. Laura watched her watching Mark—smiling in spite of herself—as he tackled his pancake with gusto, picking it up in both hands and taking big bites. Jessie sat next to her grandmother and began to describe her airplane trip in great detail: what she ate, which books she had "read," how she'd helped her daddy change Mark's stinky diaper.

"Your kids are a good influence," Christine commented as she and Laura stacked the dishes after breakfast. "Mom actually ate something."

As soon as the kitchen was cleaned up and everyone's clothes were changed, it was time to leave for the funeral.

"Can I ride with Grandma?" Jessie asked.

Laura looked down at her bright face. Her innocent excitement was a relief on this difficult day.

"She and Mom could both ride with us," Christine offered.

"I'll move the car seat," Peter said.

Mark, looking adorable in his tiny vest and corduroy pants, rode in the car with his parents, while Jessie and her grandmother sat side by side in the back seat of Dan and Christine's car. Driving behind them, Laura could see Jessie's hands waving around the way they did when she was talking a mile a minute.

A clump of her mother's friends and neighbors had gathered outside the church. Mrs. White was among them; she offered her arm to Laura's mother and escorted her inside. The casket, now closed, had already been placed at the front of the sanctuary.

Laura sat down with her family in the front pew and stared at the photograph of her father on top of the casket. It was a formal portrait, not one of her mother's lively snapshots; she wasn't sure where it had come from.

"Is Grandpa in there?" Jessie whispered.

"No, honey. Just his body," Peter answered.

I couldn't have said it better, Laura thought gratefully.

She felt herself going numb again as the service began. It went by in a blur: the organ played, the congregation sang, Mark and Jessie fidgeted, her mother wept, and Christine sniffled quietly. Peter picked up Laura's hand and held it.

"The Lord shall preserve thy going out and thy coming in from this time forth, and even for evermore," Reverend Mallory read. It was the end of the psalm her father had liked, the one about the hills. Laura thought of her father "going out" from his life. He was really gone now; whatever relationship they had was finished and she wasn't ever going to see him again.

She sat there, feeling entirely alone, as if everyone else had just evaporated. She didn't realize there were tears streaming down her cheeks until Christine pressed a tissue into her hand.

"Mommy's crying," Jessie whispered.

Peter leaned down close to her ear.

"It's OK," he reassured her. "Mommy's feeling sad."

"Does she miss her daddy?" Jessie asked.

"Yes, I think so. Shh, now," he whispered back.

After the service, Laura followed her children outside. She felt as if she were lost in a fog and they were beacons of light, guiding her. She wished she weren't going to the cemetery without them, but she and Peter had already agreed that they shouldn't stand out in the cold beside an open grave. Only a few people were going to the cemetery anyway: her mother, Mr. and Mrs. White, Christine and Dan. Peter and the kids could greet anyone who showed up at the house while they were gone.

Laura waited with them on the sidewalk, trying to shield them from the wind, while Peter went to get the car. People were drifting slowly out of the church; Laura looked up to see Michelle coming toward her.

"Hello again," Michelle said. "Who have we here?"

"These are my children," Laura said. She'd never had a chance to mention them at the funeral home. "My daughter, Jessie, and my son, Mark."

"You have children," Michelle repeated mechanically. She looked a little stunned. "How old are they?"

"Jessie's five and Mark is two."

"They're cute." Michelle spoke as if they were inanimate objects.

"Thank you." Laura could feel her children's hands through her gloves, hanging on to her as they looked up at this big, strange woman. She remembered how she and Michelle used to play at motherhood, fantasizing about their future children.

"Do you have any . . . ?" she started to ask, then bit her tongue, remembering what Christine had told her.

"No, none for me," Michelle said briskly, as if she were turning down dessert. "Too much responsibility. Besides, I never met a man whose kids I'd want." She gave a dry, forced laugh.

Peter pulled up and came around to the sidewalk where Laura stood with the children.

"This is my husband, Peter," Laura said to Michelle.

Peter put out his hand. "Pleased to meet you," he said.

Michelle shook his hand stiffly. She glanced at Laura and then away and it struck Laura that she had never seen such a look of loneliness in Michelle's eyes.

She's the one who is hurting, Laura realized with amazement, and the self-pity that had clung to her for so many years seemed to loosen and fall away. After all, she had a good husband, two beautiful children, and a best friend she loved as much as she'd ever loved Michelle—maybe even more.

Peter opened the back door of the car. "Hop in," he said to

the children.

"Are you coming over to the house?" Laura asked Michelle.

"Uh . . . no . . . I don't think I can make it. Sorry."

"Well . . . goodbye then," Laura said.

"Who's that, Mommy?" Jessie asked, climbing into her car seat.

"She was Mommy's friend . . . a long time ago," Laura murmured, as she watched the retreat of the woman whose bulk contained, somewhere deep inside, the little girl she had loved so unreservedly.

CHAPTER 16

The trip home on Monday took nearly all day. There was snow in Chicago so the connecting flight was delayed; it was late at night by the time everyone was back in their own beds.

Nevertheless, Peter was up early the next morning driven to hurry back to work. That was so like him, Laura thought, and then reminded herself that he had the same steadfast devotion to his family as to his job; it was precisely that quality which made him "a good husband," in her mother's words. As Laura poured Cheerios for the children, she found herself thinking about Michelle, all alone and lonely.

"Do I have school today?" Jessie asked.

"Yes, you do," Laura replied.

All the routines were falling into place: Peter going back to work, Jessie back to school—and soon Laura would see Julia again.

Gray clouds were skidding across the white sky as Laura parked in front of the nursery school and scanned the street for Julia's van. It wasn't there yet.

She walked Jessie inside to her classroom.

"Have a good day, sweet pea," she said, taking Mark by the hand.

He didn't want to leave the classroom; it was getting easier to imagine him going to school himself in a year or two. Laura finally coaxed him outside and they stood in the cold, waiting for Julia to arrive. Laura looked around the schoolyard, noticing how good it felt to be back.

Mark climbed onto a low wall next to the playground and walked along it, placing one foot carefully in front of the other, holding tightly to Laura's gloved hand. He was a cautious little boy; Laura hoped that would still be true when he got older. She wanted him to be brave and capable, but not reckless—not taking pointless risks or making her worry about him behind the wheel of a car. It dawned on her that she was hoping he would turn out like Peter.

At the end of the wall Mark turned around and a big smile spread across his face.

"Doolia!" he cried.

Julia was coming out of the school, hurrying toward them. Laura couldn't bear to wait for Mark to pick his way back along the wall; she swept him into her arms and ran toward Julia, half-laughing at her own eagerness.

Julia threw her arms around them both.

"You're back!" she cried joyfully.

"It's good to be home again," Laura said. "I missed you."

"I missed you, too. How are you? How's your mom?"

"I think she'll be OK," Laura said. "She has some really good friends."

"How's Christine?"

"She's such a strong person, Julia—I'd never realized that before."

"And you? How are you holding up, my dear friend?" Julia stroked one finger across Laura's cheek in a gesture of great tenderness.

Laura's throat constricted and she felt the sudden, heavy closeness of tears behind her eyes. She opened her mouth to speak but no words came.

A garbage truck rumbled noisily down the street and Mark twisted around in Laura's arms, trying to see.

"Tash tuck," he declared happily, as all three of them turned to watch it go by.

Laura cleared her throat. "I'm OK," she said.

"Shall we go to Carole's?" Julia suggested.

"Oh yes," Laura said. "I'll drive."

Julia grinned at her. "I'll buy," she said.

She bought three scones, handed them to Laura, then went back for tea and coffee, adding sugar and lots of cream to the coffee. She set both cups on the table and took off her coat. She was wearing a loose blouse Laura hadn't seen before; it looked suspiciously like a maternity top.

"You look wonderful," Laura said. "How are you feeling?"

"Not bad," Julia said. "Not sick, anyway."

"I thought the second trimester was the best," Laura recalled. "I didn't feel sick anymore but it wasn't impossible to move around yet."

Julia looked at her solemnly.

"To tell you the truth . . ." she began, then stopped. "Don't be mad," she pleaded.

"About what?"

Julia heaved a deep sigh. "I still can't quite believe this pregnancy is real," she confessed. "I haven't really accepted it." Her voice dropped and she looked down at her tea as her fingers turned the cup around absentmindedly.

"Oh, Julia." Laura reached across the table for Julia's hand.

"Are you disappointed in me?" Julia whispered. "Do you hate me?"

"Of course not," Laura said. "I love you, remember?"

Julia sighed again, a long trembling sigh.

"It will be OK about the baby," Laura said. "You'll see."

"What if I don't love it?" Julia asked.

"You will, Julia. You're so full of love you won't be able to help it."

Julia raised her eyes and looked at Laura gratefully. The emotion flowing between them was nearly palpable.

Mark's voice broke the spell.

"All done," he said, sliding off his chair.

"Looks like he's ready to leave," Julia remarked.

"The poor kid has been so cooped up: two plane trips and a funeral. I should take him to the playground or something."

"Good idea," Julia agreed. "I'll come, too."

They walked out of Carole's to see Jim Darling and his dog approaching.

"Docky!" Mark exclaimed.

Mr. Darling smiled. "Is that Taylor's pal, Mark?" he asked.

"Good morning, Mr. Darling," Laura said. She was surprised by how happy it made her to run into him. She didn't even know him, really, but in a certain way he seemed like an old friend, an important part of her world.

"Hello . . . uh, oh, I know you're Mark's mother but I'm afraid I've forgotten your name," he said.

"It's Laura."

"Laura. Such a pretty name," he said. "Well, I'd better go inside. I'm meeting someone."

"Have a nice day," Laura said.

After the door closed behind him, Julia looked at Laura quizzically.

"Since when is he such a friend of yours?" she asked.

"We've just run into him a few times. You can see how Mark loves that dog." It hadn't occurred to Laura that Julia would be surprised—even a little impressed, it seemed—but it was fun to see her react that way.

"Well, can you tell me what he does for a living?" Julia asked. "How come he's always free in the middle of the morning?"

"I don't know," Laura said. She thought for a moment. "Maybe he's a gigolo."

Julia laughed and so did Laura, pleased to have come up with the sort of thing Julia might say.

"A blind gigolo—that's brilliant," Julia said. "He wouldn't have to strain to be flattering to ugly rich ladies. And what a perfect name: Mr. Darling!" She chuckled again. "Who would imagine a gigolo working in our own boring little suburb?"

"You never know," Laura said. "There's so much you never know."

"I've got it!" Julia cried. "Our business venture: L and J's Nail Salon and Gigolo Supply Service."

"Julia!" Laura pretended to be shocked.

"We'll have to personally screen the employees," Julia added, grinning wickedly. She could always think of something more outrageous than Laura could.

The playground was chilly and deserted and the overcast sky was taking on a deep blue-gray color.

"It almost looks like it might snow," Julia said, as Laura lifted Mark into an empty swing.

"It was snowing in Chicago," Laura recalled.

"I was afraid we'd have a blizzard and you'd be stranded out there in the Midwest," Julia admitted. "I really wanted you to come back."

"I'm really glad to be back," Laura said.

"Was it a good trip for you?" Julia asked. "Even if it was sad?"

"Yes, it was. I learned a lot." Laura watched Mark's eyelids starting to close.

"What was it like for you?" she asked. "Losing your father?"

Julia was silent for a moment. "Well, complicated . . ." she said finally. "To be honest with you . . . I felt a kind of relief. Finally I felt like I could stop being a lawyer."

"Were you really doing it just for him? You didn't like it at all?" Laura asked.

"No. I found it somehow tedious and tense, both at once. A bit like motherhood—except without the sweet moments."

"Those are the moments that make it all worthwhile," Laura mused. "The big payoff."

"Being a lawyer only paid money."

"It helped you meet your husband," Laura pointed out.

"It's also how I met my ex-husband," Julia reminded her. "It was never the right career for me. But I couldn't disappoint my father. My sister is a cardiac surgeon, for Pete's sake—I was afraid he wouldn't love me as much as her."

"I never really knew my father loved me," Laura said. "He never said anything. But my mother told me he was proud of me," she added, choking up suddenly.

Julia laid her arm around Laura's shoulders. "I'm sure he was," she said.

"Why couldn't I have heard it from him?" Laura asked.

Julia shook her head. "I don't know."

Laura looked down at Mark; he was sound asleep, his head tipped sideways, his body slumped in the swing.

"You grow up to be a man who shows emotion," she ordered him in a fierce whisper.

"I don't think our children have the kind of fathers we had," Julia said.

Laura thought of Peter in her parents' bedroom: tucking Mark's toy monkey into his bed, brushing Jessie's hair out of her face.

"Hey, you'll never guess who came to the funeral," she said. "Michelle Dooley. I hadn't seen her in years."

"Who's Michelle Dooley?" Julia asked.

Could it be that she had never told Julia about Michelle: how important she had been, how painful it was to lose her, how Laura had carried around that burden of grief for so long? Laura probed her emotions now the way you might examine a scar to see if the wound was fully healed. It had been such a habit to feel hurt by Michelle; it was strange to realize she didn't feel that way anymore.

"She was my best friend growing up," she explained. "Her family moved away when we were in junior high and I hadn't seen her since."

It seemed unnecessary now—or maybe just too difficult—to describe the whole relationship to Julia. Besides, a little part of

Laura still felt guarded, self-protective. Michelle had called her a "lez," had mocked her feelings of love and attachment; surely Julia wouldn't do that, but perhaps it wasn't worth the risk to find out.

They stood quietly for a moment, looking at Mark sleeping in the swing. A fat snowflake floated through the air, landed on the sleeve of his jacket, and melted instantly.

"See? It's starting to snow already," Julia said.

She held the swing still while Laura extracted Mark, pushing each foot out carefully through its hole. A few more snowflakes appeared; they seemed to be coming down in slow motion.

"I have to thank you again for taking care of my children while I was gone," Laura said. "I don't know how I can ever repay you."

"Don't be silly," Julia said. "There is nothing to repay. I was happy to do it. I'd do it again in a heartbeat. And so would you," she added.

Laura drove straight home after picking up Jessie, eager to be off the roads before the snow accumulated. She let the children watch TV while she unpacked suitcases, threw laundry into the washer, and went through the mail. She was making beef stew for dinner when Peter appeared.

"You're home early," she remarked.

"I decided to leave before the snow got worse," he said.

Laura looked out the window. It was snowing rapidly now, a heavy wet snow; the shrubs in the yard had become weird, white lumps.

"I'll be in the study," Peter said. "Call me when dinner's ready."

Laura hadn't expected him to be home in time to eat with the rest of them; she'd figured the stew would be easy to keep warm until he arrived. The house felt cozy with her whole family sitting at the table together, while the snow came down outside.

Mark picked the carrots off his plate and squished them between his fingers. By the end of dinner, he managed to wind up with food smeared all over himself.

"Oh boy, do you need a bath," Laura said, lifting him out of the chair.

"Let me do it," Peter said.

Laura looked at him, surprised. Even when Peter came home in time for dinner, he'd be back in the study afterward, or reading the paper in the living room, while Laura took the children upstairs to get ready for bed.

Her first impulse was to say no. She loved bath time with Mark: watching him play in the water, admiring his naked body, wrapping him in a towel and hugging him close. But she remembered the regret on her mother's face as she recalled that Laura's father had never experienced that pleasure with his children—nor they with him.

"OK," she said, reminding herself silently not to offer instruction. Peter knew how to bathe his own child; Laura had just asserted that to her mother.

"I want a bath with Daddy, too," Jessie piped up.

Laura felt, simultaneously, a wistful tug of attachment and also gratitude that Jessie's father was more than a shadowy presence in her childhood. Laura couldn't remember asking her father for anything.

After Mark's bath, Laura sat in the rocking chair and read *Goodnight, Moon* twice through before putting him down. As she left his room, she heard Jessie giggling down the hall; she went back to the bathroom, opened the door, and peeked in.

Through the steamy air she could see Jessie sitting in the tub and Peter kneeling beside it. He'd taken off his shirt and Jessie was swirling shampoo around on his chest hairs. Her own hair was piled high in a big white wig of shampoo lather.

"Look, Mommy!" she said. "I'm making a hairdo on Daddy's chest!"

"That's quite a hairdo on your head," Laura replied.

Peter turned around and grinned at her, clearly reveling in the silliness of the moment. Laura looked at his wet, sudsy chest and found herself remembering showers at his apartment in their early days together: they'd soaped each other's bodies and stood under the running water, kissing as if their lives depended on it. What had happened to that passion? Laura wondered. Was it gone—or just obscured by the mundane details of parenthood?

The telephone was ringing. Laura slipped out of the bathroom to answer it.

"Hi, it's me," Julia said.

"Hello, you." The image of Julia's face, her hazel eyes sparkling, came into Laura's mind.

"I thought you might like to know . . ." Julia paused dramatically. Laura could tell it wasn't bad news, Julia was just teasing her.

"I felt the baby move this evening," Julia said. "Right after supper."

"Oh, Julia!" Laura breathed.

"I knew you'd be glad," Julia said.

"Oh, Julia . . . are you?"

"Yes, I guess I am," Julia admitted. "There really isn't anything quite like it, is there?"

"Nothing in the world." Laura remembered how it felt when her babies stirred and kicked and hiccuped in her womb, how it had made her believe the unbelievable: that there was a living child inside her body.

"You are the very first to know," Julia said. "I haven't even told Greg yet—he's busy reading to the girls."

"I'm honored," Laura said. "And I'm so happy for you."

As she hung up, Laura pictured Julia telling Greg and the pleasure he would take in the news. He'd probably be more amorous than ever.

She read Jessie's bedtime stories while Peter dried himself off and went back to the study. After Jessie was tucked in, Laura went to the window, pulled aside the curtain, and looked out. Under the glow of the streetlight, the yard was transformed, an alien landscape. In the morning, Peter would pull on his boots and shovel a path to the street, but right now they were snowbound, her little family together inside their house.

Looking out at the falling snow, Laura thought about Julia, safe and snug with her own little family: her husband, her daughters, the new child growing inside her.

"We're lucky," Laura murmured to herself.

CHAPTER 17

Snow fell heavily all night and school was cancelled for the next two days. The first day Peter stayed home and took the children sledding, but then he went back to work and Laura was on her own with them. She and Julia talked to each other on the phone every few hours.

"I hope the roads are clear by tomorrow," Julia said. "I have an ultrasound appointment."

"Is something wrong?" Laura asked anxiously.

"No, it's just routine," Julia assured her. "They'll take measurements and stuff—didn't you have ultrasound when you were pregnant?"

"Yes," Laura admitted. She'd been nervous before those appointments, too.

"Shall I come along?" she asked. "Mark and I can hang around in the waiting room."

"That's OK, Greg is coming," Julia said. "But thanks for the offer."

Of course Greg was going with her. Just as Peter had gone with Laura.

The next morning Laura took Jessie to school and then took Mark for a long walk through the snow. She kept thinking about Julia stretched out on an examining table, her shirt pulled up, her belly covered with ultrasound gel, watching the screen for an image of her baby.

Greg and Julia both came to school at the end of the morning. Julia ran straight to Laura.

"It's a boy!" she said. "He just happened to be in the right position: legs wide apart . . . it was just hanging right out there." She leaned close and added softly, "Like father, like son," just as Greg came over to join them.

"Congratulations," Laura said.

"Thanks. The baby looks great."

"It's incredible how much you can see," Julia went on. "They showed us all the organs. . . even all the chambers of the heart."

Laura remembered lying on her back, listening to the thrilling, unmistakable sound of her own baby's heartbeat. She looked down at Julia's abdomen and tried to picture a baby boy inside, his tiny heart beating as fast as a sparrow's.

"It is wonderful," she said. "Have you picked out a name yet?"

"Greg junior, of course," Greg answered promptly. He grinned at Julia and she rolled her eyes.

The weather stayed cold for weeks and the snow stuck around in icy, increasingly dirty patches.

"It feels like winter will never end," Julia complained. "I'm sick of wrestling the kids into boots and snowsuits."

"I know," Laura said, but she didn't really mind. She almost wished winter would go on forever; she loved the mornings with Mark and Julia while the girls were in school. Julia was growing more beautiful every day, her body ripening noticeably, her hair shining and thick, her skin aglow with the hormones of pregnancy.

One morning, early in March, as Laura was changing Mark's diaper on Julia's living room floor, he commented distinctly, "Go pee-pee."

She looked up at Julia. "I've never heard him say that before."

"Do you suppose he's ready to try the potty?" Julia asked. "I can bring ours up from the basement."

"Why not?" Laura replied.

Julia turned up the heat in the house, and they let Mark run around naked, Laura guiding him to the bathroom every so often to try out the potty. He was delighted to have unimpeded access to his penis; he handled it frequently and energetically.

"He has such cute little erections," Julia chuckled She didn't even get upset when he peed on her dining room floor and stood there staring at it.

"Pee-pee," he declared, pointing at the spreading puddle.

"It's lovely," Julia told him. "But it's supposed to go in the potty, remember?"

Mark headed to the bathroom, plunked himself down on the potty, and beamed out the open door.

"Mark on a potty!" he announced.

Julia laughed. "Well, better late than never."

"I love it that you laugh," Laura said. "I never thought of potty training as amusing before."

"It's only fun because you're around," Julia assured her.

"We'll go to my house tomorrow," Laura said. "There's no need to ruin your floors."

The next morning was sunny and not so cold, the snow at last beginning to recede. Laura drove Mark and Julia back to her house from the school. As they ambled up the front walk, Julia pointed suddenly toward the ground.

"Look!" she cried. "Your crocuses are coming up!"

Sure enough, a cluster of little green shoots was poking up an inch or so above the ground.

"Oh, Julia!" Laura was enchanted. It seemed so long ago that they had tucked those bulbs into the earth where they'd spent the winter forgotten, out of sight.

"I guess maybe spring is going to come after all," Julia said. "Thank God for crocuses: they make me believe it every year."

As the days grew warmer and longer, the crocuses bloomed

and then daffodils lit up a corner of Julia's yard, bright and cheerful as a patch of sunshine.

"We'll plant some in your yard this fall," Julia promised. Laura felt an uneasy flicker of doubt, wondering if she'd still be here, but she pushed it quickly out of her mind.

Julia's daughters both had birthdays in the spring: Emily's in April, Sara's in May. Emily had a party with costumes, just like Jessie's, and then of course Sara wanted to have one, too.

"If it were up to me, I'd plan a party at the beach," Julia said. "But the weather is so unpredictable in May—I could wind up with a bunch of freezing, whining little girls."

As it turned out, the day of Sara's party was warm and humid, an early taste of summer. It was too hot for costumes: Julia handed out squirt guns and water balloons instead. Afterward, Laura and Julia sat in Julia's back yard, fanning themselves with leftover party hats.

"I've never been pregnant in the summer," Julia remarked. "I'm already so hot all the time—I'll have to spend the last month stuck in my house with no clothes on."

Laura was quiet for a moment, picturing that. Then she said, "We'll get you a maternity swimsuit so you can go to the beach and show off your glorious belly."

"If you say so," Julia said. Her eyes widened suddenly. "What a kick—this guy's a soccer player for sure!"

"Let me feel, Mommy," Sara said. She pressed her hand against her mother's abdomen.

"Did you feel that?" Julia asked.

"That didn't feel like a kick," Sara said. "Is there really a baby in there?"

"There certainly is," Julia assured her. Sara picked up the edge of Julia's blouse and put her face underneath it.

"Hey, you baby," she called. "Why don't you come out?"

"It's not time yet," Julia said.

"Can I feel?" Laura asked shyly.

"Of course!" Julia lifted the bottom of her shirt and Laura put her palm down over the warm taut skin of her belly.

"You have to press harder than that to feel anything," Julia said. "Don't worry—you won't hurt me."

Laura remembered Peter's big hand pressing firmly on her own belly when she was pregnant. She pushed down a little more, looking at Julia's skin between her fingers.

"Oh! There he is!" she cried. She looked up and Julia's radiant smile washed over her.

The children came out of school on Friday carrying mysterious paper bags. Jessie hid hers under her bed when she got home, determined to keep her gift a secret until Mother's Day. She presented it to Laura on Sunday morning; it turned out to be a little flower pot, hand-painted and filled with dirt.

"We put seeds in it," Jessie announced.

"How nice . . . what kind of seeds?" Laura asked.

"I forget. Some kind of flowers."

"We'll have a surprise when they come up, won't we?" Laura set the pot on the kitchen windowsill. "Thank you, sweetie."

Peter smiled at his daughter. "Would you like to help me make dinner for Mommy?"

"You're making dinner?" Laura asked.

"I thought about going out but then I decided it might be more fun at home with the children," he said. "Don't you think so?"

"Oh yes. After all, I wouldn't be celebrating Mother's Day if it weren't for them."

Peter made an elegant rack of lamb with fresh asparagus and new potatoes. He really was a good cook, he was just too busy to do it anymore. He'd bought a bottle of wine to have with dinner and afterward he insisted on taking care of the dishes, too.

"This is supposed to be your day off," he said. "There's only one thing you have to do. . ."

"What's that?"

"I think you should call your mother," he said. "Wish her a happy Mother's Day from me, too."

"I was going to," Laura replied, but she was grateful to be reminded. Ever since the funeral trip to Indiana, Peter had kept in contact with her mother. Sometimes he'd even pick up the phone himself and call to ask how she was doing. Laura found his interest touching and a little puzzling, but Julia had declared it refreshing when Laura told her.

"It's a relief not to see the cliché of the awful mother-in-law," she'd said. "I wish I could feel that friendly toward mine."

Laura's mother sounded thrilled to hear from her.

"Hi, honey!" she exclaimed. "The flowers are beautiful!" At least Laura had remembered to order flowers.

"Did you have a nice day?" she asked.

"I had dinner over at the Whites' house."

The Whites had no children of their own; there was no one to wish Mrs. White a happy Mother's Day. She'd never received the clumsy, precious, handmade gifts of a child, carried home proudly from school. Neither had Michelle Dooley, it occurred to Laura suddenly.

"I just talked with Christine," her mother said.

"How is she?" Laura stopped herself from saying what she was thinking: that today might be especially hard for Christine.

"She's fine. Working too hard, as usual. How about you?"

"We're fine, too. The kids are growing like weeds."

"It was so good to have them here after your father passed," her mother said. "They brought some life into this sad old house."

"We'll come visit again soon," Laura promised, recalling Jessie's spirited conversation with her grandmother on the way to the funeral. It would be nice for them to know each other better.

After her mother said goodbye, Laura called Christine.

"Hey, happy Mother's Day," Christine said.

"Thanks, Chris. How are you doing?"

"Well, Dan and I are trying again—my doctor said it was OK."

"I'm glad," Laura said fervently. "I really hope it happens for you guys."

"Did you talk to Mom?" Christine asked.

"Just now. She seems OK."

"She's lucky to have such good friends helping her through this."

"I never used to think of Mrs. White as anything special, you know?" Laura said. "She was always just the neighbor across the street."

"She's been a great friend to Mom," Christine said. "It's funny how you see things differently when you grow up, isn't it?"

The nursery school sent out invitations to a graduation ceremony for the children who were going on to kindergarten. Laura showed theirs to Peter when he got home from work.

"Oh no—I'll be in Chicago that day," he said. "I'll just be getting back that afternoon."

"You're going away again?" Peter's business trips had become more and more frequent as the spring progressed. "Can you reschedule?"

"No, I really can't, not this time. I'm so sorry. You'll have to tell me all about it when I get home."

On the last day of school, Laura and Mark arrived at the designated classroom, where parents were perched like giants on the child-sized chairs. Mark made a beeline for Julia, sitting in the second row.

"We saved a seat for you," she said, picking up her purse from the chair beside her.

Laura lifted Mark onto her lap. Julia sat between her and Greg, her pregnant belly almost large enough now to fill her own lap.

After the ceremony, everyone moved to another classroom for refreshments. Greg brought Julia a little paper cup full of juice and she downed it gratefully.

"Where's your husband?" he asked Laura.

"He's away on business. He'll be back later today."

"Too bad he had to miss this special occasion." Laura couldn't decide if he was being serious or sarcastic.

"I should get back to work myself," he said. He put his arm

around Julia and gave her a long kiss, right in the midst of all the other parents. Then he flashed a smile at Laura and left the room.

"What do you think? Are you ready to go, too?" Julia asked.

Laura looked around the classroom. The place felt so comfortable to her now: the little chairs and tables, the stained linoleum floor, the faint smell of bleach in the bathrooms. She was actually going to miss it.

"Let's take the kids out for ice cream," Julia suggested.

"Ice cream!" Jessie echoed, joyfully.

Laura smiled. "How could I say no?"

After that they went to Julia's house. The children scurried inside to play while Laura and Julia sat down on the porch steps.

"Can you believe our kids are going to kindergarten?" Julia said.

"A year ago I couldn't even imagine nursery school," Laura admitted.

Julia leaned back on her hands. Her shirt was stretched tight; Laura watched the surface of her belly jumping and twitching with the movements of the baby inside.

"He's really active today," Julia said. "I think he likes ice cream." She sat up and put her hand over her belly, then took Laura's hand and pressed it against her.

"See what I mean? I'm going to have my hands full with this guy." Julia said.

"I can't wait to meet him," Laura said. "Hey, what's with the flowers?"

Behind Julia, on the floor of the porch, were several flats of petunias with huge pink and purple blossoms.

"I bought those last weekend but I couldn't seem to get them planted," Julia said. "It's too hard to bend down."

"Would you like me to plant them?" Laura offered. "I'll put them wherever you like."

Julia hauled herself to her feet, went into the house, and came back with a trowel. She sat back down on the steps and watched Laura plant the petunias in the front yard, just below the porch.

The frilly flowers danced in the afternoon sunlight. Laura sat back on her heels, admiring them, and then looked at her watch.

"We should go . . . we really ought to be home when Peter arrives."

"It would be sad for him to come home to an empty house," Julia agreed. "Thank you for planting my flowers!"

"You're welcome. Let's get together soon."

"How about tomorrow? Maybe we can go to the beach," Julia suggested.

Laura hesitated. "Peter might want to spend some time with the kids after being away," she said.

"He can come to the beach too!" Julia said magnanimously.

Laura laughed. "I'll call you," she said.

As she drove away, she could see Julia in the rearview mirror, waving, one hand on her belly, the petunias fluttering in the yard below.

Peter arrived just in time for dinner. He walked in carrying a bottle of champagne.

"Put this in the fridge," he said, handing it to Laura. "We'll have it later."

"Champagne? What will we drink when she graduates from college?"

Peter grinned. Sometimes he came home from business trips tired and distracted but this time he seemed energized, almost jubilant. Drawn like magnets, the children hovered around him as Laura finished making dinner and after dinner Peter took them outside to play. The air was still warm even as the sunlight faded and stars began to appear. Through the open window, Laura heard shrieks of pleasure from the children mixed with the deep rumble of Peter's laughter.

When they finally came back inside, Laura helped the children into their pajamas, and then Peter read to Jessie, propped against the headboard of her bed, his arm around her as she curled against him. Laura looked in at them as she led Mark to the bathroom for his ritual bedtime trip to the potty. The night before he had actually managed to pee in it, to his astonishment. Peter hadn't heard about that little triumph yet; she'd have to remember to tell him later.

The children were so wound up that it took a while to get them settled. But finally Laura and Peter came downstairs and Peter took the chilled champagne out of the refrigerator while Laura found two champagne flutes and wiped the dust out of them— they hadn't been used since the move to this house.

Peter opened the bottle with a satisfying pop and poured champagne into the glasses. The bubbles rose and hissed merrily. He set down the bottle, picked up both glasses, and handed one to Laura.

"Here's to Jessie," Laura said and took a sip. The effervescence tickled her throat.

Peter leaned forward suddenly and kissed her.

"What's that about?" Laura asked. She peered at his face. "You look like the cat who ate the canary."

He grinned. "There's another reason to celebrate," he said. "I have a surprise for you."

"What?"

"We're moving to Chicago. And this time we're going to stay put." He beamed at her expectantly. "Isn't that great?"

CHAPTER 18

Laura's stomach seemed to turn over inside her and her fingers tightened against the glass until she was afraid it would break in her hand. She set it down quickly and held onto the edge of the counter to steady herself.

"We'll finally be able to put down roots," Peter went on blithely. "I know you haven't liked all the moving—it's not very stable for the kids. Now that Jessie will be starting school, it's time to give up this gypsy lifestyle."

Laura stared down at the champagne glass, the bubbles spinning upward to burst on the surface.

"Jessie already started school," she said.

"I meant public school. It'll be good for her to have some continuity, don't you think—make some friends she can grow up with?"

"How could you?" Laura's voice was low and harsh; she felt as if an invisible hand were clamped around her neck.

Peter's smile faded.

"I thought you'd be happy," he said. "I thought you'd be glad to stop all the moving around. I went after this new job so we could live like other families. We can get a dog for the kids. We'll be closer to your mother—at least the children can get to know one grandparent before they're all gone."

"You never even asked me," Laura choked out.

"I thought you'd be glad," Peter said again. "I wanted to make it a surprise. The company was going to move me again anyway but I thought it was time for something more permanent. I thought this would be a good thing for all of us."

He seemed truly bewildered and with good reason: Laura had never responded to news of an upcoming move with anything more than a sigh of resignation. She'd never objected or even asked to be consulted; the nomadic nature of his job had just been taken for granted.

Peter put his glass down beside Laura's and started to reach for her but she backed away. She didn't mean to, but it was as if some unseen force were controlling her.

"I can't go," she said.

"Laura, what's wrong?" He stood in front of her, leaning toward her, his hands hanging awkwardly at his sides.

"I can't leave Julia." She said it so softly she wasn't certain the words had actually come out. But Peter heard them.

"What do you mean, you can't leave Julia?"

"I promised . . ." Tears began forming in her eyes. "I promised to help her with the baby."

"Isn't that baby almost due? We'll probably still be here."

"Not just for the birth—I promised to help her take care of him, to help her take care of all her children . . ." The tears were falling now.

"Surely she can find help," Peter said. "It doesn't have to be you."

"It does, it does," Laura wailed. "I want it to be me." She took a deep breath. "I can't leave Julia. I love her."

Peter stood up straight.

"You love her," he repeated slowly. "What does that mean?" Each word fell like a stone into the space between them.

Laura looked up at him mutely, her face streaming with tears. She opened her mouth to speak but nothing came out.

Peter stared at her.

"Are you telling me you are in love with her?" he asked.

Laura shrugged helplessly. "I don't know," she whispered.

"You don't know if you're in love with a woman," Peter said, incredulous. "Jesus, Laura, what's going on with you?"

"It's not what you think . . ." She broke off. Was it? She felt unsure of anything, as if the very ground beneath her feet were giving way.

"What am I supposed to think? What the hell can you be thinking?"

"I'm sorry . . ."

Laura could hardly breathe; the room seemed to be closing in around her. She turned and left the kitchen, walked through the house, and picked up her keys from the table by the front door.

Peter followed her, alarmed. "Where are you going?"

"I have to get some air." Laura swung the door open.

"When will you be back? Are you coming back?" Peter's panic-stricken voice came after her as she walked out onto the porch and down the steps. She turned and looked at him standing in the doorway and her heart felt like it would break into pieces.

"Stay with the children," she said.

She opened the van, climbed inside and sat in the driver's seat, pulling in big gulps of air.

"Don't hate me," she said aloud as she started the car.

She drove slowly down the street away from the house, afraid to look in the rearview mirror and see Peter standing alone on the porch in pain and confusion—terrible feelings that were all her fault. What was she doing, what on earth was she doing? She felt numb, her mind a blank, as she drove around aimlessly, the van lumbering along the dark streets under the canopy of trees arching overhead.

And then suddenly, without planning it, she was on Julia's street. The tears, which had stopped while she was driving, began again as Laura pulled the car to the curb and looked across the street at Julia's house.

The porch light cast a glow on the newly-planted petunias, illuminating their fragile blossoms. Laura stared at them through her open window and her body shook with weeping; every grief she'd ever felt seemed to be coming up at once, filling her to overflowing. Her head felt ready to burst, her throat ached, and her chest heaved with ragged, gasping sobs. She put her hands over her face and tears slid between her fingers.

When she looked up again, Julia was standing on her porch. She was wearing a pair of white painter's overalls, her belly large inside them, and the porch light lit her up like some kind of angel. She lifted her arms, stretching, and walked to the edge of the porch and then she spotted Laura's car. She ran down the steps, her hand on the railing, and hurried across the street, a smile of sheer pleasure on her face.

"What brings you here on this beautiful evening . . . Laura, what's the matter?" Her smile evaporated as she came close enough to see Laura's face, tear-splotched and swollen. "What's going on?"

"Julia . . . Peter wants to move. He already took a job in Chicago . . . oh, Julia, I can't stand it!"

"Stay there," Julia directed. She walked around the van, opened the passenger door and got in. That was her seat; she had spent more time in that seat than anyone else.

"When I saw how upset you were, my first thought was that you were pregnant," she said.

Laura looked through tear-blurred eyes at Julia. She seemed so solid, sitting there inside the car, more tangible than anything in Laura's reeling world. Laura took a deep breath—in and out—as Julia sat quietly beside her.

"What brought you outside?" Laura asked finally. "Does Greg know where you are?"

"I was going to take a little walk," Julia said. "He just got home from work and I've been stir crazy all evening."

"Could I walk with you?"

"Of course."

They got out of the car and met on the sidewalk, then began

walking, side by side, not saying anything. The air felt soft; a slight breeze stirred the leaves, wafting the heady fragrance of honeysuckle. A lone mockingbird was singing into the darkness, high on a chimney somewhere, showing off its complicated repertoire.

At the corner of the block, a huge new house was going up. So far, only the foundation had been poured, outlining the footprint of the house to follow. A massive earth-moving machine stood by, waiting for morning to swing noisily back to work.

Julia took Laura's hand and led her off the sidewalk into the muddy lot.

"Come sit," she said, sitting down on top of the foundation.

She patted a spot next to her and Laura sat down, too. The concrete wall was like a rough, cool bench underneath her. She stared straight ahead, breathing unsteadily, as Julia put a comforting arm around her and waited for her to speak.

When she didn't, Julia finally said, as softly as if she were speaking to an injured animal, "Is Peter leaving you?"

Laura was afraid to look at her, fearful she might come apart if she saw the loving concern in Julia's face. As it was, she could feel Julia's eyes on her as she looked at the dark ground under her feet.

"No . . . but . . . he wants us all to leave. He found a job in Chicago . . . without even telling me."

"Damn—I was hoping you'd stay here forever," Julia said. "Even though you told me Peter's job keeps moving him."

"This new job is different; he won't have to move all the time anymore."

"Oh . . . well . . . that might be good?" Julia floundered.

"It's in Chicago!" Laura cried.

"Right." Julia heaved a deep sigh and they sat in miserable silence for a while, until Julia lifted her head.

"Chicago's supposed to be a pretty fun town," she said tentatively. "I hear it's O.K . . . .for the Midwest, anyway." She managed a smile but Laura began to weep again.

"Of course, it is awfully far from the ocean," Julia went on.

"But at least Lake Michigan is big . . . you can't even see across it . . . there must be beaches . . ."

"I don't care about stupid Lake Michigan," Laura burst out. "All I care about is you!"

Julia stopped talking and looked at her. The baby must have started kicking; Julia put a hand reflexively on her belly and Laura reached over to put her hand there, too.

"You've made me so happy," she whispered. "I just love being with you."

"I love you too," Julia said tenderly.

She lifted her hand to Laura's face and looked deep into her eyes, her pupils large and liquid-looking in the dim light. Overwhelmed with emotion, Laura leaned toward her and suddenly, unbelievably, they were kissing.

Julia's lips were soft and surprisingly warm. Her fragrance filled Laura's nostrils and she could feel the child inside Julia moving under her palm. Every nerve in Laura's body felt electrified. Time seemed to be suspended, as if the earth had stopped spinning and just stood still.

Julia pulled back slowly and Laura felt the cool evening air on her lips again. She opened her eyes and stared at Julia, frightened and astonished.

"Oh my God," she said. "What are we doing?"

Julia smiled her luminous smile, her eyes full of love.

"Do you hate me now?" Laura couldn't stop herself from asking.

"Of course not," Julia said.

The memory of Michelle's twelve-year-old voice filled Laura's head: "What are you, a lez or something?"—that tiny word filled with dismissal and disgust. But here was Julia now, a woman she had just kissed, not thinking anything ugly of Laura, not loving her any less. It was a miracle.

"What are we going to do?" Laura whispered. The course of her entire life seemed suddenly up for grabs.

"I guess we'll be spending an awful lot of time on the phone,"

Julia said. "And I'll come visit you—how much is a plane ticket to Chicago, anyway?"

Laura stared at her.

"I don't want to go to Chicago," she said. "I want to be with you, I want us to be together always . . . I love you, Julia." She felt an overpowering desire to kiss her again.

"And I love you, Laura. You know that."

They turned toward each other on the wall and embraced. Laura clung to Julia, her whole body aching with grief and desire. Then they did kiss again; it was sweet and deeply sorrowful, like a final goodbye.

"I want to be with you," Laura whispered again. "Don't you want to?"

Julia sat still for a moment, looking at Laura.

"Yes, I do," she said at last. "I love you . . . and I would love to make love with you." She took a deep breath. "But I couldn't do that to Greg—I could never hurt him that way."

So Julia didn't really do whatever she wanted, Laura thought. No matter what that video might or might not mean to her.

Julia paused and then continued. "I also love my life, Laura. And you love yours, I know. Our husbands love us and we love our children and we love our precious, fragile family lives."

Now Julia began to cry, her wet eyes glistening. She picked up Laura's hand and held it, resting lightly on the concrete wall between them.

"You're the best thing that's happened to me in a long time," she said. "I'll miss you terribly."

With her free hand, Laura gently wiped the tears from Julia's cheeks.

"Suppose—just for a minute—that we didn't have families," she said, her heart pounding. "Would you . . . could you . . . really imagine?" she trailed off.

"With you? Absolutely," Julia declared. Laura let out her breath.

"Although I'm not sure how we'd have met, if it weren't for the children," Julia added.

"Wouldn't we have found each other somehow?" Laura said. "I thought you said we were soul mates."

"Maybe we were lovers in a previous lifetime," Julia suggested. "Or maybe we will be in the next one." She smiled at Laura. "Maybe even in this lifetime, after we're both widows."

It was an oddly comforting thought.

"You won't forget me?" Laura asked plaintively.

"Are you kidding?" Julia's warm gaze washed over Laura. "You are part of me now, you are inside my heart."

Laura longed to fling her arms around Julia again, to press against her pregnant abdomen and milk-swollen breasts, but she held herself back. They sat together silently for a long time. Leaves rustled in the trees high above them. Far away, on the street, a car drove by, music blasting out the window; it might have been in an entirely different world.

Finally Julia stood up.

"I should go back," she said, "before Greg flips out and calls in a missing person's report or something."

She reached out a hand to Laura who got up reluctantly. She didn't want to leave; she didn't ever want this moment alone with Julia to be over.

Her eyes filled again as they walked slowly back toward Julia's house.

"When do you have to leave?" Julia asked.

"I don't know. The conversation didn't get that far."

"I hope we can still have lots of time together," Julia said.

Laura tried to picture herself with Julia in the daylight, with all the children around, doing something mundane and normal, but at this moment such a thing seemed unimaginable. She could still feel the warmth of Julia's kiss on her lips; everything was different now. She thought suddenly of her mother, quitting the painting class to save her marriage. Could life ever just go back to the way it had been before?

She and Julia paused on the sidewalk next to the van.

"Well . . ." Julia hesitated. "I guess I should go in."

Laura couldn't speak.

"Will you be OK?" Julia asked.

Laura nodded wordlessly.

"You should probably think about going home, too," Julia said. "I expect your husband is worried about you."

Laura remembered the look of utter bewilderment on Peter's face—Peter, who was always so sure of himself. In her head, she heard him calling after her as she walked away, the sound of real fear in his voice.

"You're right," she answered Julia at last.

"Will you call me tomorrow?" Julia begged. "I need to know that you're OK."

"I'll be all right," Laura said, but she felt stunned, dazed, not at all certain.

Julia walked around the van, and opened the driver's door. Laura climbed in and put her hand on the edge of the open window; Julia covered it briefly with her own, then backed away.

"Drive safely," she admonished. She turned and started across the street.

"Julia?" Laura called after her.

Julia turned back, in the middle of the empty street.

"Yes?"

"Do you think it's possible to be in love with two people at once?" Laura asked.

"Oh, Loretta . . ." Julia answered. "Isn't it obvious?" She blew a kiss and continued across the street, up the sidewalk and onto her porch. She turned to wave, then disappeared into the house.

Laura sat motionless inside the car, watching the petunias tremble in the evening breeze. Thoughts and images entered her head, one after another in rapid succession, overlapping and merging the way they do in dreams.

She saw Mark snuggled against Julia, listening to a story, and Jessie curled against Peter as he read to her. She saw Julia watching the children, sound asleep after the trip to the beach, and Peter looking down at them in their blanket nests on the floor of her mother's room, Julia helping the children plant crocus bulbs, Peter showing Jessie how to make a snowball. And she saw Julia dancing in the bar, her slim body swaying, and then Peter's bare chest, the hair wet and soapy with Jessie's shampoo, Julia sipping brandy and listening to country music, Peter raising his champagne glass to Laura, toasting what he thought was happy news, completely unprepared for her response . . .

She really did love them both; her heart was a bigger place than she had known. After all, it had expanded to make room for each of her children: Mark hadn't taken over Jessie's place there, he had a place of his very own. Now Julia had established a place for herself in Laura's heart . . . but it wasn't the same as Peter's. And Peter's was still there, too.

Laura pulled her seatbelt around her and started the car. The route back to her house was so familiar it seemed as if the car itself knew the way home.

When she arrived, the house was dark; not even the porch light was on. Laura put her key in the lock, stepped inside, and closed the door behind her.

She heard no sound except the low steady hum of the refrigerator. She put down her keys and walked into the kitchen; the champagne bottle and the two full glasses were sitting on the counter, abandoned, as if whoever lived in the house had suddenly been forced to flee—to escape some unforeseen disaster.

She was seized with a terrible fear that everyone was gone, that the house was really empty. Her heart racing in alarm, she ran upstairs to look in the children's rooms.

They were both in their beds, sleeping peacefully. The sight of them made all the drama and upheaval of the last few hours seem inconceivable. Laura went back and forth from one room to the other, taking in the nourishing reality of their presence.

Julia's voice echoed in her head: "We love our family lives." It was the sharing of those complex, frustrating, fulfilling lives that had drawn her and Julia together from the start. Even though, for a moment, Laura had wondered what their friendship might have been outside those intricate webs of love and attachment, she couldn't really imagine anything else. They were both mothers, both wives; that was part of what they loved about each other. Laura felt her pulse calming, her breath becoming steady and regular again as she watched her children sleep.

But where was Peter? He must be somewhere in that dark house; he would never have left the children alone. Laura began to look for him, upstairs and down, and then she realized that the door to the study was closed. She put her hand silently on the knob and turned it.

Peter was sitting at the desk, his head down on his folded arms. He didn't even look up when she opened the door.

"Peter?" she said softly.

He didn't move. Was he asleep? Was he still breathing?

Laura crossed the room and approached him, filled with remorse and trepidation.

"Peter?" she said again. She laid her hand gently on his shoulder.

He sat up then and in the glow of the streetlight leaking through the sheer curtains, Laura saw the tears on his face.

Peter was crying. It seemed as improbable, as incredible, as the thought that she had just kissed a woman. Laura had the sensation of her heart opening up inside her chest.

"I'm sorry," she whispered.

He turned his chair to face her.

"All I ever wanted was to take care of you and the children," he said, his voice ragged with grief. "I don't want to lose you, you're all I have in the world." A sob escaped him.

Laura bent down and wrapped her arms around him. He buried his face between her breasts and cried like a baby. She was awestruck. She'd never seen him fall apart; somehow it made him so much more like herself, someone she could identify with, could feel truly close to.

"What happened to us?" he asked mournfully. "I only wanted

to be a good husband, to make you happy."

"You are. You have," she said, beginning to cry, too. She wouldn't have guessed she had any tears left but here they came.

"What am I supposed to do?" he asked. "What have I done wrong?"

She held him close against her, feeling his tears soak through her shirt. He hadn't failed her; it was she who had failed to account for him, to hold open his place in her heart.

"Nothing," she said, looking down at the thinning hair on top of his head. "I love you, Peter."

The words came out of her unbidden and as she heard them she realized how long it had been since she had spoken them.

Peter's arms tightened around her.

"I need you," he said, still weeping.

"I need you, too," she murmured.

He looked up. "What about . . . her?" he asked, painfully.

Laura heard Julia's voice again: "We love our precious, fragile family lives," and she knew that it was true, for both of them.

"You are my husband," Laura said aloud. "My life is with you."

Peter rose and pulled her into his arms. They stood there, exhausted, leaning into each other, for a long moment. Finally Laura raised her head to look into his face; he was gazing down at her, his blue eyes full of love and sorrow. She stood on tiptoe and kissed him; his lips were almost as soft as Julia's.

Holding hands, they made their way wordlessly upstairs, shed their clothes, and crawled into their bed. Laura laid her head on Peter's bare chest, his hair tickling her cheek, and listened to the steady beating of his heart.

CHAPTER 19

Laura woke in the middle of the night. She rolled onto her back and lay there, eyes open, as the evening replayed hazily in her mind. She turned to look at Peter in the bed beside her; he seemed, at the same time, foreign and familiar.

She put out her hand to touch his face. His cheek was rough, the whiskers he shaved so thoroughly every morning growing back furtively as he slept. Laura felt like she was encountering him for the first time, discovering things she had never taken notice of, or had forgotten from some earlier life.

Peter opened his eyes and they stared at each other for a long moment. He lay perfectly still as Laura began to trace the contours of his face with her fingers, exploring him as if she were blind. Her hand traveled down to the soft hairs on his chest, down over his belly, and toward his naked thighs. A sound escaped him, a sigh emerging from deep inside.

Laura climbed on top of him, pressing the whole length of her body against his. His penis stirred helplessly underneath her as he closed his arms around her. She lifted her head and kissed him, softly at first, then with increasing passion, moving slowly down his body as he twined his fingers into her hair. She felt simultaneously generous and aroused, giving and taking in equal measure; all thoughts left her except what was happening at that moment, in her husband's body and in her own. He reached for her, urging her back up, until they were face to face again. Laura gazed into his eyes, watching them blur into a sea of blue as his lips came toward hers. They kissed for what seemed like hours and Peter's hands caressed her everywhere, as her desire rose and crested. And then he was inside her, and she clasped him close, holding him so tightly it was as if their two bodies were merging into one, transfigured. Afterward, still naked, she lay against him, breathing him in, until at last she slept, wrapped in his arms.

In the morning, Jessie walked into the bedroom.

"I'm hungry," she announced.

"I'll be right there," Laura said, pulling the sheet up quickly. "Go pick out some clothes, I'll meet you in the kitchen."

Jessie hesitated.

"Go on, honey," Peter urged. "We'll do something fun together after breakfast."

"Aren't you going to work?" Jessie asked.

"No, I'll be yours all day," he assured her. "Go get dressed."

"OK," she agreed, swayed by the promise of his company, and left the room.

"We'd better get dressed now before she comes back," Laura said. She swung her legs out and put her bare feet on the floor.

"Laura . . . wait," Peter said urgently. She turned back toward him; his face was serious, his body still hidden under the sheet.

"That's the reason I took the new job," he said. "So I could spend more time with the kids . . . and with you," he added.

"I know," she said.

"I thought I could do more for the family—be around more," he went on.

"Yes, I know."

Peter pulled himself up on one elbow, the sheet falling away from his chest.

"But is that really what you want?" he asked. "Or should we . . . ?"

"What?" Laura prompted nervously.

"Should we stay here? Will you be miserable in Chicago?"

Laura's eyes filled. After all that had happened, he was still trying to look out for her. She was deeply moved, even as the thought flew into her mind that maybe she could stay, maybe she could have it all, not leave Julia or her marriage.

But looking down at Peter's earnest face, she knew it would never work. That line she'd been afraid of crossing for so long had been crossed; she had to choose a path—and whatever she chose would be a new, untraveled road.

"No, we should go," she said. "We need to go."

She could see his body relax, ever so slightly. She tried to smile but her mouth was trembling.

"I still don't understand what's happening," he said.

"I know. I'm sorry."

"Are you really in love . . . ?" he broke off as Laura put a finger to his lips.

"I love you, Peter, and we are going to Chicago. Please, can we just leave it at that?"

They looked at each other for a long, silent moment. Then Laura bent to kiss him and he put his arms around her and opened up his hands against her back. To her astonishment, she felt herself becoming aroused again.

"I thought you were getting up." Jessie stood in the doorway, wearing a pair of red shorts and a clashing orange tee shirt that was too small, the pale skin of her belly showing between them.

"We are, sweet pea," Laura said. "Get yourself a bowl and some Cheerios. I'll be right down to pour the milk."

Jessie disappeared again; this time Laura got up and dressed promptly.

"You can sleep in for a while," she said to Peter just as Mark began calling down the hall, "Mama, get me!"

"I'll get him up," Peter said.

"It's probably time to think about putting him in a big bed," Laura said. "Then he could get himself up."

Peter looked startled to hear her suggest such a thing; Laura was a little surprised herself. It even crossed her mind that maybe they should sell or give away the crib, rather than taking it to Chicago, but she didn't say so because the thought of moving made her throat close up too much to speak.

She went downstairs and emptied the champagne into the sink while Jessie ate her cereal. She glanced up at the painted Mother's Day flowerpot on the windowsill; a spindly seedling had begun to grow but she couldn't tell yet what kind of plant it was. Peter brought Mark downstairs and they both had breakfast but Laura couldn't muster any appetite. She poured juice for everyone and made a pot of coffee for Peter.

"Can we go to the playground, Daddy?" Jessie asked. "You promised to do something fun with me."

"Sure, honey. Hey, Mark, you want to go the playground?"

Mark's eyes lit up. "Paygown!" he echoed.

Peter turned to Laura. "How about you?"

"No . . . I think I'll stay home and clean up a little," Laura said.

"Are you sure?" Peter asked. She could see another, silent, question in his eyes.

"Yes. It's OK," she assured him.

After they left, she sat down at the kitchen table and leaned her head on her hands. She was drained, spent, as worn-out as if she'd run a marathon.

The phone rang and she knew immediately who it was.

"Hello?"

"Laura, it's me, Julia."

How she would miss hearing that voice every day!

"I just had to see how you're doing," Julia said. "Are you all right?"

"I guess so."

"Is Peter there? Are the two of you OK?"

"He took the children to the park."

"Would you like to get together? I could meet you at Carole's."

What a comfort it would be to sit across from Julia at one of those little tables again, Laura thought. But it might feel like a tryst now, something sneaky and clandestine—the sort of thing they joked about Mr. Darling doing there.

"No, I don't think so," she said sorrowfully.

"Shall I come over? Laura, are you really OK?"

Laura knew Julia only wanted to ease her pain—but seeing her now might make that pain unbearable.

"Julia . . ."

"I know, Laura. I'm sorry. I'm just missing you," Julia admitted.

"I miss you, too." Laura struggled not to cry.

"I think I need a little time," she said. "I . . . I'm afraid to see you right now."

"Oh, Laura . . ." Julia sounded so miserable Laura felt herself weakening.

"I'll call you as soon as I can," she promised and hung up the phone.

It was so strange to put limits on the friendship now. What Laura really wanted was to spend every minute she had left here with Julia, like a dying woman who has only a few weeks to live.

When her family returned from the playground, she made lunch for everyone: little crustless sandwiches for the children and a fancy tuna salad for Peter.

"This is delicious, honey," Peter said. He was being cautious, keeping an eye on her, out of either suspicion or concern. Laura knew she'd given him cause to feel both.

That evening, after the children were in bed, they circled each other uncertainly, as shy as if they'd just met.

"Shall we talk?" Laura suggested.

"OK. You want a glass of wine or anything?" Peter asked.

"I don't think so," Laura answered. "You should have one if you want."

"No, I'm fine."

They sat down side by side on the couch. Peter's hands rested on his knees as he stared straight ahead. Laura looked over at him, observing little details: the protruding tendons on the backs of his hands, the tiny lines around his eyes, the silver hairs scattered among the brown ones, like touches of gilt. He really was a good-looking man and he was liable to age handsomely. He'd probably turn out to be one of those men who are even more attractive in their fifties than in their forties.

She took his hand and he turned toward her as his fingers curled around hers.

"I think we should tell the children," she said.

A look of alarm crossed his face. "Tell them what?"

"About the move. Let's talk to them about it tomorrow."

"OK," he said, with wary relief.

"And let's plan a trip to Chicago as soon as we can, to look at houses."

"OK," he said again. He looked away for a moment and then back at her.

"Laura . . . you're sure about this?"

This was hard. It had been eye-opening—even exciting in a way—to see Peter's confidence shaken, but she was beginning to understand how much she had depended on his certainty. Now she had to be certain for herself, even when she wasn't quite.

She squeezed his hand. "Yes," she said.

She wanted to tell him not to ask her again, but she knew that wasn't fair; he might need to hear it again . . . and she might need to say it. After all, nothing in life—or in a marriage—was really unshakeable. The truth was that you decided over and over again, day after day, whether to leave or to stay. She'd been making the choice unconsciously all along, but now she had to make it with awareness, out loud, knowing what she could lose and what she could keep.

They told the children about the move the next morning. Mark was still too young to have much reaction but Jessie had plenty of questions: Where will I go to school? Can we get pizza in Chicago? Can I have a kitty? Who will be my friends?

Laura cleared her throat. "We'll make some new friends," she said. "And we can call our old friends on the phone."

Jessie pondered this. "Can I call Emily? She's my best friend."

"Yes, of course. Her mom is my best friend." Laura glanced at Peter as she said this, but he didn't flinch.

"I wish they could come with us," Jessie said.

"I know. Me, too."

Laura called Christine that evening.

"Guess what?" She wanted to tell it like good news. "Peter got a new job . . . we're moving to Chicago!"

"Chicago!" Christine echoed.

"I'm going back to the Midwest—can you believe it?"

"At least Chicago's a city. Not like that sleepy little town we came from."

"It feels like a big change," Laura confessed.

"You must be used to change, though, with all the moving you do."

"This is supposed to be the last time. The new job won't require all that upheaval."

"Oh, that's good, don't you think? Better for the kids?" Christine suggested.

"That's right." Although the children could thrive anywhere, Laura thought, as long as their family stayed together.

"I have news, too," Christine said. "I'm pregnant again. I just found out."

"I'm so glad!" Laura exclaimed. Maybe she wouldn't get rid of the crib just yet.

"Pray for us, won't you . . . for everything to be OK?"

"I will." Laura had never talked about prayer, but it seemed natural to acknowledge it now. She'd prayed for her own babies to come safely into the world, and for Julia's; now she would pray for Christine's, too.

For over a week, she resisted calling Julia and Julia stayed dutifully out of touch. Laura tried to occupy herself with her children, the way she used to do, but it was different now: they'd gotten used to having other people in their lives—and so had she. She was keenly aware of loneliness that had once been unconscious.

When she finally couldn't hold back anymore, she called Julia while Peter was at work. At the sound of her voice, Julia burst into tears.

"I'm sorry," she spluttered. "I'm just so glad to hear from you."

Laura's eyes filled.

"I'm glad to hear your voice too," she said. "I miss you so much already," she added, daring herself not to cry.

"How are you doing? What's going on?"

"We told the children about the move," Laura reported.

"What do they think?"

"Jessie asked if she could call Emily from Chicago."

"That's sweet!" Julia said. "Did you say yes?"

"Of course. We'll need a hotline between our house and yours." Laura took a breath. "We're going out to look at houses next week."

"Oh! . . . well . . . I hope you find something you love. Housing is a lot cheaper out there—you guys can probably afford a palace."

"I suppose." Laura expected to feel impoverished without Julia, no matter what kind of house they found, but that thought lay unspoken inside her.

"Laura . . . ?" Julia began.

"What?"

"I'm wondering how things are with you and Peter. Was he mad when you came home that night? What did you say to him?"

Poor Julia had been living with those questions all this time, Laura thought contritely.

"He was pretty upset," she admitted. "The truth is, I've never seen him that upset."

"Oh, Laura." Julia's voice was full of compassion. "He was afraid of losing you."

Laura's throat ached, remembering the pain in his face, his un-precedented loss of composure.

"If I thought Peter was unfaithful, I don't know what I'd do," she said. "I'd be so hurt."

"It's a terrible feeling," Julia agreed.

Laura was starting to lose her battle against tears.

"I never meant to hurt anyone," she whispered.

"Of course not," Julia soothed. Laura could feel her love coming right through the phone. It made her long to see Julia again, wanting it so much she didn't dare.

It was true that you could get more house for the money in Chicago, and there were plenty of houses to choose from. Laura and Peter drove from one neighborhood to the next in a rental car, the children restless in the back seat. They looked at houses with swimming pools, finished playrooms, three-car garages, houses with green lawns and mature, majestic shade trees.

Laura had a hard time finding any reason to prefer one over another; they all ran together in her mind. But the children were captivated by a house with a tree house in the backyard: meticulously built by hand, with real windows and ivy trailing gracefully from real window boxes. Jessie couldn't stop talking about it as Laura tucked her into bed at the hotel.

The realtor took them back for a second look the next day. They walked through the house again; the children raced into the yard and danced exuberantly around the tree house. Laura tried to see it through their eyes instead of thinking about how much fun her children and Julia's could have playing here together.

"It looks like the kids have made their choice," Peter said. "What do you think, honey?"

Laura scanned the yard, trying to picture where she would plant bulbs. She wanted crocuses to come up in the spring.

"It's very nice," she said, stalling. She knew it was up to her to make the decision but she was still resisting, holding out.

"The schools here have an excellent reputation," the realtor commented.

Laura already knew that; Peter had carefully researched all the neighborhoods they were considering.

"Let's look inside one more time," she said.

"You go ahead—I'll stay out here with the kids," Peter offered. He was ready to commit and so were the children. What was she waiting for?

She went around to the front of the house and then stopped abruptly: a man was walking along the sidewalk with a guide dog. For one crazy moment, she thought it was Jim Darling—he was about the same height, and his walk was similar—but this dog wasn't a husky like Mr. Darling's; it was a rich brown chocolate Lab, its smooth coat glistening in the afternoon sun. They went through the gate of the yard next door and up to the house, where the dog sat down, waiting, as the man unlocked the front door. Then they disappeared inside.

It was completely irrational, Laura knew, but the thought of having a guide dog next door was inexplicably reassuring. It seemed like a favorable omen, as if the benign spirit of Jim Darling were letting her know that life could go on somehow, wherever she landed.

She returned to the back yard. "I don't need to go inside again," she said to Peter. "Let's go ahead and make an offer."

"You're sure?"

"Yes."

They spent a few more days in Chicago, finalizing the deal. Before they left the hotel, Laura called her mother.

"We're in Chicago," she told her. "Peter has a new job and we're buying a house—we'll be moving here in August."

"That's great news, honey! You won't be quite so far away."

"As soon as we're settled, we'll bring you up for a visit," Laura said. Now that her mother didn't have to take care of her father anymore, maybe she'd really come.

"You could bring Mrs. White along," she added. "I don't think she's ever seen Chicago."

"What a thoughtful idea," her mother said. Laura had forgotten how easy it was to please her.

On the plane back to Boston, Laura thought about the last time she'd flown home from Chicago, after her father's funeral. It had been winter then, with a snowstorm on the way; now it was summer—and everything had changed. She was heading home, but soon she would be leaving again and home would be somewhere else. Somewhere without Julia.

But she'd been wasting the time she had left with Julia, holding back, keeping a fearful distance. Until she'd gone to Chicago herself, she hadn't been able to actually picture living there. But now that a house was bought, the upcoming move finally seemed unmistakably real. Surely she could risk making contact with Julia again.

The next morning, after Peter had left for work, Laura plunked the kids in front of the television and called her.

"Laura!" Julia exclaimed and Laura knew she'd call from anywhere just to hear her name said in that joyful way.

She swallowed. "We found a house," she said.

"I guess this means you're really leaving, huh?" Julia sighed. "Is it nice?"

"Yes. And big—there's enough room for your whole family to visit." Laura hadn't even dared to think of that before the words came out of her mouth.

"There's a tree house in the back yard," she added. "And the oddest thing: a blind man and his guide dog live right next door."

"Mark must love that," Julia said. "What's his name?"

"I don't know. I haven't actually met him yet."

"Oh . . ." Julia sounded puzzled. "Well, I'm sure you will."

She didn't seem as struck by the coincidence as Laura had been. It didn't carry the same symbolic weight for her.

"When are you moving?" Julia asked.

"The end of August." It would be almost exactly a year since the move to Massachusetts.

"The baby should be here by then—unless this turns out to be the world's longest pregnancy." Julia laughed wryly.

"Julia, I feel terrible that I won't be here to help you with the children," Laura said.

"It's OK."

"But I promised . . ."

"Sometimes one promise overrides another," Julia said. "It's really OK."

A wave of love surged through Laura.

"You're wonderful," she said.

"So are you."

They were both silent for a moment, as Laura gathered her nerve.

"Shall we get together?" she asked at last.

"I'd love to!" Julia replied. "When?"

Laura took a breath. "Why don't you and the children come over tomorrow? We can fill up the kiddie pool and stick our feet in it while they splash each other."

"Sounds heavenly. You're on."

The next day was hot right from the start. Laura checked to be sure the freezer was stocked with popsicles and then dragged the plastic pool out of the garage and into the yard. It occurred to her that the new yard in Chicago would have more shade on a hot day like this, but she pushed the thought away. She didn't want to think about Chicago.

She put on her favorite swimsuit, wondering what Julia was going to wear. They'd never gone shopping together for that maternity bathing suit but maybe Julia had bought one on her own.

A new thought struck her; she picked up the phone and called Julia. "Maybe we should just go to the beach," she suggested.

"I'd love to, but I'm actually not feeling very good. I was just about to call you," Julia said. "How's that for lousy timing?"

"Oh, Julia, I'm so sorry." Laura thought for a moment. "Would you like me to take the girls so you can rest?"

"I really wanted to see you," Julia said mournfully.

"I want to see you, too," Laura declared. "I'm coming over to check on you. Do you need anything?"

"I don't think so."

"I'll be there as soon as I can."

Laura changed quickly out of her swimsuit, but it still took forever to get out of the house: first Jessie had to go to the bathroom, then Mark wanted to use the potty, too. Laura forced herself to be patient, although she felt almost ready to jump out of her skin until they were finally buckled into the car.

Laura hadn't driven down Julia's street since that unforgettable night. She felt suddenly empty-handed now, wishing she'd brought flowers or some little gift for Julia.

Mark and Jessie marched into the house and headed straight for the playroom. Julia was lying on the couch; the children walked right past her without even noticing the strained expression on her face.

"Thank God you're here," Julia said.

"I'm sorry it took so long," Laura said. "Are you all right?"

Julia's eyes met hers. "I think I'm in labor," she answered.

"What? It's not time yet, is it?" Laura cried.

"No, it's early," Julia said. "Sudden, too."

"Are you sure? Why didn't you call me?"

"I only just realized what was happening and I already knew you were coming. I tried to call Greg but—wouldn't you know?—he's in court all morning."

"Did you call your doctor?" Laura asked.

"Not yet."

"I'll bring you the phone," Laura said.

She left Julia alone to make the call and went to look in the playroom. Jessie and Emily were kneeling together in front of the dollhouse, Sara was chatting into a toy telephone, and Mark was pushing a little car around on the rug. It all looked so harmonious, Laura wondered if they were appreciating each other more after the separation of the last few weeks. Or was she just ascribing her own feelings to the children?

"My doctor thinks I should go to the hospital," Julia wailed, hanging up the phone. "She said a third child can come a lot faster."

"That's what I thought." Laura tried to sound calm.

"How am I going to do that? What am I supposed to do with my kids?"

"I'll stay with the kids, Julia, don't worry about that," Laura reassured her.

"But I need you to come with me!" Julia cried.

Laura's stomach jumped. "You do?"

"I always wanted you there," Julia insisted. "Didn't we talk about this?"

They hadn't, Laura was sure, but of course all their conversation had been suspended for a while.

"I always thought I'd stay with your children," she said.

"I figured Greg could do that—or Mrs. Nixon or somebody. I just knew I wanted you with me for the birth."

"Oh, Julia . . ."

"Here comes another one," Julia said. Concentration gathered on her face.

"I'll call Mrs. Nixon," Laura said. She took the phone and hurried to the kitchen; a list of frequently called numbers was posted on the refrigerator. Her own number was listed, along with Greg's law firm, the pediatrician, and Mrs. Nixon. Laura's hands shook as she called.

"Hello?"

Thank heaven: Mrs. Nixon was home.

"This is Laura Donovan. . . I'm at Julia's. . . she's in labor. . . can you come and babysit all our kids?" The words poured out in a rush.

"I'll be right there," Mrs. Nixon said. "Tell Julia not to worry. I'm leaving right now."

Dear Mrs. Nixon—she was more wonderful at this moment than any fairy godmother. When Mark was born, Laura hadn't had a regular babysitter to call; Peter's secretary had stayed with Jessie. She was pleasant enough, but Laura had hated leaving her daughter with anyone.

It struck her that she should call Peter and tell him what was happening.

"Hi, honey!" he said, surprised. "You just caught me, I'm on my way to a meeting—is everything all right?"

"I wanted to let you know I'm taking Julia to the hospital. She went into labor this morning."

"Where are the kids?" Peter asked.

"We're all at Julia's. Mrs. Nixon is coming to babysit."

"Should I pick them up?"

"They'll be fine. I'll call you again from the hospital."

"O.K . . . .Laura?"

"Yes?"

"Wish Julia good luck for me."

"I will," Laura said, touched.

The children came out of the playroom, curious, when Mrs. Nixon arrived. How fortunate that they were all at ease with her, Laura thought. She recalled the reassuring presence of Mrs. White, making her blueberry pancakes, when Christine was born.

Julia stood up carefully, gripping the arm of the couch.

"The baby's ready to come out," she explained, the brave smile on her face dissolving as another contraction seized her.

"Is Mommy OK?" Sara turned to Laura, her eyes wide with alarm.

"Yes, honey, she's OK," Laura assured her. "But she needs to go to the hospital now to have the baby. Mrs. Nixon will take care of you and we'll call you as soon as your brother is born."

The four children watched solemnly as Julia staggered out the door, leaning heavily on Laura's arm. Laura guided her into the passenger seat, then ran around to the driver's side, climbed in, and started the engine.

As she backed out of the driveway, Julia gasped. "My water just broke! I'm making a mess in your car!"

Laura stifled an urge to laugh. "Don't worry about it," she said.

She drove to the hospital as fast as she dared. At every stoplight she glanced at Julia, who sat rigid, eyes closed, clutching the shoulder belt across her body. She was in heavy labor now, not even trying to speak.

Laura pulled into the emergency lot, beside an ambulance. She helped Julia out of the van and supported her across the driveway and through the automatic doors.

"My friend's in labor," she told the receptionist. "Her doctor's meeting her here."

Julia collapsed into an empty wheelchair in the corridor.

"If you could step over here and fill out some insurance information?" the receptionist replied.

I don't know Julia's insurance information, Laura thought wildly. An attendant stepped behind the wheelchair.

"She's coming with me!" Julia hollered hoarsely. "I need her!"

She tried to rise just as another contraction came on; Laura caught her and eased her back into the chair.

"We'll deal with insurance later," Laura declared.

She hurried along beside the wheelchair as the attendant pushed it toward the elevators. While they waited for one to open, Julia reached for Laura's hand and squeezed it hard. Laura looked down at her tenderly, remembering how overpowering labor was, how you had no choice but to surrender to that primal drive of your body. Julia was entering a different kind of consciousness now— an intense and personal place that would contain the astonishing drama of birth.

They took the elevator to the maternity ward, where a nurse ushered them into a delivery room. Julia struggled out of the wheelchair and clambered onto the bed.

"Laura?" she said weakly.

"I'm here," Laura replied, taking her hand.

A young woman in a white coat walked in.

"Hello, Julia," she said. "Isn't it lucky we had an empty bed this morning?"

Julia mumbled an incoherent response, and the woman turned

to Laura.

"I'm Dr. Campbell," she said. "You must be Laura." Her speech was calm and measured; it seemed almost in slow motion after the frenzy of getting Julia here.

"How did you know?"

"Julia told me you'd be with her."

They both turned toward the bed as Julia let out a loud, throaty groan.

"Oh, it's coming, it's coming!" she cried.

"Hang in there . . . hold on," Dr. Campbell said, grabbing a pair of gloves. "Laura, can you help take off her clothes?"

The delivery nurse pulled off Julia's sandals, then she and Laura scrambled to get her shorts and underpants out of the way. They were soaked with perspiration and amniotic fluid and they clung to her skin but Laura finally managed to pull them free of her feet.

Julia's shirt was bunched up around her breasts but from there down she was naked. Laura hadn't seen her naked since the night of the Valentine's dinner; she looked completely different now—her belly huge, her skin splotchy and sweaty. Still, she looked beautiful to Laura.

"Oh, my God, I have to push," Julia gasped.

Dr. Campbell placed herself between Julia's legs.

"Let me just check . . ." she said, reaching her fingers inside Julia to feel her cervix. Laura watched, shuddering with recognition.

"It's coming! I can't wait!" Julia hollered.

"OK. Go ahead and push now." Dr. Campbell backed up a little.

Julia's face went crimson with effort as she bore down.

"It's so fast," she panted.

Laura was thinking the same thing: it had taken her such a long time to push her babies out but Julia's was ready to just burst forth.

"Your body knows how to do this by now," the delivery nurse pointed out. "Oh, the baby's head is crowning!"

Laura didn't know whether to concentrate on Julia's face or to watch her baby actually emerge. Julia gave another mighty push and groan and the nurse cried, "Oh, look down, look down!"

Laura knew Julia was too focused to look anywhere but inward. When she'd been in that deep trough of labor herself, she hadn't been able to see the births of her own children, but now she could be a witness for Julia.

Below the huge mound of Julia's abdomen, the patch of pubic hair was parted by her swollen, straining genitals. How could something as big as a baby ever come out of there?

The doctor's gloved hands were waiting, the nurse hovered beside her, and Laura peered between the two of them. Julia cried out again and—incredibly—there was the baby's head between her legs. Dr. Campbell reached forward and tears sprang to Laura's eyes as Julia gave another cry, another push, and out followed the baby's body, pallid and still.

Laura looked up at the doctor's face in horror. Something was wrong: the baby was too blue, too quiet. Laura felt as if her own heart had stopped.

Unperturbed, Dr. Campbell lifted him clear of Julia's legs, the rope of the umbilical cord still connecting them inside her. Julia sighed and then her son took in a breath and began to cry. He made a surprising amount of noise for such a tiny creature.

Julia reached for him reflexively. The doctor clamped and cut the cord, then laid him on Julia's stomach—outside the belly that had sheltered him until now. Julia's hands came down gently over him.

Laura looked on, awestruck, brushing away tears.

"Oh, Laura," Julia whispered. "Isn't he perfect?"

"He is perfect, Julia. He's wonderful and you're wonderful."

They gazed at each other, enraptured.

"Can I touch him?" Laura asked.

"Of course."

Laura stroked his waxy skin with her fingertips. It was already turning rosy, as his lungs pulled in oxygen. Julia groaned again and the nurse said, "Here comes the placenta. I'll clean up your baby and weigh him while you push."

Julia let go reluctantly and labored to deliver the placenta. The baby wailed loudly as he was carried to the scale. Laura was torn between staying next to Julia or keeping a protective eye on her baby—and then suddenly Greg strode into the room.

"Am I too late?" he asked.

"Your son has arrived," Julia told him, a radiant smile breaking on her face as the placenta slithered out of her into the doctor's hands. "I'm sorry I couldn't wait for you—it all happened so fast."

The nurse brought back the baby, wrapped in a blanket, and placed him in Greg's arms. Greg slipped his big hand gently under the tiny head and looked down at the scrunched-up, crying face.

"He's beautiful," he said, his voice husky. Laura could see tears in his eyes.

He walked gingerly over to Julia and sat down on the bed beside her.

"Here—let me have him," Julia said. She tugged her shirt up, lifted her bra, and placed the baby at her nipple, coaxing it into his quivering angry mouth until he latched on and the room was suddenly quiet.

Laura stared at Julia's full breasts, the nipples huge and brown. She imagined the weight of them, heavy with milk, and her own breasts tingled with a memory of the letdown sensation, as if the baby were hers, too.

Julia looked down at her child, adoringly. "Hello, Benjamin," she cooed.

"What was that?" Greg asked.

"His name is Benjamin," Julia said, lifting her shining eyes to her husband. "OK?"

"It's a fine name," Greg said. "I've thought so all along."

"It's my father's name," Julia told Laura. "I couldn't make up my mind about using it."

"It's a great choice," Laura murmured.

Greg leaned down to kiss Julia, his hand resting lightly on the baby's head.

"I guess Benjamin decided to be your birthday present," he said.

"It's your birthday?" Laura asked. "Why didn't you tell me?"

"It's not until tomorrow, really," Julia said.

"You should have told me," Laura chided. "I wanted to give you something special."

"Oh, Laura. You already did," Julia said. She looked up at Laura, her eyes full of unguarded love. Laura drew in a deep breath and let it out again.

"I should probably leave now," she said.

She began to back toward the door but Greg reached for her suddenly and pulled her into an unexpected embrace.

"Thank you," he said.

"For what?" Laura mumbled, feeling small against his big body.

"Taking care of Julia—getting her here and helping her—and the baby. We're all grateful to you."

Laura raised her eyes cautiously to his face. There was no sign of his dazzling smile; he looked perfectly sincere, his expression tender with appreciation. She'd never before felt really seen by him.

"You're welcome," she said.

"Don't leave yet," Julia said. "Don't you want to hold the baby before you go?"

Benjamin's mouth was growing slack against Julia's nipple as he drifted into sleep. As exhausting as it was to give birth, Laura thought, it must be even more strenuous to be born. She went back to the bed, leaned over, and lifted the baby from Julia's breast into her arms. His downy head lay in the crook of her elbow, his body barely longer than her forearm. He wrinkled his forehead and pursed his lips as he settled against her, eyes closed, his tiny lashes sticking straight out above his cheeks.

Laura held him close against her heart, feeling joy and loss all jumbled together. Love wasn't always simple, she knew—but it was rich and it was boundless. She looked up and her eyes met Julia's. Laura stood perfectly still, trying to memorize this moment to hold in her mind forever. Soon she would call Julia's girls—and Peter—just as she had promised. Life would continue: she would move away, the children would grow up, things would change, and people she hadn't even dreamt of would enter her life and find space in her heart. There was no knowing what might lie ahead, but right now Laura wanted nothing more than just exactly what she had.

ACKNOWLEDGMENTS

I am deeply grateful to – and grateful for – many people who helped me bring this book into the world.

Thanks, first of all, to my family, for their patience, love, and unwavering support.

Thanks to Bonnie Hoke-Scedrov for proofreading, to Alida Castillo for the interior layout, and to Jill Breitbarth for the cover design.

Thanks to Jessie Brown for her perennial enthusiasm, and for the cover photograph – and to Kickstand Café in Arlington, Massachusetts, for the photo location.

Thanks to my early readers – Holly Abernethy, Jessie Brown, Debora Hoard, Kevin McCarthy and Jennifer Opp – for their feedback and encouragement, and for asking to see more.

Thanks to my fellow tap dancers at Studio Ten Tap, who have been an unexpectedly rich network of resources and a wellspring of kindness and joy.

And last, but certainly not least, profound and heartfelt thanks to my dear friend of so many years, Grace Gillespie Carter, without whom the journey of writing would be far lonelier and this book might never have been born.